The Greatest Sin

I0663772

Harbinger

Published by Tangled Sky Press
www.tangledskypress.com

First printing, October 2014
Second printing, July 2016

Harbinger is a work of fiction. Names, places, and incidents are either products of the authors' imaginations or used fictitiously.

ISBN: 978-0-9911965-8-6

Harbinger

The Greatest Sin #2

Lee French & Erik Kort

TANGLED
SKY
PRESS

Acknowledgments

Lee French

I wish to thank the Worcester Writer's Collective and the Olympia Writer's Coop for all the support both groups have given me. Also, thanks to my parents, specifically for babysitting and making lunch.

Erik Kort

Few people ignore Chavali—I'm not one of them. She hasn't forgiven me for the last book, so I've given in. According to demands, I have a few people to thank. First is Alex, who sometimes cooked (my job) AND cleaned (our job) when I was deep into plotting hell. Next, my sister, who is about to embark on her own journey: Andrea, marriage is a song—I've always been off key, so perhaps you ought to seek to look to others for harmony advice. Finally, Mom, I don't call and I don't write. I'm a horrible son. Maybe stories other than my own will sustain you until again I figure out how to work my cell. I love you all—Chavali would too if she could be bothered.

Other Books by the Authors

The Greatest Sin Series
epic fantasy

The Fallen

Harbinger

Moon Shades

Illusive Echoes

Lee French
In the Ilauris setting
standalone fantasy tales

Damsel In Distress

Shadow & Spice (short story)

Al-Kabar

Spirit Knights
young adult urban fantasy

Girls Can't Be Knights

Backyard Dragons

Ethereal Entanglements

Ghost Is the New Normal (coming 2017)

Maze Beset Trilogy

superheroes in denim

Dragons In Pieces

Dragons In Chains

Dragons In Flight

Anthology Appearances

Into the Woods: a fantasy anthology

Merely This and Nothing More: Poe Goes Punk

Unnatural Dragons: a science fiction anthology

Missing Pieces VIII: short stories from GenCon's Authors Avenue

(coming August 2016)

Non-fiction

with Jeffrey Cook

Working the Table: An Indie Author's Guide to Conventions

Erik Kort

(as Erik Marshall)

Wards of the Thicket

adventure fantasy

Children Without Faces

Children Without Voices (coming 2017)

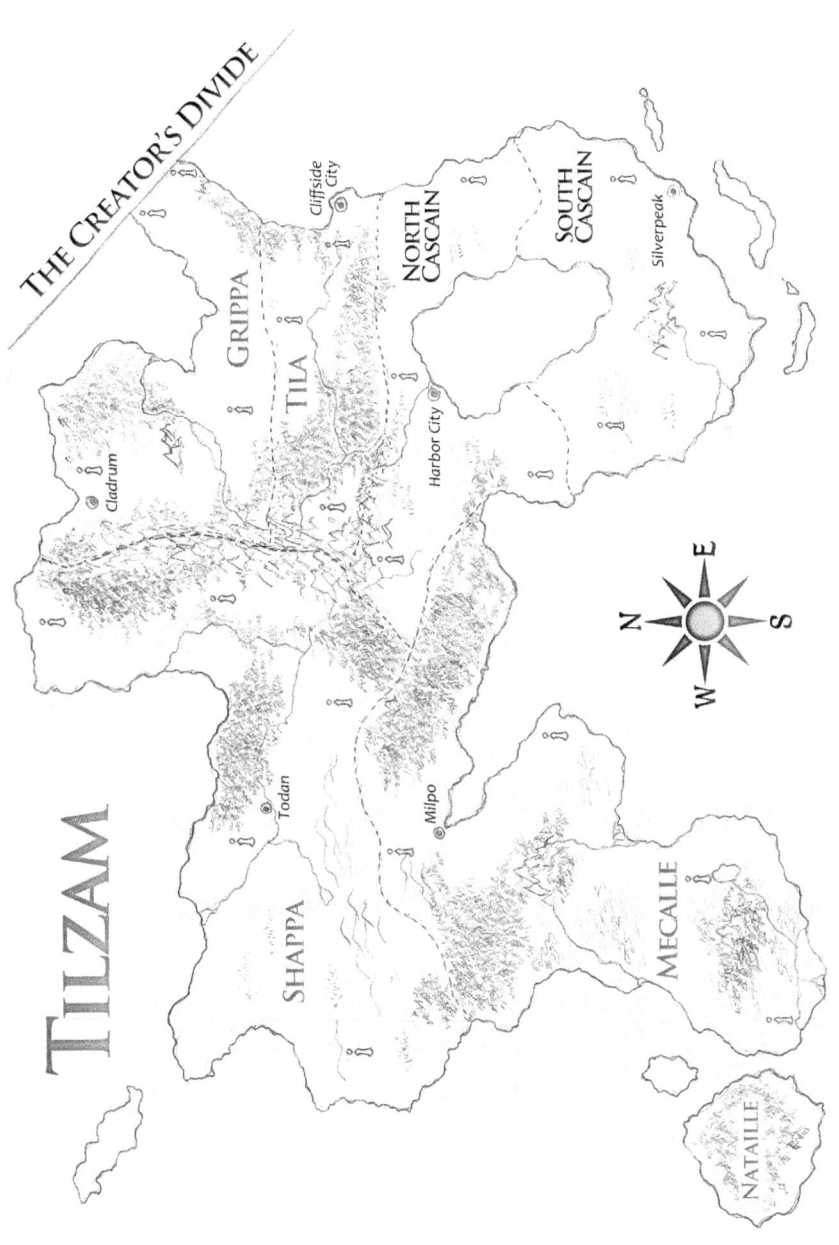

Chapter 1

"Excellent."

Chavali did not consider this a proper response to the current situation. Why Eldrack sent her with this madman, she had no idea, because he clearly suffered from at least four kinds of derangement. Although she'd carefully avoided touching him, and thus hadn't sampled his thoughts, he played the part of a lunatic more than half the time. Such as now.

"This is a grand opportunity to get some hands-on experience with everything you've been practicing, Chavali." Algie smiled brightly, holding his hands up in surrender. He did this because three men with blades held weapons on the pair of them. Another two stood in the tall grasses off the side of the road with bows ready to fire.

Chavali held her hands up, too, facing the five men. "Is it?" Although she had no intention whatsoever of giving anything up to some band of thieves, Algie's desire to fight them left a sour taste in her mouth.

"Yes," the more senior Fallen nodded gleefully, "I think so."

"Shut up," the apparent leader snarled as he approached. "Quit yer yapping, halfbreed, and hand over what you've got."

"His manners are quite poor," Chavali observed dryly. She had fear of these men. If any of them had great skill, they wouldn't be out here, harassing travelers for whatever coin they might carry. Choosing her and Algie as targets did give her concerns about how far they might go, given they had neither horses nor any other outward signs of wealth. Care needed to be employed. Algie might not agree.

"This," the leader shouted, "is a robbery! You give us whatever you have, and we let you live!" He desperately wanted them to take him seriously. Desperately.

Instead of doing so, Chavali lowered her hands and clenched them into fists, which she planted on her hips. "So you say. What if we intend to rob you instead?" Her eyes flicked about, noting the position of the sun in the cloudless sky, judging the distance to a stand of trees nearby, and considering if that low hill ahead might be close enough to use somehow.

"We certainly could," Algie agreed, sounding serious and thoughtful for the first time since they left the Tower yesterday. "I could take three of them, that leaves two for you. You can take two of these idiots. Rush the archers and I'll handle the rest."

The leader's eyes popped with indignation. "You can't just stand there and discuss—" He made an angry, frustrated noise. "Tactics!" The word exploded from his mouth. "You're talking about tactics for fighting us right in front of us!"

Snaking her hand out, Chavali patted the leader's cheek hard enough to smart. "You poor thing. All out of control and about to die." In the brief snatch of contact, the spirits showed her his thoughts: no different from his words and actions. This bandit bit off more than he could chew and groped for how to handle it without losing face among his men. They wouldn't follow a leader who couldn't lead.

Algie took that as a signal and wrapped an arm around her waist. A blast of magical power pushed outward from them, knocking the three men back on the dusty road. He shoved her towards the archers, and since she expected it, she used the momentum he provided to throw herself at the remaining two men. Too stunned to react, the idiots stood there as she plowed into both—one with a shoulder and arm, the other with her hip and knee.

Tumbling to the ground with them, she pulled her knife and rolled to be clear if either managed to attack in return. One of the archers hit his head hard enough to make him slow to stir. The other dropped his bow and rolled onto his hands and knees. "Head up, Chavali," Algie called out cheerfully, "don't lose your advantage!"

She ignored him and flung herself at the archer again, keeping him on the ground with her. All she'd learned so far covered only the most basic ways to use the small blade in her hand. If it got to be a fair fight, it wouldn't go well for her.

"The most important thing to remember is, unless you're up against a child, you're probably going to be facing someone bigger and stronger than you." Eliot's gloved hand wrapped her fingers around the dagger she didn't want to be holding, because it reminded her too much of the knife she killed herself with. He understood that, but still wanted her to use it. She'd tire too easily with something heavier. *"You have to learn to use*

3

their strength against them instead of relying on your own. Surprise and distractions are your best friends. And when all else fails, kick them in the balls."

If only Eliot traveled with her instead of Algie. Not only did the more subtle and sensible man not cackle like a mad goat, he wouldn't have been ambushed in the first place. Even if it did still happen, they would fight side by side, not separately. He'd have her back. Algie's actions did not, in her opinion, constitute "having her back."

This archer was, as she already knew, bigger and stronger than her, and she didn't bother trying to resist as he grabbed her forearms, safely covered by her long sleeves, and rolled her onto her back. He made the mistake of not pinning her skirts down, which left her free to use her knee on his most sensitive parts. His reaction to the impact struck her as somewhat comical. She took advantage of his momentary weakness to stab her dagger into his side as he curled up and rolled off her.

Without checking his thoughts, she couldn't be sure he meant to kill her. Not that she cared in the heat of a battle. He went down for the moment and the second archer came around. She swung her legs around to kick him wherever she could reach. It turned out to be his hip, which fouled his still disjointed efforts to get up and made him grunt.

"No, Chavali, stab two or three times, not once." Algie's voice grated on her nerves, rising up over the sounds of his own struggles with the other three men.

"You bitch," the one now curled up and bleeding wheezed out. While he scooted farther away and the other archer got to his hands and knees, Chavali threaded her fingers through the spirits, willing them to create a copy of Eliot, running up to help.

Algie, as it turned out, had expertise in the matter of crafting illusions. After merely a day and a half of putting up with the half-elf's idiotically over-pleasant instruction, the quality of the images she could produce had vastly improved. Before becoming Fallen, she used illusions only to enhance storytelling. Now, she needed to use them to enhance her fighting skills. That took precision and control over shading and tone, two things she actually could see. The colors themselves...she couldn't perceive any of that, but Algie enjoyed helping her fine-tune them (enjoyed it a little too much, in her opinion).

This illusory Eliot had flaws. She didn't have time to put enough concentration into his creation for perfection. That would take an hour, at least, until she had more practice. It could still fool two men already hurt and distracted by an angry armed woman. The one with the stab wound gasped and wriggled away from Illusory Eliot, which brought him back toward her. The other stared stupidly at the fake newcomer, eyes wide and fearful.

With a new opportunity, Chavali swung her dagger and applied a second stab wound to the already bleeding archer, then a third, higher up where it would hopefully hit something important. Three freely bleeding gashes ought to finish him, she thought, and if they didn't, they certainly ought to keep him out of trouble long enough for her to take care of the other one. That other archer scrambled away from the still approaching Eliot, enough sense recovered to keep him from heading straight for Chavali, too.

No matter how daft it seemed to chase the man down, Chavali got to her feet to do it anyway. Eliot circled around to keep him off balance. She threw a kick at his neck, but it missed and only clipped his shoulder. If she wore lesser footwear, it probably would have hurt, but her sturdy walking boots could take such abuse. The man flinched with a whine and grabbed his shoulder.

"Please don't kill me." His voice cracked in high pitched panic.

"Be silent." Grabbing his hair with her free hand, Chavali pulled his head up and back. This restrained him well enough, but she reached around his neck and lay her blade across it for good measure. Only then did she check on Algie. There he was, having the time of his life, beating the snot out of three men at once as they surrounded him. His stick—not nearly long enough to be a staff but too thin to be a club, and possessing a handle jutting out perpendicular to its two foot length—whipped around him, clacking on their blades and thumping on their bodies. He used his skill with magic to augment the stick's impact and his own ability with it, or so he claimed.

If nothing else, she did have to admit he used his chosen weapon with artistry. They had no hope of getting through to hit him, yet they stayed in the fight. Perhaps that was his true talent: duping his foes into thinking they had a chance. He employed it with obvious relish. His eyes caught hers for a moment and flashed with a rather disturbing amount of bloodlust and far too much madness in his gleeful grin.

As soon as they broke eye contact, he ducked down and flung a hand out, a thin line of blue-white power whipping out from his fingertips. That line flew from him and hit each man half an inch above the knees, cutting deeply into their flesh and forcing them all to the ground with shrieks of pain. Algie's expression went wild and feral for a moment, then he shivered with pleasure and settled back into pleasant cheer.

"Why did you not do that in the first place?" Chavali kept the blade at the archer's throat and her fingers curled in the man's greasy hair.

"Efficiency." Plucking a sword from a bandit's hand, he used it to stab the man in the chest. "Why did you take a prisoner?"

Turning away to avoid watching Algie butcher the three men, Chavali sneered in distaste. "Dead men have very little to say."

"Ah, yes. Good thinking." She heard him stab the next man, and the third blubbered, begging for his life. "You'll want to get him on his knees," Algie said loudly, talking over the noise. "It's proper information gathering stance. You can slice his throat from behind easier, then, which is how you avoid getting blood all over yourself."

Chavali saw a distinct difference between killing a man who actively tried very hard to kill you first and slaughtering a man who offered no resistance or true threat. She could live with the former. The latter bothered her. No doubt, these men all deserved it ten times over for what they'd done up to now, but the notion of sitting judgment over them when she knew nothing of their other crimes left a distinctly unpleasant taste in her mouth.

Despite her feelings on this, she yanked her prisoner by the hair to get him to kneel for her, dismissing the illusory Eliot as she did so. "If he cooperates, he need not die."

Algie giggled at her. "They're animals, Chavali. Men who choose to prey on those weaker than themselves aren't worthy of mercy."

"Perhaps not," she admitted, "but if anyone understands the notion of second chances, it should be us." Letting go of his hair, she put her hand on his neck and let the spirits wash over him. They drank greedily, shoving his thoughts at her. For the moment, he did nothing more than panic and pray to the Creator.

Giving a little shrug, Algie stooped to rifle through the pockets of the men he just killed, blood still oozing from their fresh wounds. "This is a distraction and we have nowhere to chain him up."

"Quiet," she snapped at the half-elf, then turned her attention to her prisoner. The man perched on his knees, head hanging as much as he dared to let it with her knife at his neck, hands resting on his thighs to help hold himself up. Putting her mouth close to his ear, she murmured, "The Creator will not save you now. How long have you been doing this, robbing people on the road?"

I've been doing this so long I don't know the answer.

He managed nothing more than a whimper from his mouth, but his mind said enough. "Long enough not to remember. I see. You must be, what, twenty-some summers?"

I don't know that for sure, either. Twenty-one is my best guess. With the thoughts came fleeting images of life in a city, where he had to beg and scrape for everything.

"Ah, an orphan."

How do you know that?

"So, you have been doing this for perhaps ten or fifteen years, and somehow, we are the first travelers you ever encountered willing and able to fight back. And now your brothers in spirit are dead." Her eyes flicked over to the other archer, still breathing heavily and ignored by Algie. "Or dying," she added. "You beg for your life, why should I spare it? My partner will be happy to feed your blood to the ground. It is only me standing between you and your death."

"Please don't kill me." His voice, barely more than a whisper, cracked, and she could see his eyes dart all around to match the rising panic of his thoughts. "I'll..." *I'll do anything, agree to anything.*

"Yes, I believe you would agree to anything at all if it would save your neck." Crouching down beside him, she pulled the knife away while leaving her other hand touching him. "I less believe you would *do* anything."

The man kneeling on the ground looked up at her, pathetic submission plain on his face. "Please," he managed to force himself to say out loud. His thoughts couldn't calm down now that he knew she could sense them. His mind jumped around, a jumbled up mash of awe and terror and begging and despair.

"If I grant you your life," she asked him in a purr, "what will you do with it?"

Whatever you tell me to. "I don't know."

She smirked. "As honest an answer as I could hope for." Looking over to Algie, who watched with amusement, she raised her voice to address him. "How far is it to the town?"

He shrugged. "Atrica is an hour's walk, give or take." With a bright smile, he added, "I have rope."

Chavali snorted. "That will not be necessary." Her attention went back to her prisoner and she raised an eyebrow, still choosing to be amused over bothered by Algie. "Will it?"

He shook his head almost violently. "No. No, ma'am." *Life debt. You have mine.*

"Good. First, let us speak for a moment about your soul." In her periphery, she caught Algie actually looking surprised, swiftly followed by keen interest. "You have noticed I can tap your thoughts if I wish to."

His mind admitted he grasped this, his head nodded, and he started leaping to all the conclusions she wanted him to. "Yes, you understand well enough. Keep that in mind as you consider what options are open to you."

He would chase nightmares of her eating his soul and similar such ideas for some time to come, so she pulled her hand away. "Come," she stood and beckoned for him to do the same. "We have a town to reach and only our feet to take us there."

"You know, you're really just delaying the inevitable," Algie said as he stood also, having finished checking through the other archer's pockets. "As soon as they see him, they'll realize what he is and take him off our hands for execution."

The archer gulped and put his hands up. "He's right. You could—" He licked his lips nervously. "—let me go. By myself, I can't do any harm."

"You must take us for fools," Chavali huffed. Both men did have a point, but for the moment, she refused to acknowledge either. Instead, she chose to see the archer as an impudent child in need of management. She grabbed his ear and pulled. "Get moving."

The archer made a few distressed noises but obediently heeled. His thoughts showed disappointment that she didn't fall for the notion of letting him go, but not surprise. The idea of actually working for a living at a regular, grinding job grated at him, even though the alternative seemed to be death. She let go of his ear when his mind settled on a plan: he would cooperate at least until they reached the town. At that point, he would try to run away, and she couldn't say for sure that she cared.

"I love working with you," Algie chirped in his most annoying, singsongiest voice.

"Wonderful," Chavali sighed as she set the fastest pace she could manage. The sooner this wretchedly ridiculous mission ended, the better. "What is your name?" she snapped at their prisoner.

"Harris. Um, will I be able to have my bow back before you let me go?"

Chavali said "yes" at the same time Algie said "no", and the two of them stopped and looked at each other. She lifted an eyebrow and glared, he smiled cheerfully. "At least let him have something," she grumbled. "A man with nothing covets everything."

"I like that," Algie told them, and he repeated the saying a few times. "It has a nice ring to it, sounds lofty without being pompous. Where did you hear it?"

"Who cares where I heard it?" Chavali's temper danced on the edge of exploding and she knew it. He didn't, of course, mean to remind her of her clan—who were nearly all slaughtered not so long ago—by asking such an idiotic question, as he didn't know about her clan. Or, if he did, he knew very little and had no reason to ascribe sayings to them. This did not assuage her anger with him in the slightest. "The point is that he needs a means to survive."

Apparently unfazed by her continuing to snap at him, Algie shrugged and started walking again. Chavali and Harris followed. "He can have a knife. I have an extra."

Delicately, Harris cleared his throat. "I'm an archer." Chavali had to give him credit for not whining.

"Seems it's time to learn a new weapon, then." Algie beamed at him. "Stagnation is death, after all."

The statement dealt Chavali a body blow, a much fiercer reminder of everyone she lost the day she died. It formed the basis of the clan's entire philosophy, their entire outlook on life. Stagnation is Death, the creeping doom that climbs into your lap and smothers you like a warm pillow. To have it slip out of his mouth made her steps falter as if she tripped over a rock. Everything else she wanted to do, she stifled down to keep inside. No need to hand Algie this kind of information about her. That went doubly for the other man.

Harris sighed heavily, a sound of defeat and acquiescence. If he noticed her falter, it didn't show. "What are you actually going to do with me, then?"

Algie shrugged, unconcerned. Chavali rubbed her forehead to mask the effort she made to hide her emotions, but she didn't bother trying to hide the wince. With the fight over and the short walk ended for the moment, she noticed all the aches and pains creeping up from the frenzied minute of action. Her shoulder and hip, where she initially hit the two men, throbbed. Somewhere in there, she managed to cut her lip and hit a few other parts. Even her foot hurt inside her boot, probably from kicking the man whose life, more or less, now rested in her hands.

"Do you have any other skills at all, besides shooting people and taking their things?" She asked to stall him while her body ached more with each passing moment.

Harris gulped and flicked his eyes to Algie's knife, which he hadn't been given yet. "I know how to deal with the unpleasant aftereffects of combat."

Algie tittered with amusement. "Poor Chavali."

She took a step and slapped Algie across the face. He more than deserved it. "You are coming with us," she growled at Harris and stalked off.

Behind her, she heard Algie say, "I think I'll go ahead and agree with her." The ass still sounded pleasant and cheery. She must not have hit him hard enough.

"That seems like a good plan," Harris said with a little cough.

Chapter 2

The two men kept quiet the rest of the way to the town, which Chavali considered a blessing. Algie didn't even hum to himself. They could see and smell Atrica well before reaching where it perched beside a swell in the river running down to the ocean in the distance. "What did we need here? The word Eldrack used, I do not remember it."

"The cobbler," Algie supplied. Perhaps that slap had done its job after all, because he sounded much less irritating than before. "It's a person."

Harris flicked his eyes up to Chavali's face as she glanced over her shoulder to check that he didn't now have Algie at knifepoint. He'd probably spent the last half hour examining her backside in detail. The dress she wore didn't particularly outline her rear, but it did give a man something look at. "Why are you going to Atrica for a shoemaker?"

"None of your business," Chavali threw at him.

"It's just that Atrica is a tiny little place in the middle of nowhere. There are lots of better places to get shoes. Bigger places, places with more skilled craftspeople, places where they infuse shoes with magic, all kinds of things. Why come to this dinky fishing village when you could go anywhere?"

Algie let a giggle slip. "My dear boy, do use your head."

"What do you mean?"

"Chavali, dear, he's good looking, but not too bright." Algie giggled again, edging toward hysterics. The man must have snorted something that killed half his mind at some point, or maybe he died from having his head split open. Some of his brains may have been irretrievably lost when the Fallen collected his body. She could certainly see why someone would want to crush his skull.

"I'm right here, you know."

"Yes, you really are."

Chavali glared at the ground ahead of her and growled at them both. "We are going to Atrica to visit a cobbler because we are going to Atrica to visit a cobbler." Thankfully, this shut them both up for a minute.

"Have you decided what to do with me yet?"

Stopping in her tracks, Chavali threw a dangerous smile on her face and clapped her hands together while she turned around. "Yes. I am going to kill you myself, with my bare hands."

He had the gall to grin at her. "I'm down for that, so long as there'll be rolling around on the ground as part of it." Pulling the collar of his shirt down, he stretched his neck to offer it. "Take your time, because I want to watch you sitting on top of me with your hands on me for as long as I can. Preferably enjoying it."

Chavali had no answer for a reaction so ridiculous. She hated that feeling. A quiet growling noise hung in the back of her throat as she stared him down, unwilling to let him have the last word. To her satisfaction, his grin faltered and he stopped holding his head and shirt to make it easier for her to choke him. "You can come with us, but only if you stop asking questions about why we are here and what we are doing."

"Is that wise, Chavali?" That Algie would question her wisdom felt farcical, but she considered his point anyway. Despite the singsong voice.

Her eyes didn't leave Harris, who continued to wither under her gaze. "Letting him go will only get him killed or others robbed, and I would rather see his soul bound and him used than either of those outcomes."

"Wait, what?" He put up his hands to ward her off and took a step back. "No one said anything about binding souls."

Chavali matched his step and gestured to Algie. Thankfully, he nodded and slipped around behind Harris. "You have a choice in the matter, of course." While she crowded him from the front, Algie did the same from behind, leaving him nowhere to go. "We can kill you instead."

She had his attention, fully and completely, and he gulped. "Uh, no, I'd really rather not do that."

"I am glad to hear this." Close enough now to touch him, she reached out and tapped his nose, then leaned in to be face to face with him. To convince him to police himself, she needed to be close enough to kiss him. Or hit him with her skull. "Algie is right, you are good looking. It would be a shame to waste that. Just remember, Harris, I have tasted your soul. There is no rock you can crawl under, no place you can hide that I will not be able to find and drag you out. If I have to do that," she lowered her voice to a soft whisper, "you will wish you were dead. For a very long time."

She watched his eyes go wide, felt his breath come out in short little puffs, and heard his heartbeat speed up. With this skill, the manipulation of people, she had few peers. It was wrong and she knew it and she didn't care. Some people were meant to be shining beacons of righteousness, like Colby. Everyone else lived in the real world, where people had to get the job done with whatever tools happened to be at their disposal.

He nodded, definitely terrified of her. Under that, he also found her attractive. "I understand," he whimpered, and she believed him.

"Good." Pulling away, she flicked her eyes down to his feet and back up to his face to give him the impression she thought about what she might do with his body. His mind would fill in her intentions with things both pleasant and unpleasant, and it would be a mistake on her part to clarify which she actually considered. With that, she turned her back on him and started walking again, knowing he'd follow like a whipped dog now, especially with Algie there to provide incentive.

A grin curled her lips when she heard him scramble to keep up with her, and the lack of chatter following in her wake lifted her mood tremendously. The noise of the small town a short time later actually felt welcome, in a fashion. People busied about their work, pausing only to take a quick look at the strangers, then returning to their tasks. Certainly, the three of them would be the stuff of rumor tonight, but the townsfolk could make up whatever they wanted without wasting time gawking.

The town lay on one side of the river with farming fields on the other. The three of them crossed the stone bridge draped with fishing nets to reach the cluster of buildings huddled together that comprised the town. It surprised Chavali that it had no ring of even a small stone fence or some other sort of minor defensive structure. In all her years traveling with her clan, they encountered very few places where no sort of precautions were taken at all. These people were likely open and trusting, then, and this would be a very simple matter.

In the center of all the buildings stood an open air market. The cobbler probably wouldn't be found there. A long building ran down one side of it, but Chavali didn't see any obvious shops. The town wouldn't get visitors here often enough to care about whether travelers could find anything. She scanned the market and didn't see anyone selling shoes or shoe-like things, so she went for a boy she spotted doing nothing in particular.

He probably stood guard over the covered basket at his feet, and seemed to be watching for someone, likely whoever put him in charge of the basket. "Excuse me," she said with a very fake friendly smile, "I am looking for your local cobbler."

The boy, probably twelve or thirteen years old, stared at her. He said something to her in Meccallish, but she didn't speak more than a few words of it, only enough to recognize it. Behind her, Harris answered him, and he and the boy had a short conversation, ending with the boy pointing at the long building and Harris thanking him.

"He says it's in there, towards the other end. Master Pratic." Harris nodded towards the building.

"More than a pretty face," Algie chirped.

"Indeed." She had nothing else to say at the moment, and found herself mildly pleased she didn't kill the archer. Also, threatening his soul had been a good idea. Leading the way into and through the building, she passed shelves and tables with wares of various types, mostly for fishing or farming or weaving. As Harris said, she found the cobbler towards the other end.

Master Pratic sat in the middle of an array of shoes and boots, half new, half awaiting repair. His cramped "shop" had crates of shoes instead of tidy arrangements, and tools scattered about him. The cobbler himself had a shock of white hair sticking out at odd angles and didn't appear to have been cut all the same length. Bushy eyebrows, a sparse beard, numerous creases in his face, and small, beady eyes made him seem an elder lunatic in Chavali's eyes. The leather apron attested to some amount of sense, at least.

Chavali walked right up and rapped with a knuckle on his work table to get his attention. "Do you speak Shappan?"

Blinking rapidly, he looked up from his task of patching a heel and nodded. His eyes scanned her body, lingering rather longer on her chest then she considered polite. "Yes, miss, some. Not too fast."

"I am here for wood carved roses." Two days ago, Eldrack told her to come here and ask for this, specifically, and not to leave until the cobbler produced them. She had a very exact number of coins in a small pouch for the express purpose of paying for them. "They are ten gold pieces, five silvers, and three coppers, yes?" Why this thing from this man in this place, she had no idea. Her job, however, did not include worrying about "why."

More blinking left her wondering if Master Pratic had an infirmity in his eyes. "You want what?"

"Harris, translate," she grumbled.

The archer did as he was told, and the two men had a conversation that went on rather longer than Chavali thought necessary. She crossed her arms and gave Harris a pointedly impatient look, one that made him put up a hand to stave her off. The discussion went a few exchanges longer, then he shrugged and told her, "He's confused why you came to a cobbler for that. I don't have an answer for him."

Although she didn't feel particularly impatient, she made herself look such as she addressed the cobbler again. "Do you have them or not?" To emphasize her unwillingness to be waved away by a refusal, she pulled out the money pouch and dropped it on the table with a clink of coins. Master Pratic's attention, as expected, focused on the pouch, and Chavali put her hand on it. "It is for you, to pay for them."

For a moment, he seemed torn, then he turned and rummaged in a crate at his feet. When he resurfaced half a minute later, he had a cheap wooden box in his hands which he set on the table and pushed towards her. "Ten gold, five silver, three copper."

Chavali pulled the lid off the box and checked inside. It held several of what appeared to be wooden roses, exquisitely carved by a deft, skilled hand with painstaking attention to detail. To be sure it wasn't an illusion, she dipped her hand in and pulled one out, lifting it up to examine it. Oddly, it carried a rose's sweet musk, but she could think of several possible explanations for that. More importantly, it appeared this box contained what they came for, and she replaced the rose, covered the box again, and picked it up.

"Thank you. Good day." With that, she walked away, leaving the pouch behind. This strange mission didn't end until they got the box to Eldrack and made a report. Then she wouldn't have to deal with Algie anymore. If only this town offered horses for sale, the trip home could be faster. Another day and a half of his insanity might drive her to murder him.

21

"What was that about?" Harris's voice didn't break the silence between them until they'd crossed the bridge and gotten far enough away to not be overheard by anyone working in their fields. With him around, she might actually be able to avoid killing Algie, if only because someone else could take his attention part of the time.

Algie giggled. "We may never know," he told Harris. "Our masters are a mysterious lot. They send us here and there, most anywhere, and we do as we're told without asking too many questions. Questions can get you killed, you know. Here, watch. This one might be the end of me. Chavali," he said louder, "do you mean to take Harris to the Tower?"

Did she? "Yes," she nodded without looking back.

"How fascinating." Algie sounded delighted, and he clapped with all the excitement of a toddler gifted a new toy. "Allow me the honors of explaining what he's gotten himself into."

Instead of answering verbally, she waved a hand to signal her acquiescence. As the senior Fallen between them, Algie technically had the lead on this mission, but he'd deferred to her for almost everything since they started out. Perhaps his leadership style involved forcing someone else to make all the decisions, though she rather suspected Eldrack told him to treat her this way for one reason or another. It may have been solely a consideration for Algie's personal safety.

"Excellent. You see, Harris, we have stolen your life along with your soul. The moment you chose to participate in an attack on us, you were doomed, one way or another. All your friends died there, but you get to sacrifice your life for a cause. Isn't that wonderful?"

"Uh." Chavali grinned at Harris's response, and even had to stifle a chuckle. He had no idea what he stepped in, and now found himself in it for the long haul whether he wanted to be or not. Better yet, he'd taken Algie's attention. "I don't quite...uh...follow."

"That's alright," Algie told him cheerfully. "Eldrack will explain it in more detail, provided he doesn't decide to kill you, and then you can work for us under threat of a horrible disease that will kill you slowly if you so much as think too hard about betraying us. The basic idea is we're working towards Reunion, following directions that are sometimes just as odd as those we came with today, and sometimes make perfect, complete sense."

Harris didn't answer that right away, but something made Algie stay quiet and let the poor man think. Chavali glanced back, saw both men's faces, and smirked. As annoying and insane as Algie was, he could be rather pleasantly competent and capable. Those were two traits the Fallen tended to have, a fact she found rather balanced out that she had to die once to become part of it.

Only Algie's madness broke the quiet in spurts for the rest of the day. Chavali distracted herself from him by practicing her illusions, making horses clop alongside them. Sound made the images much more complex and difficult to produce properly, and she didn't quite have the hang of it yet. As soon as the sound started up, the image faded, and when she tried to get it back, the sound died. Algie's random observations about things only he could see or hear didn't help, but she knew she needed to be able to do this under duress and so didn't snap at him.

Algie picked out a spot for camping. Harris let himself be tasked with starting a fire while Chavali and Algie went about setting up a camp around him. Harris finally had something else to say after a dinner of smoked meat, apples, and cheese.

He stared at the flames, a mug of warm tea in his hands. "Why did you guys join up with this group you're taking me to be forcibly inducted into?"

Chavali looked at her own mug. "Until you are bound, we cannot tell you the specifics. Suffice to say that few agents join because they genuinely want to. One woman's chaff is another's treasure, though, yes?"

Nodding, he took a sip of his tea. "I suppose so. What did you do before you got this job?"

Her eyes lifted again, to study his face. One eyebrow arched suspiciously as she flicked her gaze to Algie and back. The half-elf pretended not to be listening, and he did so well, but she could see the conversation amused him. Now she had to decide whether to lead Harris on or squash him flat. At this point, it would serve her best if he believed she saved him because of interest in him, rather than only to avoid the unpleasantness of killing in cold blood. It could be considered a reward of sorts, for being helpful in Atrica, though he'd only enjoy it until she dropped him into Eldrack's lap.

"I was an entertainer, part of a troupe."

"Ah." Harris nodded. "And they wanted you for this job?"

"I was not *only* an entertainer. That is merely my most marketable and pleasant skill set."

That answer satisfied him, and he had to think his picture of her complete, or nearly so. "What's with the feather?"

Frankly, it surprised her that it took him this long to say something about the pink feather grafted into her forehead and surrounded by a floral tattoo. People frequently stared at it while speaking to her, and given more than a few minutes of exposure, nearly everyone said something about it, either as a question or a comment. He lasted a few hours. "I am eccentric."

He stared at her for a few seconds, then laughed. Algie took the opportunity to fall over giggling, which made Harris laugh more. She drank her tea and let them laugh and giggle to their hearts' content.

A few minutes later, Harris calmed down and Algie muttered to himself in his blankets. At least they only needed to put up with some random noises from him at this point, and only until he fell asleep. Harris watched her while she sat and ignored him, sipping her tea and mulling over the fight. The illusion worked, it did the job she needed it to do. Still, she got lucky. If the two archers hadn't already been distracted and disoriented, they wouldn't have been fooled by it.

"You look really serious." His words made her look up at him, to see he had that softened expression of a man considering how best to put space between a woman and her undergarments. She let him see a hint of interest, but not enough to make pressing his luck tonight seem plausible. The mug in her hands also sat as a buffer between them. Assuming he picked up on subtleties. In her experience, men rarely did.

"I have been accused of this before."

He grinned. "I'm sure. Can I ask you about your accent? I've never heard one like it before."

"Have you been many places?"

"No," he admitted, his grin faltering, "not really. Just Meccalle. But I've heard a lot of different travelers, and you're unique."

"That I am." She smirked behind her mug, choosing to focus on how much she looked forward to seeing Danel, Haizea, and Biholtz after she reported to Eldrack. The visit would be pure pleasure, a time to revel in what little she truly had in this second life.

He waited, amused by the answer and watching her expectantly. "And you're not answering the question."

Giving a light snort of amusement, she pulled her mug away to let him really see the smirk. "This is also true."

When she said nothing else, he sat and stared at her for a short time, then cracked a grin. "I see. That's how it's going to be. Alright, I can roll with that. I guess you're staying up for the first watch, so I'll get some sleep."

On the way down, she and Algie hadn't set watches. Instead, they'd slept in out-of-the-way holes others wouldn't stumble over. With Harris here, though, she could see the value and wisdom of not merely leaving their necks exposed to him. For all she knew, he would pretend to sleep and run away from them as soon as she drifted off.

She watched him make a show of bedding down—pulling his shirt off and making sure she got a good eyeful, fluffing up what he had that passed for a pillow, and wriggling around to be comfortable. He thought he had her attention. He didn't. While he had pleasant features, even with the scars that only made sense given what she knew of his life, she felt close to nothing towards him. Harris held no more interest for her than a cheap piece of art.

Chapter 3

Eventually, once she felt certain Harris actually slept, Chavali followed suit. When she woke, Algie had breakfast ready and Harris still lay there, stirring from sleep. Not long after, they walked again, Chavali still leading the two men. The time passed with Harris making stabs at idle chatter intended to get her to talk about herself. He failed. She gave him nothing to work with. By midday, he gave up and she suspected he spent the rest of the walk until they reached the Creator's Tower watching her behind.

"I'm afraid we don't have any spare cloaks," Algie said with a bright smile, as if this amused him a great deal. "We're going to Shappa."

"Which had plenty of snow on the ground when we left." Chavali showed her ring to the guardians of the Tower, then pulled her own cloak, scarf, and mittens out of her small pack. "It is only an hour walk or so, though. You are man enough for this, yes?"

If the guardian found that amusing, they'd never know for all the armor covering him up. Harris, on the other hand, tried to fake bravado for her. "Sure, that's not such a big deal. Hey, I prance naked in weather just a little warmer than this."

Algie slapped him in the face. It took Chavali off-guard, as it he didn't do anything of the sort up to now. Aside from the fight that yielded Harris in the first place, he barely hurt a fly for the whole trip. His hand dropped to his side and Algie gave Harris a mad grin. "Don't disrespect the weather, little boy!" He darted into the Tower with an odd skipping gait.

Blinking, Chavali watched him go, but she'd been stoic in the face of worse before. Reaching over with her already mittened hand, she grabbed Harris and tugged to get him going. "They will loan you something on the other side. We have an arrangement with them."

Harris stared stupidly after Algie, rubbing his face and letting her pull him along. His eyes slid up the hollow Tower to the blue crystal five hundred feet overhead like he'd never seen any of this before, so she let him cling to her hand despite the gleam in Algie's eyes as they reached him, waiting impatiently to trigger the transport.

"Aw, that's so cute," Algie said. His eyes fixed on their hands and he gave a little sigh that reminded Chavali of matchmaking teenage girls. She ignored it. Harris didn't say anything, but a fool's grin spread across his face.

As with the few other times she'd traveled this way before, something hooked into her belly and pulled with a twist for a second or two, then they stood in the frigid cold. Harris made a soft gagging noise as he glommed onto her, presumably for warmth. Someone else might have enjoyed the closeness; Chavali did not. Without giving him a warning, she started moving, jerking him along behind her.

Getting him a cloak to use required nothing more than pulling a mitten off and showing her ring. The guardians knew it would be returned within a few days and didn't make a fuss. Once he had that, she pushed to get him going and they followed a plowed path in the snow straight to Cloverdale. Horses like Colby's Karias, a behemoth of a creature well suited to such labor, made this path. Fallen agents on missions comprised most of the traffic through here. The villagers also went places from time to time, for trade or other purposes.

Harris wound up walking beside her, sending Algie to the rear and giving her a buffer that muffled the half-elf's obnoxious humming. With the cloak, she knew the archer's had nothing to stare at from behind, which explained him electing to travel beside her. About halfway through the woods between Cloverdale and the Creator's Tower, he finally said something.

"This would be a really good place to set up an ambush."

Chavali laughed at the idea. "That would be a mistake of the kind a person does not recover from. Tell me, would such an ambush fare well against people such as myself and Algie?"

He opened his mouth, but shut it without saying anything and looked around more, thoughtful. "I suppose it depends on the ambush."

"Indeed." Her laughter faded in the face of his gravity. "We are not so foolish as to leave the wood unguarded. Anyone attempting to stage anywhere near here would find it no easy task. Between our efforts and those of the Order of the Creator's Path, this is not a place to worry about personal safety."

Harris nodded his understanding. "We must be getting close, then? This is a lot of ground to cover."

Something struck her as odd about the question, something that made her wary. Instead of following her impulse to yank off a mitten and grab him by the neck, she gave him a smirk and kept an eye on him. "Indeed." Did she meet him by chance after all? No one could have guessed she would choose to spare this one of those five men, nor that in doing so, she would bring him back with her. Not unless they had a gift like hers, but that didn't seem probable from how people reacted to her.

Pulling her mitten off, she took his bare hand in her own on the pretense of warming it. "You keep asking about me and my employer, yet you say very little of yourself. Do you feel there is nothing of interest in your background, or are you merely disinclined to reveal it?"

"I'd be delighted to reveal as much of myself as you want." His thoughts traveled along the familiar paths of a man interested in a woman for everything below her neck and very little above. Nothing of import lurked under this. He felt the chill, had a bit of pleasure at the fact she seemed to be warming up to him, and hoped he didn't find his death at the end of the journey.

"Really. What pushed you into banditry? Besides the overall unpleasantness of your youth, there must have been some specific event that triggered the decision to join that band, to learn archery and use it to rob people." Scenes pushed the playful lust away, of a childhood spent on the streets. His mentor, an older boy he thought of as a brother, kept him safe until he could take care of himself. A guardsman caught a younger boy and the rest of the gang attacked to get him free. The leader of a bandit group came along as they hid to avoid the aftermath and promised willing women to teenage boys. He and his brother signed up at once.

His expression went somber and he sighed. "There was a boy,

Caleb." His thoughts focused on the incident with the guardsman, about which he felt both justified and horrified at the same time. The memory lay deep in his past, dulled by the passage of time, and he felt it had been pivotal. "We were just dumb street kids, no parents, no one but each other. There were eight of us. We looked out for each other. You probably grew up thinking the streets are pretty safe, but I didn't. There's a stinking underbelly in any city, a place where kids are toys, bought and sold under the noses of the city guard."

His free hand reached up to scratch idly at his cheek, a gesture showing his general discomfort, showing how much he didn't want to talk about it. He pressed on only because he thought she genuinely wanted to know, and this might earn him more of her favor. Some people might consider it rude to keep manipulating him this way, but Chavali considered it business. Eldrack would do worse to him, though he'd do it politely and with a sympathetic smile. Her way was superior, if only because Harris got to fantasize about something pleasant in exchange for selling his soul to her. So to speak.

The memory played in his mind. Caleb disappeared, and the rest of the boys tried to expose those who'd taken him. The guardsman who arrived too late missed all the obvious evidence, instead blaming Caleb and, to a lesser extent, Harris's gang, for the depredations of an unscrupulous man. They killed the guardsman and then turned on each other in the aftermath. The path of his life made sense in that context, though he surely could have made different choices if he wanted to.

Into the silence he left, not wanting to put the incident into words, Chavali said, "This is a particularly dark memory. Can you overcome it to dedicate yourself to the service of the Creator?" She gave him no time to answer the question. "The main difference between what you did before and what you will do now is that you will be paid to do things that generally do not involve robbing or killing people. Scruples are optional."

"Ah." *That doesn't sound so bad. I only ever wanted to survive.*

Since none of the questions he wanted answers to had been voiced, she refrained from behaving as if he asked them. He remembered she could tap his soul, but had more or less forgotten she could access his thoughts. She had no reason to remind him. Almost no reason, actually. Once he became an agent of the Fallen, she would feel compelled to treat him more fairly. Until then, she would continue to treat him as a prisoner, and avoid burning this bridge. Who knew when they'd meet again in the field.

Beyond that, she had no reason to invest in his problems. He could be dead later today, which didn't matter to her, aside from a sense of having wasted her time and effort bringing him all this way. Because his thoughts devolved into distracting rambles, she let go of him and replaced her mitten, uninterested in how he felt about that.

Cloverdale came into view before he had anything else to say. Without the forest to shield the ground, a thick blanket of snow covered the fields and houses, though the road had been properly cleared starting a half mile from the edge of the fields. The road became wide enough here that Algie moved up to walk beside them, putting Chavali in the middle.

"I've had a grand time, Chavali, dear. Harris is your idea, that makes him your problem. Since you have to take care of that anyway, you may as well report to Eldrack."

"And you can write it up." She turned to see the farmhouse where the rest of her clan lived. It had only a narrow path to the front door cleared. Later, she'd come up to see them. If any of them watched, they wouldn't recognize her under the hood, so she didn't wave.

"Very well, yes I can do that." He grinned at her, eyes flashing with amusement. "I'll be sure to include how charming the two of you are together." He hurried ahead at a brisk pace, giggling madly.

She saw no point to doing anything at all about that remark, choosing only roll to her eyes. When he got out of earshot, she muttered, "I swear, he is insane."

Harris chuckled. "I was starting to think you didn't realize that."

"I think even the snow realizes that."

"Probably." He grinned and kept his attention on his footing. "Why do you work with him?"

"Our employer makes such decisions." She waved off the subject. "You will learn about it soon enough. Come, we are almost there."

He looked up from his footing, nodding at the houses they walked past. The road went to the middle of town, and she pushed open the door of the tavern. "You work in a bar?"

"Yes, in addition to my other talents, I am also a *shepoína*, a dancer without clothes." The warmth of the tavern embraced her, and she hurried to shut the door behind Harris.

"You're joking, right? That's a joke." His eyes danced down her body as she pulled off her cloak and hung it over an arm.

She might have answered, but the bartender's voice distracted her. "Who's that?" Looking at Chavali, the spindly man wiping down a glass with a clean rag nodded at Harris. The intensity of his dark eyes bothered her in the same way a mouse might be bothered by a piece of cheese smelling of cat.

Of course, she had never brought someone back to the Tower before, and didn't know the proper protocols and procedures. If he expected some specific answer, she had no idea what it might be. "My guest."

"Really." The bartender shifted his attention to Harris. Everyone else in the bar, some fifteen people (no one she recognized), now openly stared at him.

"Is...that...bad?" Harris gulped and his eyes darted around.

The moment Chavali thought about this turn of events, it made sense. This tavern stood as the first line of defense against any attack. She smirked. "I vouch for him, and not under duress. Come." She beckoned to Harris and went for the back door. He grabbed her arm and followed, a frightened boy clutching his mama. The door opened onto a set of wooden stairs down into the cellar. Once down among the barrels of beer and other provisions, she found the lever for the hidden door and held it open for Harris.

"This is like a smuggler's hideout." He took a step into the darkness and a soft white magical light flared to reveal a narrow, spiraling stone stair going down.

"And you know much about such things?" Nothing in his thoughts so far pointed to that in his background.

He shrugged. "More than's probably healthy."

She pushed him in and shut the door with the lever on the inside. "Are you concerned that you have been pulled from a mule's behind to a horse's?"

"I...can't say I've ever heard it put that way, but I guess so. I'd say 'from the frying pan and into the fire.' "

She walked down the stairs, and heard him scramble to follow seven steps later. "Then let me be very clear." Without knowing how recruitment worked for people who weren't dead already, she only had a guess to go on, and hoped it came close to the truth. If not, Eldrack would set him straight and make sure she understood the process for the future. "Nothing I have told you about this place was false. It is a serious thing you have stumbled onto and been lucky enough to learn of without losing your head."

"The dancer thing was a joke."

"Very much so, yes."

"That's a shame."

Men. She smirked and shook her head. "At least you have a full appreciation for the value of your life."

"Survival is one of my favorite vices."

Later, he would appreciate the irony of making that statement here. Chavali pushed open the door at the bottom of the stairs, revealing a vast, cavernous, boring, empty room. She hurried across it to the next set of stairs down, a wide flight-and-a-half of steps too large for her gait. At the bottom of those, they wound through a twisting, turning tunnel too narrow to walk side by side, and going on and on and on. After that, they finally reached the main stairwell, a wide, brightly lit spiral descending into the depths of the earth.

"I take it back." Harris took the stairs beside her, watching his footing. "This is too big for smuggling."

Three people Chavali didn't know passed them on the way up. She gave them a polite wave, and all three returned it. "Indeed."

They went down and down and down. Each floor had a number

next to its open doorway. When she first arrived, she couldn't see them because of the colors used. At her request, they recently carved each into the stone and inlaid the numbers with white stone to contrast with the blue-gray. No longer did she need to count as she went from floor to floor.

"This place just kinda keeps going. How many floors are there?"

"Actually, I do not know. I have never been to the bottom." Unless, that is, she woke up at the bottom after being revived from death. Which didn't matter, because she still didn't know how many floors there were.

At the thirteenth floor, she took him through the doorway and to a door. She knocked out of politeness and walked in. They entered a small sitting room, which she ignored in favor of knocking on the next door. At this one, she waited until a voice inside invited her in.

Eldrack sat behind his desk, closing a folder and setting it aside. With lines in his face, comfortably worn clothing, and gray in his hair, he looked like what he was: a clerk of advanced years with adventures well behind him. His office suited him with small potted plants, books on shelves behind him, and worn, comfortable furniture. "Ah, Chavali." He smiled at her and gestured to the chair across from him, then saw Harris. His smile didn't falter and he showed no surprise at seeing the man. He gestured for Harris to sit in the chair beside hers. Lacing his hands together on his desk, he looked at her expectantly.

"The mission went smoothly." Digging in her pack, she pulled out the wooden box with the roses and slid it across the desk to him. "This man and his companions were bandits. They tried to rob and kill us. He survived. I did not think it wise to turn him loose. He has an interesting and useful skill set, as well as a base of knowledge in certain unusual areas, and I thought perhaps he might be a valuable asset for us."

Eldrack opened the lid of the box as she spoke, then shut it without touching the roses. His eyes flicked over Harris. "I see. What do you think of him otherwise?"

Chavali shrugged. "He has issues with authority not derived from fear and strength, but also a quick enough wit and knows better than to stab the hand that feeds him. He can be counted on to hold secrets close so long as he is treated fairly and fed well."

Harris stared at her. "Uh, thank you?"

Eldrack's smile grew broader, and suggested he stifled down amusement. "I'll take that to mean you feel her assessment is fair. I trust your judgment, Chavali. You can leave him here."

Taking that as a dismissal, Chavali stood and nodded to him. She had nothing else to say and left the room, shutting the door behind herself. At the doorway to the stairs, she paused and looked up, then down. On the one hand, she could use a good meal. On the other, she wanted a bath and to go see her clan.

"Chavali! Welcome back." Eliot came down the stairs in fresh, clean clothes. "We should spar."

Her shoulders slumped. "Not now. I returned only minutes ago. Tomorrow."

"Bah." The short, slim man cuffed the air in front of her with a rough hand. "Do you expect your enemies to sit down and wait while you fill your belly and take a nap? Tired and cranky is the best time to practice what you already know." He ignored the withering glare she gave him and grabbed her hand. "It's good for the digestion you'll do later, when you get a chance to eat."

His thoughts informed her that if she didn't cooperate, he'd follow her around until she gave in. "Fine, fine," she snapped. He only wanted to help her protect herself. "At least go to my floor, so I have a short walk to my room when we are done." So much for seeing the children today. She yanked her hand away and climbed the stairs to the tenth floor with him. "How long have you been lurking, waiting to ambush me?"

Eliot gave her his sly little smirk, the one that spoke of mischief. "One of the things I like the best about you is your ego."

She stuck her tongue out at him. "Do you expect me to believe this meeting is chance?"

"I'm wounded, Chavali." He clutched at his chest with a fake grimace of hurt. "Why would you ever think me a schemer?"

After suffering with Algie, Eliot made her laugh. "Let me heap upon you the apologies of my wagon for daring to question your tactics."

"I accept," he sniffed. They passed through the doorway of her floor and walked down the hallway to the practice room at the end. On the way, she paused at her own room—marked by a string of dark beads dangling from a small hook mounted on the door—to drop off her pack. He lunged at her, knife bared, the moment she walked into the practice room.

The sparring session lasted until he knocked her off her feet for the umpteenth time nearly an hour later, and she struggled to motivate herself to get up again. Panting, she lay on the floor, unable to speak. He waited a few seconds, then sheathed his dagger and crouched beside her. The bastard barely even broke a sweat.

"Did something happen on your mission?" He smiled at her, full of genuine pleasure.

Seeing he meant to let her give up for now, she dropped her wooden practice knife. He had the skill to keep a real blade from cutting her. She used a fake one to practice following through properly. "Why do you ask?"

His smile quirked into a smirk. "You're favoring your shoulder and knee, but there's something else. You've shed the hesitation in your strikes, and even though you started tired, your eyes followed my movements more closely than before. It's the change that comes from having to fight for your life, instead of for your tutor's approval." He offered a her a hand. She used it to sit up.

"We were attacked once." At his gesture to continue, she told him about the fight, recounting it as well as she could remember, while stopping short of informing him she left a survivor and took him prisoner. She didn't want to talk about that.

"It sounds like you did well enough, and everything you already know looks good, so we'll add new strikes and defenses now."

She groaned. "Because this is what I need: more new muscle aches."

"You asked me to teach you, Chavali." His mouth drew down, becoming serious. "I'm not going to settle for basic competence, and neither should you. I want you to be good enough to have at my back, not just able to defend yourself if someone gets past me."

She nodded and heaved herself to her feet. "This is what I want, too." She smirked. "After I have a chance to rest and eat and bathe."

He chuckled and straightened. "Yes, I've abused you enough for one day. See you tomorrow."

"Tomorrow," she agreed. She left him behind and took as quick a pace as she could manage in her exhaustion to find her room again. The beads on the door clacked against the wood as she opened it, and again when she closed it. Everything remained as she'd left it, though someone dropped off a basket with her clean clothes by the bed. She had a rug on the floor, woven from a dozen or more ends of dyed yarn. The screen set up on one side had been made from fabric once used as a painting drop cloth. She asked for such things, knowing no one else would want them. Her bed, dresser, table and chairs, and chest were all the Tower's standard issue light colored wood.

Despite her weariness, she took the time to pull the beads and second feather out of her hair, and grabbed her robe and soap. The bathing room had no other occupants while she washed in the luxury of hot water, and she saw no one else around when she shuffled back to her room again. The bed claimed her, throwing her into nightmares, as usual. Her stomach woke her later.

So far underground, Chavali hadn't yet determined how to judge time here. The dining floor had food available all the time, and she rarely wanted to meet with anyone other than the children, who she could see at any time. When she woke, she dressed and went down to eat. By the muffins and juices and pancakes, she guessed it to be morning. She took a few fruit pastries with her after eating her fill.

As she passed the thirteenth floor on her way to get her cloak and boots, she nearly collided with a white-clad servant hurrying out. The woman stopped short and apologized, then saw her face, smiled with recognition, and pointed through the doorway. "Chavali, wonderful. Eldrack asked for you, fourth door down on the left."

Chavali frowned, but waved a hand to show she got the message and turned to head for the door in question. Perhaps Harris chose to be a problem and Eldrack wanted her to know. Were that the case, though, why not meet in his office? She opened the fourth door on the left, finding a meeting room with a large round table surrounded by half a dozen chairs. These rooms were used to assign missions.

Two of the chairs already had occupants: Eldrack and Harris. She arched an eyebrow, taking in the sight of them sitting across from each other. "Good morning, Chavali." Eldrack smiled as he usually did, full of warmth and understanding. Except when he showed sympathy, which was, by far, much worse.

Harris lifted a hand in an uncertain greeting. His lips moved to form words, but no sound came out.

She looked from one man to the other. "What is going on?"

"I gather you were on your way to see your children. I'm sorry for interrupting that. This mission is somewhat urgent, unfortunately."

Harris looked at her, surprised and confused. "Children?"

Ignoring him, she furrowed her brow and pointed at the archer. "Mission? You are sending him on a mission? With me?"

"And two others," Eldrack nodded, "yes. He doesn't need to adjust in the same way others do, and he's accepted the binding, so he might as well get to work already. I'd like you to supervise him and build on the basic understanding I've given him already about our work here."

"Algie will not be one of the others, will he?"

Eldrack chuckled. "No, he won't."

She narrowed her eyes at the Administrator. This had to be revenge for bringing Harris instead of killing him. Oh, he would call it something else, something pretty, but it came down to turnabout being fair play. "What did you tell him?"

"Mostly, he told me not to be an ass to other Fallen," Harris said. "You have kids?"

"No." Chavali flicked her hand at him. "Shut up. I meant about—" She gestured around herself, meaning the spirits that gave her the power to read thoughts and create illusions. Eldrack didn't know it worked that way, but he knew enough.

"Ah." Eldrack nodded his understanding. She suspected he understood quite a bit more about his conversation with Harris than he did five minutes ago. "Only that he's safe from you trying to eat his soul now, or however you put it. You are, after all, on the same side."

"I'm not allowed to stab you, either, so we're even." Harris gave her a bright smile that wilted under her lack of response to it.

Someone entered the room, distracting her from the situation. Colby's large frame filled the doorway, and she gave him a nod of greeting, then took a seat. Standing in some sort of protest would be silly. Eldrack chose to assign her to this mission, binding her to it.

"Morning," Colby said, full of bright cheer. He walked up to Harris and offered a hand. They exchanged names and polite greetings. When he sat, his chair groaned in protest. The man had muscle packed onto every part of his nearly seven feet of height. He looked ready for anything, as he always seemed when she encountered him.

The last person to join them arrived shortly after. Portia shuffled in wearing loose pink pants and a gray shirt that didn't obscure her athletic figure, with fat, furry slippers. Her long brown hair hung loose, some sticking out at odd angles. She rubbed her eyes and yawned, dropping down into a chair without preamble.

"Now that we're all here, let's get started." Eldrack produced a folder and set it on the table, leaving it where anyone could take it. As Chavali expected, Colby set a hand on it first and drew it to himself. "As some of you know, we have multiple informants in every country, keeping track of various situations for us. Each reports on a regular schedule, even if they have nothing to report.

"Our agent in Ket has missed three reports in a row. Hers came monthly, so she hasn't been able to get word to us for a long time. This could probably wait another day or week, but I feel now is the time to move in and determine what happened." Chavali couldn't be sure if her imagination played tricks on her, but she thought his eyes flicked to her, implying he chose now instead of tomorrow because of her. Why that might be, she had no idea.

"The mission is to go to Ket, find out what happened, and deal with it. If she's dead and you can, bring back her body. Carry out any justice the situation calls for; the Fallen take care of our own. All the information I have about her is in that folder. I've never met her, and the Fallen who recruited her are not available right now, so I have no additional insights to offer about her. I suggest you get on your way as soon as possible. Harris is new, please keep that in mind. There's no way to know how long this mission will last. Pack accordingly.

"For this mission, you have the authority to present yourselves as agents of the Crown, if needed." Eldrack produced four silver medallions on thin silver chains. Each had an image of a fierce bear with a crown of leaves, which Chavali recognized as the symbol of the Crown of Shappa. "They're enchanted so only the bearer can actually be recognized by it, making them useless to steal."

With a gesture, he got Colby to hold out his hand. He took one of the medallions and used the edge to slice a tiny cut in Colby's finger. "Nobility and members of the City Guard should recognize the authority granted by this." Pressing the medallion to the blood, he shut his eyes and breathed out through his nose. Chavali felt a whisper stir in the air, a tiny fraction of the same kind of Something Other she felt when she took her oath and bound her soul to the Fallen.

Eldrack stayed that way for three seconds, then opened his eyes and smiled. "And it's done. These are optional, and you surrender them when you return." He gave Harris a meaningful look while still smiling. "I keep close track of them."

"I'll pass," Harris said, holding his hands away from the table. "Not interested."

Portia took one and endured the same swift procedure. Chavali watched and frowned, feeling that swish of power again. She saw Colby tuck his under his shirt, and it barely showed. With winter clothes, it would even be a hassle to pull it out at need. Did she want this kind of authority? Would it be more of a hindrance than a help? Given how few missions she'd handled, she chose to err on the side of caution. In the future, she might turn it down. Now, she held out her hand.

The cut made her hiss. When he pressed the medallion to her finger, the sting vanished and the power bowled her over, forcing her to slump over in her chair. Neither Colby nor Portia showed any sign of being affected by it, yet she needed to catch her breath after brushing against that presence for the second time.

Eldrack studied her with concern etched on his face as she blinked and straightened. "Are you alright?"

Turning her hands over and noticing she had no cut on her finger, she felt her strength return in a steady flow. "Yes, I think so."

"Good. I have other duties to attend to. Good luck, and the Creator guide you."

Chavali's eyes slid to the pastries sitting on the table as Eldrack bustled out of the room. If she hurried, she could at least see them for a few minutes. "I will meet you all at the stables," she said as she stood up. "Where is Ket? Will it be cold there?"

Colby flipped the folder open and scanned the top page. "Shappa, on the western coast. Looks like maybe half a day's ride from the nearest Creator's Tower. I doubt they get much snow, and it's probably a little warmer than here."

"I'm gonna be a little bit," Portia said with a yawn. "Woke me up for this."

Colby put out a large hand to stop Chavali from leaving the room. "We'll meet you at the house. It's on the way anyway."

"Thank you." She gave him a small smile and hurried out. If Harris didn't have the sense to speak up and ask for help when he needed it, he was an even bigger idiot than she thought. In her room, she dumped her pack out and stuffed fresh clothes and things inside it. She did one quick check of her room to make sure she hadn't forgotten anything important, then grabbed up the pack and pastries and headed for the surface with as much speed as she could manage.

Chapter 4

The sun marked the time as mid-morning when she finally saw it. She panted and puffed from climbing all the stairs, yet still pushed herself to jog through the town and up the narrow path in the snow. At the front door, she took a minute to catch her breath, then knocked. Marcus answered the door, his weathered, aging face lighting up with a delighted smile when he saw her. He immediately stood aside so she could come in.

"I'm glad to see you're back. Penny made a pie last night, and it even turned out good." Still out of breath, she shook her head to refuse the offer and held out the pastries. He took them and looked her over. "Are they sending you out again already?" When she nodded, he grunted. "Short visit, then. Come on in and have some tea, at least. Kids! Chavali is here!"

Pulling her mittens off, she sat down on the couch while Marcus disappeared deeper into the warm, cheerful house. A little girl ran into the room, with her arms out and a delighted grin. "Chavaaaaaaaaaaaaaaaaaaali!" Haizea flung her small body at Chavali, knowing her Seer would catch her. Danel ran all the way to Chavali and flung his arms around her knees. Biholtz entered the room at a more sedate pace, a broad smile showing her pleasure with the visit.

"I can only stay for a little bit." The moment she met Penny and Marcus, she found them to be such pleasant, friendly people that she quashed all misgivings about the people who would foster the remaining members of her clan. They proved accommodating and pleasant, and had more than enough patience to handle the three of them. "I only returned last night, I know, but they are sending me out again already." She switched to the clan tongue to make the children more comfortable. "Colby and his giant horse'll be here soon, and I'll have to go with him."

Danel climbed up onto the couch. Biholtz sat on her other side. Chavali settled Haizea on her lap and hugged all three of them at once. "So we're not going to waste our time on how unfair it is," Biholtz said with all the authority of a clan Elder despite being only twelve. "We're going to enjoy the short time we have."

"Tell us a story," Haizea begged.

"A short one, I suppose." She let go, and they stayed close, touching her. Marcus shuffled in and pushed a steaming cup into her hands. His wife, Penny, stood in the doorway, watching them all with a wistful smile. The two of them treated her as the daughter they never had, the rest of her clan as their grandchildren.

She sipped the tea while Marcus handed out the pastries to the kids, each now on a plate and warmed enough for the drizzled icing to have melted into sticky, sugary goo. "Once upon a time, the four goats slept for the winter in a cave. A heated spring in the back made it warm and cozy, and when they woke to check if the snow passed yet, it gave them water to drink.

"One time, Mendeba woke by herself. She got a drink and went to the cave mouth to look out. Pine boughs covered the entrance, lifted into place with their teeth. She peered out through a gap and saw something that made her freeze in place. A monster sniffed near the mouth of the cave. She didn't know the name for this thing, but it terrified her.

"And yet, the only thing that stood between it and her was nothing. A few tree branches. It would tear through them and then her to get at the rest of her clan. What did she have to defend herself with? Her hooves and her small horns. Ekia and Hegoa, of course, had much bigger horns, but they weren't awake. If she went to wake them, the monster might see or hear her. So she stood still and tried not to breathe."

Chavali couldn't hide a smile at how everyone in the room held their breath, even Marcus and Penny. She had taught them a few words of the clan tongue so they could handle the children, but not many. Biholtz must be teaching them more, because they seemed to understand the story. She should have discussed that with her Seer first.

"The monster snuffled closer and closer." She sniffed at Haizea and then Danel, exaggerating the sound. "Then it reached the pine branches and it nudged them aside to find itself face to face with Mendeba. She was scared, of course. Terrified. But she stood tall and proud, filling the space to defend her clan from the monster and staring it down. It would have to go through her to get to the others, and if it chose to attack, she would scream to wake them.

"It bared its teeth, and she bared hers. It stomped a foot, and she stomped hers. It snorted out a breath, and she snorted out hers. She thought the monster meant to bite her next, so she darted her head in and bit its nose as hard as she could. She tasted blood and it yipped in pain, skittering back and protecting its nose. It glared at her and she hissed at it.

"Making it shy away in pain bolstered her resolve, and her fear receded. 'We are not food for you,' she rumbled at it, her voice heavy with menace and anger. The monster fled."

Haizea used her fingers to make horns on her head and roared with her small voice. "No monsters!"

"You're such a gifted storyteller," Penny said with glow of pride. "I didn't understand all the words, but I still enjoyed it."

"Thank you." Chavali had something else to say, but a knock on the door cut her off. She hugged the children again while Marcus answered the door. "Biholtz, ask for me if Penny and Marcus will consent to joining our clan. We shouldn't be teaching them so much of our language if they won't."

The girl bowed her head, duly chastised. "I'll mention it," she promised. "You can talk to them when you come back."

A rush of cold air came with the door opening, and Colby stood there with a smile on his face. "Hi, sorry to interrupt, but we need to get going."

Marcus shook his hand and everyone else but Chavali waved to him. Chavali kissed the children on their foreheads and cheeks, then sighed, reluctant to leave so soon after arriving. Duty would not wait, though, and she waved from the door, then pulled her mittens and hood on as Marcus shut it behind her. The children would watch her from the window until she left their sight, and she waved one more time without looking.

"They seem to be doing well," Colby said.

"Yes." She didn't want to talk about it, and did want to get to Ket and get this all over with. Portia and Harris sat on horses. She looked comfortable, he did not.

"We decided to ride. I'll give you a hand up." Colby lifted her onto the broad back of his large beast, then vaulted up behind her. This arrangement made her feel small and helpless, which soured her mood. "Here's what we know." The horse jumped into a trot without Colby's direction, leading the other two down the road.

"The agent's name is Elise, and she's never been aware of the Fallen, thinking instead she was working for the Crown. We set her up as Seran Garrian's clerk in Ket, where she's been paying attention to the books."

"What an awful name. Seran Garrian." Chavali grimaced at how little thought must have gone into such an artless pairing.

Colby chuckled. "Seran is a noble title in Shappa. It's the male form of Sera, which is the lowest rank granted by the Crown. Garrian is his family name. His first name is David."

"Ah. Continue, then."

His gloved hand offered her the folder about the mission. "Do you want to read this for yourself?"

"No, I cannot read very much. We did not need to."

"No time like the present to learn." He flipped the folder open in front of her and held the pages with one hand while using the other to point to the words as he read over her shoulder. "The woman in charge of the city is Lady Amelia Mardis. This is a high rank, so it's best to assume she's responsible for a large area around Ket. The Lady is married and has a deceased brother. Not sure why that's relevant. Her daughter, Luna, is sixteen and the heir to her title.

"She has five councilors, Garrian is the only man. The rest are Konti Jore—Konti is another title, a step above Sera. Sera Wessin, Sera Malora, and Sera Drune. Ket is divided into three sections, the east, west, and south. Konti Jore represents the east, Sera Wessin the west, and Sera Malora the south. Seran Garrian is the Minister of Finance and Administration. Sera Drune is the Minister of Civility and Law. Seran Garrian is married and—"

Chavali frowned and interrupted him, as it seemed he now intended to discuss each person at length. "Why do we care about these people and their arrangements?"

"Elise works for Garrian. He's a councilor. We may need to talk to him and the other councilors at some point, so we should know something about them before we get there."

She shrugged. "You cannot tell me what I need to know about them with a piece of paper. What do we know about anything that might have led to Elise disappearing?"

Colby left a short silence, which she interpreted to be disapproval. "Nothing. Whatever may have happened, she didn't have a chance to get a message out about it. If there were any irregularities in the books or her duties, she either didn't notice them or considered them beneath attention."

"Then that seems to be the extent of what is necessary to know about prior to arriving."

"That'll leave you at a disadvantage in dealing with them."

She twisted in the saddle to see his face and found the expected exasperation along with disapproval. "You were military, yes? Something like this. For you, everything is about having a plan and sticking to it, and knowing as much about the enemy as you can before engagement." He nodded cautiously. "I was a fortune teller. I meet someone, appraise them, and deal with them in the span of seconds. I must be adaptable and have vague plans that can suit many circumstances."

That shut him up. He stuffed the papers out of sight.

Chapter 5

Hours later, as the sun set that evening, they reached Ket. It perched on the edge of the sea, a large city with walls of blue-gray stone twenty feet high. A few inches of snow covered the flat land surrounding the city. Trees lined the well-used and cleared strip of packed earth they rode down, until they got close to the city walls. For two hundred feet, the land lay clear of notable structures and plant life. One lonely guardsman, covered from head to toe against the chill, huddled in the gated arch straddling the road, beckoning them to hurry.

"Good thing I saw you," the guard said as they reached him. "We were just about to close the gate for the night. What's your business in Ket?"

Portia sat with regal bearing and patted a saddlebag. "Messages and some other matters for our employer. We expect to be here for a few days, conducting his business, and then we'll be on our way." She pulled off bored impatience rather well, enough to impress Chavali.

"We need an inn," Chavali told the guard, expecting the request to distract him enough to answer and send them on their way without taking further interest.

"Sure." He pointed down the road, his pike held loosely in his other hand. "Only place in the city with a stable big enough for that beast, aside from the Lady's keep, is Cander's Lodge. Not far down the road. Tell them I sent you." As she hoped, he stood aside and waved them through without further delay. The sound of the gate creaking shut for the night soon was swallowed by donkeys braying, dogs barking, people chattering, hooves clopping, axles groaning, hinges squeaking, and the rest of the cacophony of a large city scrambling to finish the day's chores.

As promised, the stable behind Cander's Lodge had beams high enough and a stall wide enough for Colby's horse to be comfortable. Colby helped Chavali climb down. She groaned when her feet reached the ground, aching from head to toe. Between the ride and Eliot's sparring and the walking and fighting to and from Atrica, she wanted to soak in a tub for a week, then lie down for a month.

Harris dismounted with a grimace. "Man, who knew riding was so tiring? I always thought the horse did all the work." He stretched and squatted.

Portia grabbed her saddlebags and pack. She flipped a gold coin at the teenage boy who approached with a smile. "Take good care of them. They've had a long day." While he agreed and took the two smaller horses into stalls, Colby's horse claimed the largest and walked himself into it.

"I'll stay and take care of Karias myself," Colby said with a wave.

That horse wasn't right, and Chavali knew it, but not why or how. She watched Karias stomp in the fresh straw and kick it around. Shaking her head to push away the thought, she followed Portia inside the inn,

Harris right behind her. Some part of him brushed her bottom. She decided to treat it as accidental and unworthy of note. If he did it again, she would slap him.

The common room of Cander's Lodge looked more like a good quality tavern than an inn, with booths along two walls, a bar, and round tables in the center. Three strategically placed magical globes of yellow light made it obvious the staff took care of the place and kept it clean and inviting. The employees wore clean uniforms and didn't seem surly as they slipped through the room. None of them had to evade the patrons, who behaved well. Perhaps that would change as the night went on and men fell into their cups.

Chavali surveyed the room with a predator's eye. People, grouped together after a long day of work, would talk. And talk. And talk. They would spill gossip and rumors, secrets and lies. With some effort, she could learn a great deal here. A quiet cup of tea did hold great allure, but the mission began the moment they left the tower. Dallying would accomplish nothing.

Handing her pack off to Harris (Portia had enough to carry already) with her eyes stuck on the crowd, she asked him to take it to whatever room they got for her. Then she went to work. It would be different than having people come to her specifically to have their fortune told, but similar enough. She scanned the crowd as she pulled off her mittens and tucked them into a pocket of her russet cloak, watching for the right person, the right mark.

That one had too much wander to his eyes—he'd only think about bedding her the whole time. This one? Too sour. Another sat with his mistress (she could tell). Ah, there. She would do nicely. A woman sat by herself at a smaller round table, absently eating soup from a bread bowl and looking up hopefully every time the door opened. The sigh of disappointment she heaved into her half-eaten meal spoke volumes.

"Excuse me," Chavali gave her a polite smile, "the place is very full, do you mind if I sit here?"

"Oh." Close up, the woman had the light wrinkles of middle age without the gray of advancing years. She probably hadn't quite reached forty yet, and from the ring on her finger, waited for her husband. "I'm, er, kind of waiting— But he... Well." She sighed again and shrugged. "Sure, have a seat."

"Men are often disappointing," Chavali said, echoing the woman's sigh. "Never where you want them when you want them there."

A waiter stopped by and took Chavali's order for hot tea without being intrusive.

"He's always late," the woman agreed. "Always."

Behind her, Chavali heard the conversations swirl around, picking up words and phrases she could use for this one. "Mine insists upon tending to his horse personally." Colby's head would explode if he knew she used him for this. "He takes better care of his mount than he does of me. Right now, he brushes it himself instead of letting the stablehand do it. Then he'll harvest the oats himself," she said with a roll of her eyes and a heavy dollop of sarcasm, "and heat the water to make a mash with his special spoon. For me? 'Go get something to eat, Chavali. I'll be up later.'"

The woman copied the eye roll and nodded her sympathy. "They're so self-absorbed. Sometimes my husband ignores me while I'm talking to him. He can't even be bothered to talk to his own wife for five minutes!"

Perfect. "Unless it is about *his* thing, yes? Mine will talk about horses forever. But a problem with the house? No."

"Exactly." The waiter dropped off Chavali's tea, making the woman stop talking and return to her soup. Now, though, resentment simmered in her shoulders and a fellowship had been established. "Chavali is a pretty name. It sounds like an exotic flower."

"Thank you. What is your name?"

"Jody."

She drew Jody into idle chatting, using both the conversation and the things she overheard to figure out what sat on everyone's minds right now. It all seemed very normal and boring to her. At some point, Portia and Harris returned to the room without their bags. They ignored her, probably deducing she needed to be left to her devices. More specifically, Portia probably guessed. A little while later, she noticed Colby walking in, and he went to sit with Portia and Harris.

A man approached the table after a half hour or so, sitting down with a heavy thud. "I'm sorry I'm so late, dear." He reached over and kissed her cheek, which she let him do with pursed lips and a mild glare. "I got an unexpected order, and it was urgent."

Jody stood up in a huff and threw the bread bowl she'd been picking at for the last ten minutes into his face. "There's always something unexpected and urgent," she spat, and then she stormed out.

"You must be Ivan." Chavali offered her hand to shake with him.

He took it, his thoughts too preoccupied with the state of his marriage to ask for her name or question her presence. "Yes." He pulled out a handkerchief and wiped at spots of soup on his coat. "I take it she's very upset."

"Yes, quite." She pulled a bit of bread off her own bowl. Casually, she asked, "What kept you?"

Ivan sighed as if he carried the weight of the world on his shoulders. "This wretched funeral." He waved his hand irritably. "Seran Garrian is going so overboard with the preparations, a person might think he has something to hide. It's terrible, of course, but good for business."

"And what is good for business can be bad for the merchant's private life," Chavali said, pouring on the sympathy. "I am new here, though. Who died?"

"Oh, his wife. She'd been ill for some time, so I've heard, and there're some rumors about the usual sorts of unpleasant things people say when a wealthy man's wife dies. I doubt any of it's true. Seran Garrian is a noble man, serving his country, and it's shameful to spread malicious lies about dalliances with no proof." The waiter came by again, and Ivan ordered the soup for himself. "Where are you from?"

"I travel so much, I am from everywhere at this point." She grinned, offering the statement as a joke. "When would it be proper to for a commoner to pay respects to the deceased woman?"

"The burial. The funeral starts at mid-morning, so I expect the burial itself will be at midday." He rubbed his face with both hands, probably still thinking about his wife.

Chavali had no interest in his marital problems and pretended to recognize someone across the room. "Ah. Excuse me. My friend has arrived." She stood and found Colby watching her, tensed to spring into action should she need rescuing. While she appreciated the sentiment on some levels, he made it so blatant that anyone watching would think her a whore or con artist, or perhaps a wayward spouse.

She carried the remains of her dinner on a winding path through the room that took her past the front door, then to the table where the others sat. Colby and Harris both pushed out the same chair for her. The former did it out of politeness. The latter... She had no one to blame but herself for whatever idiotic infatuation he'd developed.

Portia rolled her eyes while the two men looked at each other, each a little confused by the other's action. "What did you find out," she asked, leaning in and keeping her voice low.

"Many things, few of them useful." Chavali dropped into the chair, ignoring both men. "That man's wife hates him for being so focused on his business, there is a woman with too many cats bothering her neighbors, the price of wheat is too high, much snow fell this winter, people are bracing for a shortage of wool, a problem with disease is forcing a renovation at the docks, and Seran Garrian's wife is dead. Her funeral and burial will be tomorrow."

Colby, she noticed, glanced over at Ivan, then back to her. Harris watched her with an idiotic smile.

"Good work." Portia flashed her a grin. "Anything about how she died?"

Being appreciated made Chavali return the grin. "A long illness." She shrugged, mulling over what Ivan said. "It is possible Garrian killed her by poisoning over a long term, or a mistress did it, or she genuinely may have been sick. Perhaps her sickness advanced or she had a shock. With another hour or two and a walk, I can find out more."

"It's after dark already," Colby said. "In an unfamiliar city. See what you can find out here and the rest can wait until morning."

That sounded like an order regarding how to do her job, which made Chavali's lip curl. It would be amusing, in some respects, to follow Jody's example and splash him with gobs of soup. She restrained herself for the benefit of the mission. "It can all wait until morning. The ride was tiring, and it is cold out."

"We should go to the funeral regardless," Colby said, not perturbed.

"Not all of us." Portia met Chavali's eyes and flicked them subtly at Harris. Chavali agreed. He needed to be away from her if they wanted to get any usefulness out of him. Maybe Portia could hit him with a club to get some sense into his head. "Harris and I'll snoop around the city tomorrow while the two of you crash the funeral."

"I agree." The alternative? Leaving the two men to their own devices. Chavali could well imagine what disasters that might cause. A knight and a bandit walk down the street... A bad joke might start this way.

Colby opened his mouth, probably to disagree, but Portia stood up and cut him off. "Harris, let's go chat about what we'll be looking for, and that sort of thing. Don't want to wind up making lots of dumb new person mistakes, do you?"

At the sound of his name, Harris blinked and turned to give Portia his attention. "Oh. Sure, yeah. That's probably a good idea." He stood and gave Chavali an apologetic look that she waved off, then he followed Portia away from the table.

Colby rubbed his chin as he watched the two of them thread their way through the room. "What do you know about Harris?"

Chavali nibbled at a small piece of bread, watching the crowd itself. People leaned in and out, sat together and apart, left separately and in groups. That woman over there was a whore. A man sitting in the corner circulated and picked pockets every twenty minutes or so—two of the waitstaff knew and shielded him from discovery. "More than you."

"Are you going to share?"

She shrugged, still not paying attention to him. "It is not my habit to share the secrets of my clan without a good reason. Ask him if you want to know."

"I did. He said he has a shady past and I look too much like a former guardsman to talk about it."

"That seems to cover the subject." Chavali pushed away the half-eaten bread to stand.

He put out a hand to grab her arm, but changed his mind halfway there and only gestured for her to wait. "I just want to know what he's good at."

"Only time can reveal this," she said with a smirk. "Is there anything else, or may I go now?"

His hand dropped to the table, his entire body showing exasperation. It made her want to laugh at him and slap him at the same time, for reminding her of her clan. "Are you going to help that man?"

"Harris? I already helped him as much as I intend to."

"No, I mean the man you sat with over there."

"Why would I help him?"

He blinked slowly at her, eyebrows raised. "Because you know about his problem and how to fix it?"

"And?"

Frowning, he held his hands out in confusion. "And? What do you mean 'and'?"

"Is it your assertion that every time I meet some stranger with a problem," she crossed her arms, "I should make an effort to solve it for them?"

He sighed. "No, of course not."

"Do not treat me like I am a child you must lecture. My duty is to my clan, not to the world. I accept you as 'clan' because of this thing we are bound by. These other people, they are not my concern."

Colby stared at her for a beat, then rubbed his face wearily. "Would you please just go say something to him about how to solve his problems? Consider it a favor for me."

If he wanted to owe her for doing something so worthless, so be it. "Fine," she said with a roll of her eyes and a wave of her hand. "You will pay me back for wasting my time."

"Thank you."

She stood up, dismissing him, and slipped through the room. Ivan still sat, dragging his spoon through his soup, leaning his head on his hand with his elbow on the table, staring at nothing. Pathetic. Stealing up behind him to hide her sneer, she put a hand on his shoulder and leaned over to whisper to him.

Her cheek brushed his ear, showing her his thoughts. He was miserable. He missed his wife, but had no idea what to do to get her back in his arms. Because he was also stupid. "If you want her, you must show it. Go now, get her some flowers or a favorite treat. Spend the evening with her, and make it about her. Listen. Surprise her. Do it again and again. Remember what you love about her the most and tell her."

Since she knew he heard her and also had no interest in whatever might come out of his mouth after that, she turned and walked away. Colby watched her without getting up, making it difficult to blend in. She'd get little else from these people tonight so long as he insisted upon doing that, and doubted he'd agree to stop.

The last time she worked with him, she needed that kind of protection. This, however, was not a compound of telepaths trying to keep what remained of her clan locked away. The tavern had no hidden threats, no assassins lurking in the walls waiting to pounce.

She tossed him a glare that he seemed surprised by. The next step she took, one of the waitresses walked into her, spilling the contents of her tray all over Chavali's dress. A glance at the waitress's face at least gave her the reassurance this had nothing to do with the pickpocket.

"Watch where you step," Chavali snarled. "Stupid, careless—" She cut herself off, confident it had been an accident.

"I'm sorry, ma'am." The woman gave her attention to picking up the cups and plates from her tray.

In her clan, focusing on things over people in such a circumstance had been the height of rudeness, an insult. She could have been burned, or stabbed by a flying knife, yet the waitress didn't care. Chavali stayed her hand by force of will and stormed to the bar. "Your girl has ruined my clothes," she spat at the bartender.

The man flicked his eyes at the girl and nodded. "I'm very sorry, ma'am. Are you alright?"

His calm and concern infected her, dulling her anger. At least the man in charge had the right priorities. "Yes, I am fine."

"I'll have the clothes laundered for you, ma'am, no charge. Set them outside your door and I'll take care of it myself."

"Thank you." In the face of his professionalism, Chavali had nothing to complain about. With a nod of satisfaction, she went upstairs to let this day finally end.

Chapter 6

"Rough night, huh?"

Not ready for morning yet, Chavali sat there, her feet dangling off the edge of the small bed in the bland room she shared with Portia. She mumbled out a wordless noise of incomprehension, having no idea what the woman meant, and unwilling to try thinking about it.

"It sounded like you had some nightmares. They go away after a while, you know. It's not forever." Portia sounded much too bright and cheerful. She reminded Chavali of her little sister.

Pushing away painful thoughts of Pasha, Chavali rubbed her eyes and yawned. "I always have nightmares," she grumbled.

"You could try talking about them. It always helps me."

"No." The effort required to explain annoyed her. She pushed her thick, red-brown hair back, noticing she forgot to string the beads and feather into her hair again after her bath at the Fallen tower. How did she not notice until now? Between the hood of her cloak, the noise of the tavern, and her weariness, it didn't register. The children probably didn't say anything because it happened from time to time, even before. Did it look strange to have only the one grafted into her forehead and its surrounding tattoo? More strange than with the beads and second feather, that is.

She stood up and noticed Portia frowning at her. "They are not new," Chavali explained. "I had them before I died. I am used to it."

"Oh. That sounds unpleasant."

"Life is like that." Chavali changed her clothes while Portia laced up her boots. Both went quiet for several beats.

"You know, your name is really unusual sounding. You should maybe use a fake one. To avoid standing out so much."

"Colby will never be able to handle that." The idea of him twisting his morality to lie about her name made her smirk.

Portia grinned. "Tell him it's your middle name, or a nickname."

She didn't have a middle name, but did have a nickname. Being reminded of it made her scowl. "My parents used to call me 'Chala.'"

"No, that sounds exotic, too."

"Good." She hated the pet name when they lived and used it, and hated it more now they were both dead. "I have no idea what to use."

Portia sat down to wait for Chavali to finish dressing. "Easiest to remember would be something that sounds similar to your name. Hm. 'Cha' isn't very common. The only thing I can think of is 'Charlie,' which could be short for Charlotte."

"Charlie?" She rolled the word around in her mouth, finding it ugly and distasteful. "Can you think of nothing else?"

"Hm." Portia pursed her lips and slid them around, thinking about it. "Chastity? Charity? Chelsea?" She shrugged. "That's all I've got."

In no way would Chavali ever allow herself to be referred to as "Charity." She sighed. "I suppose Chastity is fine."

"I've known a few girls named that. Anyway, all you have to do now is convince the brute squad to use it. By which I mean Colby. I doubt Harris'll have a problem with it."

"No, I expect not." Chavali pulled her boots on and grabbed her cloak, trying not to keep Portia waiting too long. "Thank you."

"No problem." They found the two men sitting down to breakfast in the common room of the tavern, and shared hot oatmeal and fruit before splitting up. It passed without chatter, as all four wished to be on their way. Soon enough, Chavali and Colby walked up the street, stopping to buy flowers from a wretched woman who probably stole them. Even Chavali knew that nothing of the sort grew outdoors this time of year, so she certainly didn't pick them herself as she claimed.

"Why do you want me to call you 'Chastity'?" He handed her the flowers, a small bouquet of tiny white stars on leafy stems.

"Portia says my name is too memorable. This is the closest to what it translates to." This lie removed the burden of duplicity from his shoulders, keeping it on her own. For the mission and for the Fallen, she had no problem accepting it.

"Really? It sounds a lot alike. I thought your language was really very different from Shappan."

"Some words are this way." No other examples came to mind, so she shrugged and didn't offer any. "It seems a sensible thing to me."

"Alright, if that's what you want. I can do that." His lips moved to form the word in silence several times. Chavali would also have to remember to respond to it.

She nodded and mulled over what excuses she could use to speak to Garrian. "Do you wish to speak on the story I will weave to get us into this thing, or would you rather nod and agree as if I am your keeper?"

Colby sighed. "Maybe I should be your bodyguard."

"That will make things easier, I suspect. Watch, then. Not just me, but everyone around me. Do not follow me around closely."

"I know how to guard someone." He seemed focused rather than annoyed.

"Good." They reached the city graveyard, a fenced-in expanse of trees and greenery. Although she'd seen such places in other people's minds before, the concept of putting a body in the ground made no sense to her. Her clan burned its dead on a pyre, letting the spirit free to soar with the sparks of the flames and to roam Tilzam evermore. Two scoops of the ashes would be mixed into the next batch of the clan's wagon paint. Nature scattered the rest according to its whims.

Two guards at the gate stopped people, turning many away. Chavali and Colby waited in a short line, hearing the reason after a few minutes. "The funeral itself is private, ma'am. The burial will be open, at noon. Come back then." The guard sounded bored and tired of repeating himself. He began to speak these words again to Chavali, and she put up a hand to stop him, holding the flowers at her side, subtly suggesting they were only a pretense.

"I appreciate the duty you hold close, but I am here on an errand for the King." She pulled her Crown medallion out and let him examine it. "I was told Lady Mardis could be found inside?"

"Oh." The guard looked around with uncertainty. "I don't know that this is really the right time for that, milady. She'll be free this afternoon."

Chavali nodded in sympathy for him and tucked the medallion away again. "However inappropriate the moment, the business of the Crown does not pause for sorrow. I need to deal with this matter and be on my way swiftly. Please stand aside for me and my guard."

The guards both flicked their eyes to Colby, who must have nodded or shrugged, then back to her. "Yes, milady. Go right ahead. Sorry to delay you."

She gave them both a warm smile and entered the copse, following the stone path from the gate. Hoping to have a chance to read someone of note, she pulled her mittens off and tucked them into her belt, behind her back where they'd be hidden by her cloak. To keep her hands warm, she stuffed them into the pockets of her dress.

They found the small gathering near the center, where the oldest and largest of the trees stood. At the base of a sturdy, sprawling oak, three men had the solemn work of digging a hole in the ground, made possible in the winter through the use of heated water. Only one person paid them any attention as they toiled, a man who stood facing the grave with his head down. The rest of the four dozen or more guests formed clumps and circulated, black and gray clouds drifting around him. A scattering of guardsmen formed a perimeter.

It surprised her to see the body sitting out already. She thought they would keep it out of sight until the last minute. The woman had been wrapped in linen and laid on a stand, ready to be lifted and lowered in. Rumors of sickness had to be at least partially true, as the corpse seemed shriveled even through the cloth.

Chavali moved in, noticing it when her hulking shadow stopped and took up a watchful position near a guard. Good. He wouldn't screw anything up there. She strolled past the cliques, listening and watching for the best time to insert herself somehow. Two of them each had a woman the others looked up to. One of these women wore a brocade cloak trimmed with silver and lined with pure white fur, some kind of rounded symbol interwoven in the cloth. The other's cloak had no trim, and the fur seemed one step less fine. Chavali guessed them to be the Lady Mardis and Konti Jore, who would logically be the most important people present. The three Seras could likely be found here too, though she couldn't pick out one candidate to fit any of the names.

A thin man hurried up to Garrian and presented him with some papers and a pen. He took off his glove to sign. She saw her chance and slipped through to his side. When he handed the papers back, she presented herself with her hand offered. "Excuse me for intruding. I wish to offer my condolences."

Though his hand automatically took hers to shake, his eyes moved away from the grave with reluctance. He saw the feather in her forehead and gave no outward reaction to it. "Thank you." *I don't know you. Why are you here? Did Drune send you?* The handshake was brief. He pulled his glove back on as soon as he let go. None of his suspicion showed on his face, kept at bay by weariness and grief.

She needed a way to get him to talk, and keep him talking. "The tree is magnificent."

He gave the oak his attention and nodded in agreement. "This is her family's tree." He left a short pause. As soon as Chavali opened her mouth to say something else, he raised his hand, cutting her off. "I appreciate the impulse to try to comfort me, but I'd rather have silence now. If you'd like to talk later, you can make an appointment with my assistant." He pointed to the thin man standing a dozen feet away.

"Of course. I apologize if I have upset you." She set the flowers on the ground at the end of the grave and backed away to his assistant. Something about that conversation felt off to her. Perhaps the difference in customs skewed her perception. Her clan grieved for lost members, yet they held a feast and a dance around the pyre, celebrating those who still lived. It might help her with her own lingering grief if she did something of that kind with the children.

She secured an appointment for tomorrow morning. Before walking away, she asked, "How did she die? I have heard only rumors so far."

The assistant sighed, shaking his head, and glanced at his employer. Turning his back on Garrian, he took her into confidence. "She's always been fragile, getting sick all the time and never managing to carry a child to term. The nasty rumor about Elise gave her a shock. I think it pushed her over the edge and she didn't have the will to recover from her latest illness."

"So sad." She couldn't think of a way to ask more about Elise without revealing she knew nothing. Worse, she caught someone noticing them chatting, so she thanked him and moved on. Next, she concerned herself with the task of finding Sera Drune. If Garrian thought she might be working for Drune, she had every intention of confusing the matter by making it appear that could be true.

After circulating through the crowd again, she found Drune and approached. Much to her frustration, nothing else of substance had been revealed in a quarter hour of mingling. None of these people seemed to want to talk about rumors here. They'd save it for later, when Garrian and the dead body had gone and they could cackle to their hearts' content in relative safety.

Drune stood in a mixed group, the five of them bored and cranky. Chavali couldn't fault them for that. If they had to stand around and pretend to feel sympathy for someone, anyone would rather do it in warmth, with tea and cake. The woman herself dressed the same as those around her: well, but not to be noticed. She had sharp eyes, dark hair up in a tight bun, and a severe nose, and held herself with a precise sort of stiffness, that of a stern teacher who brooked no disobedience.

Given what she wanted to portray, Chavali stopped nearby, standing alone. Her feather stuck out of the hood of her cloak, as she'd arranged it moments ago. She stared down the slight incline at Garrian, flicking her eyes over at Drune once, then twice, then a third time. After the second time, she noticed the group of five watching her. The third glance got Drune to walk over and stand next to her.

"If you work for Garrian, you're very bad at being subtle." Her voice suited her appearance: clipped, precise, and disapproving.

It took effort not to smirk. "Thank you for letting me know."

"What do you want?"

A poor attempt at subterfuge had been fabricated for the crowd, and she had no further need for Drune. While there, though, she might as well ask a useful question. "Do you know anything about Elise, the woman who used to be Garrian's assistant?"

Drune didn't answer right away. She crossed her arms and scanned Chavali up and down. "Who are you?"

"No one important. You can call me Chastity."

"I see. All I know about Elise is that she was competent." From

Drune's inflection, she considered this high praise. "She did her job well and it took Garrian two weeks to find someone even close to her skill to replace her."

Chavali saw Garrian notice her there, and then watched him gesture to his assistant. Interesting. "What of the rumors about her?"

Drune huffed and dropped her arms. "I don't discuss that kind of nonsense, Chastity. Go find street gossips if that's what you're looking for." She stalked back to her circle of people.

She needed to leave. In a tavern, the feather marked her as entertainment. Here, it made her easy to recognize and identify. By the time she met with Garrian tomorrow, he would know her by the fake name. She collected Colby as she strode out, not hiding her haste to be elsewhere.

Chapter 7

On the way back to the inn, Chavali ignored everything except where her feet went while she picked away at what she'd learned. Given what she knew and saw, there were conclusions to leap to, and she could spew out a vague, useless "fortune" that would certainly turn out to be fitting of the truth. That wouldn't help. They needed concrete information to work with, not fragments of rumors spiced by her impressions.

She sat down at a table in the corner with Colby, expecting Portia and Harris to return soon. Hot tea would suit her well enough. She ordered a small meal anyway. Colby, predictably, ordered much more.

"I'm not sure," he said when the waitress left, "but I think someone might have followed us here. He didn't come inside, so maybe not. When we leave, we should keep an eye out."

Nodding, Chavali rubbed her thumb across a scrape in the table's finish. She should make a new Seer's table. The destruction of the old one didn't mean she couldn't carry the tradition on. "I did not learn as much as I hoped to."

"It looked like you were trying to stir up trouble." He laced his fingers together, resting his hands on the table. "I don't really see how that's helpful."

She shrugged. "You can tell a lot about a woman by how she behaves under siege."

"You can catch more flies with honey than vinegar."

"Do not be stupid. We have no honey here. We *are* the vinegar."

The common room held only a handful of patrons, so the door opening and Harris walking in cut off Colby's response. Portia followed, and the pair wove through the room to sit at their table. Both looked satisfied, but grim.

"Elise is dead." Portia sat and waved a waitress over. "Also, it turns out he's useful." She pointed to Harris.

Harris flashed a grin at Chavali. "I have a few marketable skills."

They placed orders and waited for the girl to leave. "Apparently," Portia leaned across the table, "Elise was infatuated with her boss, Garrian. So much so that he had to pry her off with a crowbar. They had a confrontation, a rather public one. He pushed her off. She was so upset, she killed herself."

"Jumped off Lover's Leap," Harris said. "It's a specific part of the seaside cliffs where a few people have jumped from time to time, same sorts of stories. We saw it from a distance. You can walk right up to the edge and fall straight down into the water, instead of crashing into rocks. I guess it seems romantic or something. Looks like a slow drowning death to me."

The thought of some kind of death being considered "romantic" made Chavali's lip curl. "I met her replacement. No one really wanted to talk much. People spoke of tragedy. The dead woman was not a healthy person overall, and her husband cared about her. He did not weep or show much, though he did stare a lot. I made an appointment to speak with him tomorrow morning."

"If she's been presumed dead," Colby said, "we should see if we can get a look at her home and possessions. Until we have proof she jumped of her own accord, we should assume she was murdered."

"How?" Portia paused while the waitress brought their food over. She picked up her fork and took a bite, enjoyed it, then continued. "We can't walk up and say 'let us in to see her stuff.' It won't work."

Harris asked, "Do we know what she looked like?"

"Not exactly," Colby said. "There's a vague description in the file: five foot four, brown hair, brown eyes, and a few comments about her preferred clothing."

Chavali watched Harris think and guessed his idea while he girded himself to suggest it. "Harris is not unusually tall."

"I also have brown hair and brown eyes, and I speak Shappan just fine," Harris nodded. "And I can stand around looking sad."

"No one will buy a distant relative popping up a few months after she died," Portia said.

"How about..." Harris tapped a finger on the table, thinking. "A brother? One that's been traveling, or living in Meccalle for some reason?"

"A half-brother," Portia suggested. "We have her family name. Make it the same father. You can have wildly different looks and still be believable. We shouldn't have to fool anyone important who really knew her well, so that's good enough."

Only one thing didn't make sense to Chavali. "How do we find her home?"

"Her address is in the file," Colby said.

"Why did we not go there first?"

Colby shrugged. "We were tired when we got here, and the funeral seemed more important."

At least the answer wasn't "I didn't think of that." Chavali ate the last bite of her meal and finished her tea. The others were ready to go, too, and they hurried off in the chill air to find Elise's apartment. Colby led the way, with Portia in the rear.

A few blocks from the inn, Portia murmured, "Don't look, but there's someone following us. Black coat, nice shoes, black hat." Chavali turned to look and spotted him. "I said *don't* look." Portia rolled her eyes. "Honestly. Don't let him know we spotted—"

Her Papá could boom his voice when he wanted to. It carried over a crowd to announce the dancers taking the stage, or an acrobatics show, or whatever else the clan wanted to highlight. Chavali missed him, but she could bring him back to life for a fleeting moment by using that voice when she wanted to. "Who are you," she bellowed at the strange man, "and why are you following us?"

Portia covered her face with a hand. Colby's head snapped around. Harris took off running without a word, headed straight for the man Chavali managed to stun into submission with the power of her voice. The man recovered, but not fast enough to get away from Harris. Colby pounded up the street right behind him, moving with speed despite his size, catching up when Harris grabbed the man by the coat.

By the time Chavali and Portia reached the spot, Colby and Harris had the stranger on the ground, Colby pinning him down with a knee on his back and Harris holding his head up to talk to him.

"This situation seems kind of familiar," Harris said with a smirk.

"It is missing something," Chavali said. She crouched down in front of the man, pulled off a mitten, and grabbed him by the neck. "Why are you following us?"

He gurgled, so she and Harris both loosened their grips. "The guards will arrest you for this." *And Garrian will be angry I got caught.*

This came as no great surprise to Chavali. "He works for Seran Garrian."

What? How did you know that? "No I don't. I'm not following you. Why did you attack me?"

"Do not waste your breath. Lie to me again, and I will devour your soul."

Colby blanched and went still, his body rigid with disapproval. Harris, on the other hand, paled and gulped. "I don't think I want to see that."

Chavali shrugged. "Then you should encourage him to answer truthfully."

Can you really do that? Creator, I don't know. The panic showed. "Wait, I do, yeah. I work for Garrian. He asked me to find out more about you, that's all. I swear." *Drune's spy must be watching this and laughing her ass off.* An image of a woman lurking near the inn flashed in his mind.

"Drune sent someone to follow us, too? Do you know her?"

The man gulped, his eyes bugging out as he realized she must know his thoughts. "How did you—? Creator's mercy," he breathed. "I only know her in passing."

Portia bent down, getting into his face. "We know who you both are now, so there's no real point to either of you following us. Go tell her to back off, and do the same yourself, or we'll get unpleasant."

Colby stood up, letting him go, aside from Harris still holding him by the hair. "He's got the message, let it be delivered."

Harris whispered into the man's ear. Chavali got the gist from the spy's thoughts: the former bandit knew how to deliver a real threat. He let go, so did she. The spy scrambled to his feet and hurried away. Scanning the street, Chavali spotted the woman, casually inspecting a shop window. Not bothering to hide it, she pointed at their other shadow.

Harris looked, waved at the woman with a cheerful smile, then turned to follow Colby. Chavali and Portia fell in behind them again. She hadn't expected the two councilors to have her followed. In retrospect, it made sense, as that would be the only way to learn anything about her. Both had their curiosity piqued, so both did something about it.

"You know," Portia said after they turned the next corner, "usually when you realize you're being followed, you don't shout out and chase them down."

"No? What is the proper way to handle such a thing?"

"Cleverness. Quiet. Distraction. Leading them on a merry chase until you lose them."

Chavali considered the point, then shrugged. "I will remember this for the next time. This kind of work is strange to me."

"Yeah, it took me a while to get the hang of it. Pig farmers don't exactly live and breathe subterfuge. A lot of people showed me a lot of patience when I first started. The key is, you have to know what your goals are. Sometimes, the most important thing is for them to not know you know they're following you. Other times, it's for them to not know what you're doing. Still others, you need them to know and be scared and go away."

"And what was the most important thing here?"

"Right then? Probably we wanted them to not realize we knew." She smirked and put an arm around Chavali's shoulders. "Don't worry about it. We'll make it work. I've done worse and not blown missions because of it."

The contact reminded her of Pasha again, and Chavali squirmed under it. Portia withdrew her arm without looking hurt.

"You know," Portia said a short time later, "there's something else you could learn that might help you a lot."

Chavali arched an eyebrow. "I am sure there are many things I can learn now. What in particular do you mean?"

"Your accent. The way you speak Shappan. It marks you as foreign, which will always make people hesitant to trust you. Listen to the way people talk and try to emulate it. Learn more words in Shappan."

"Ah. Hm." Chavali nodded, thinking the suggestion wise. As her clan's fortune teller, she wanted to sound different on purpose and so never made an effort to do more than learn words. In this new role, she needed to blend. One more thing to practice.

Chapter 8

Colby took them to a large house. Inside the unlocked front door, they found a wide hallway with two more doors and a set of stairs. He led them up the steps to an identical wide hallway, and then to the further of the two doors. A metallic number four had been bolted to the dor. Below it hung a sign in the shape of a dog's paw print with the word "welcome" painted across it in blocky letters.

He used the small brushed iron knocker mounted above the number, sending two sharp cracks echoing through the hall. Chavali didn't understand why he expected anything here with Elise dead. Still, they had no other leads to pursue, so she waited behind him with Harris and Portia. About a minute later, the handle turned and the door opened far enough for a young man, probably in his early twenties, to peer out. A dog barked in the background.

"Excuse us, we're looking for Elise Milden. Is she here?"

The man looked the four of them over. "Uh, sorry. I didn't know her, but I think that was the name of the woman who lived here before me. I moved in two months ago."

Chavali stepped forward, pushing Colby aside and dragging Harris with her. "My husband is her brother, and we learned she died a few days ago. We hoped perhaps she had a roommate and so her things might still be here. Do you know anything to help? He would appreciate very much to find a memento of her to take back to their father."

Beside her, Harris's reaction presented a passable impression of a grieving brother. With coaching and some warning, he could probably hold up the act under the scrutiny of someone who knew her. "Anything you could tell us would be appreciated, sir."

"I'm sorry." He lowered his eyes in sympathy. "Um, I don't know... Actually, now that you ask, I remember the landlord saying something. He'd been able to rent it out again quickly because someone packed up and took her things right after she died." His brow crinkled as he searched his memories. "Men working for Seran Garrian, if I recall correctly."

"Thank you for your time," Chavali said, tugging Harris away. He also thanked the man, and Colby and Portia followed them out. "Good job. My apologies for doing this without real warning."

"It's fine." He kept holding her hand, making her glad a mitten and a glove stood between their skin. "You can say we're married any time you want."

She yanked her hand away with a roll of her eyes. "Is it common for an employer to do this?"

"Not that I know of," Portia said with a frown and shake of her head. "Especially not when there are rumors about an affair circling around. It'll be something else to ask him about." She checked up and down the street. "Do we want to play up the brother angle? If anyone noticed us coming here, it makes the most sense for why."

"I'm up for it," Harris said with a shrug. "I can do better with a little time to prepare."

"I don't like lying to Garrian about that. It's one thing to pass him off for some random person," Colby waved up at the building. "No one's life is affected by that lie but your own. Telling someone who really knew her about a fantasy brother and pretending to be married, and this nonsense about a memento? It's too much fabrication. I can't condone it."

Harris gave him the kind of bemused look one gives for sympathy with naïveté. Chavali felt the same way. "We can discuss your brilliant alternative plan at the inn, since we have no other leads until the appointment tomorrow." She started walking without checking to see if the rest followed her. They did, of course.

In the tavern again, the common room had only a few patrons, making it unsafe to discuss anything in depth. They went to Harris and Colby's room, where Chavali turned down offers by both men and sat on the floor to avoid making any statements she didn't want to make. Portia dropped down beside her with a grin.

After she explained what exactly she said to Garrian, she ended with, "I cannot shake the feeling—"

"Can't," Portia interrupted. "Most people use 'can't' instead of 'cannot.' "

"Can't." If she intended to interrupt for that a lot, Chavali might start snapping at her. "I *can't* shake the feeling something with him about this is not right."

"Use 'isn't' instead of 'is not.' "

Chavali gritted her teeth and repeated the sentence how Portia wanted her to. "The grief seemed superficial to me. He is good, but his thoughts held no taint of it."

"He's," Harris suggested, grinning. "Don't worry, Chavali. We'll have you talking like a crusty Shappan sailor in no time."

"You're one to talk." Portia snorted. "Your accent is pure Meccalle city slums. I had to work hard to get the rural Cascain out, and you'll have to work just as hard to make yourself difficult to place on a map. For right now, Chavali is fine, because she's only passing herself off as your wife. Colby doesn't matter, because he's hired muscle, and hired muscle doesn't talk. You, on the other hand, need to sound at least somewhat Shappan."

"Wait a minute." Colby put a large hand out to stop the discussion. "I still don't agree with that plan."

Chavali crossed her arms. "We still await your alternative."

He gave her a flat look. "Just because I don't have another idea doesn't mean we should use this one. It's not right to do things this way. Lying *is* the worst thing you can do, it *is* the greatest sin, and I won't stand by while you all plan to do it on purpose because it's the easiest way to go."

"That's dumb." Harris crossed his arms, too. "What Order preaches that? The Order of the Morons? Backstabbing your friends is a lot worse than lying."

Colby glared at Harris. "It's not that simple, don't pretend that you think it is. You have to be honest about who you are and what you want, and treat others fairly. It's about integrity and—"

"And getting slapped for telling a woman her rump really is fat when she asks."

Portia cleared her throat. "Gentlemen. We're not here to argue about which sin is the greatest. Colby, I respect that your beliefs make this kind of operation difficult for you to participate in."

"It still must be done," Chavali said. "The alternative? We walk in there and say we came to investigate Elise's death for the Crown. Why now? It has been months since she died. To all appearances, the matter was handled and is closed. The Crown having a sudden interest in a mere assistant's suicide makes no sense. Keep in mind, we have no intent to steal from him. This is about finding the truth."

Colby's mouth puckered up in distaste. "You shouldn't use the ends to justify the means."

Chavali narrowed her eyes. "It is easy—"

"It's," Portia hissed.

"*It's* easy to be uncompromising," Chavali snapped, "to live as if nuance does not apply to you. Acting these parts may not be the only way, but it is—it's the best way we have at our disposal to learn what we must. With more time, or resources, or something, we could do otherwise and adhere to your narrow needs. We have what we have, and if the methods we employ are too upsetting to you, then perhaps you should stay here instead of doing your job."

Colby glowered and looked away. "Fine, do your play acting. I don't approve, but I won't stop you." He rolled to his feet. "I should check on Karias and brush him down, maybe take a ride to get him some exercise." No one objected as he left the room.

"He needs a woman," Harris reflected after the door shut. "Too tense."

Chavali smirked and Portia laughed. "Probably close to the truth. We should work on your accent. Chavali, you can stay or go, but I don't think you'll get a lot out of it. We're going to work on beating Meccalle out of him."

"I will go." She stood and smoothed her dress down, ignoring Harris's disappointment. "I wish to watch people here." They both wished her well and she made her way down to the tavern again. Dropping onto a stool at the end of the bar, she got hot tea and turned so she could see most of the room. The place had few customers still, and her attention drifted around, her thoughts pleasantly vague.

She noticed the girl who bumped into her last night, working and steering clear of her. Good. She had no interest in dealing with someone so thoughtless. Her eyes slipped over to watch the girl several times, and she noticed a similarity in features to one of the staff helping the pickpocket, though the girl didn't seem to know about the theft happening. Interesting.

Eventually, the room filled. When most of the various tables had been taken, someone sat beside her, despite there being a number of empty seats farther away. The middle-aged woman walked up without paying the tables any attention and claimed the next seat over, blocking most of Chavali's view. Something about this person felt familiar, though Chavali couldn't say what, exactly. She had the look and lines of all the other Shappans around, with dark hair mostly gone to gray, crow's feet around medium colored eyes, and tanned pale skin.

The woman sat in silence, and the bartender ignored her. Chavali watched her without bothering to hide it. If she didn't want to be stared at, she should have sat one seat farther down. After several minutes, the woman suddenly spoke into the relative quiet. "Did you notice the pickpocket working the room tonight?"

A direct question surprised her, but Chavali nodded. "Yes. He is good, but not *that* good. The waitstaff should toss him out, since they know what is going on."

"He's paying them from his take. The payoff is high enough for the risk, and they aren't thinking about how it'll affect the future."

Disconcerted by an uncanny echo of her own opinion on the subject, Chavali studied her neighbor. No rings or other jewelry, no unusual marks—nothing set her apart from the norm. That in itself somehow made her strange when it should have made her fit in. "It's foolish to expect no one will catch on to a rash of thefts at one particular place," she agreed.

Her clan avoided direct stealing such as this, because people talked. A reputation of pickpockets and muggers would precede them. Overpricing for their goods and services was another matter entirely. Everyone expected to be parted from their money by a carnival. They merely wanted to see it happening and know it paid for a good time.

"Perhaps we should tell the bartender." The woman looked at her, inviting her opinion. It made her feel they shared some kind of sisterhood, a connection.

Chavali smirked, recognizing the tactic to create the appearance of friendship and applauding the deftness with which the woman employed it. She liked this woman, but would take care to keep her secrets close. "I do not care enough. It is not my home. If he cannot see it for himself, and does not treat his waitstaff well enough to prevent it, the fault is his and on his shoulders be it."

The woman grinned with amusement. "If you came here often, you would say something?"

"Yes. Once people notice, the place will lose customers. The quality of the food and service will degrade, perhaps even forcing it to close."

"So, then, your concern is only for yourself."

Chavali nodded, feeling this assessment to be fair, if incomplete. "Myself, my friends, and my family. What does not affect us does not concern me." The bartender came by to refill her mug.

"Ah, that looks pleasant. I could use something hot."

"Another hot tea, please," Chavali said, "the same as this one." The bartender nodded and slipped away.

The woman stayed quiet while they waited, and still said nothing after the tea arrived. Chavali sipped at hers, disappointed that conversation had ended, but not enough to restart it herself. It surprised her when the woman spoke again, several minutes later. "What if it does affect you, but you can't see how?"

"How would a pickpocket working a tavern I intend to spend only a few days in affect me? He takes money from the unwary and foolish, and is smart enough to not come within ten feet of me. Those he targets can afford to spend their coin on food of good quality, and should not find the loss of a few from their pockets to be devastating. Those who protect him get a few extra coins of their own to spend elsewhere, and he is not living on the street. The bartender, who owns the place, loses nothing until word gets out, and if his inn closes, another will open in its place."

"If he targeted the poor, would you take issue with that? How about those on the edge of poverty?"

How Chavali would love to sample this woman's thoughts. She

asked interesting questions, and actually listened to the answers. The conversation stimulated her mind in a way no one in the Fallen tower had yet managed. "Stealing from the poor is foolish, as they have little of value and immediately miss whatever is taken from them. I am not familiar with the edge of poverty in a city, and have no opinion on that."

"What if I told you that couple," the woman pointed to a man and woman sitting together at a small table, "is here to celebrate five years of marriage? They've been saving for this dinner for a while now, wanting to pass the evening and night in a cheerful place with good food so they can go back to their difficult lives with a warm, bright memory of something better. If the pickpocket steals from them, he takes with him the only coin they have to pay for a room, and they'll have to go home to their drab, labor-filled days and nights well before they intended to. Would that be fair? Would that be acceptable to you?"

Chavali lifted an eyebrow, skeptical of such a claim. How could this woman possibly know all of that? She'd watched her companion walk in the door and go straight to her current stool without pausing. Clearly, this was meant to be hypothetical. Shifting her attention to the couple, she judged the story to be plausible. Both young faces looked thin and worn, the same as their clothes, but not boldly or wretchedly so. Subtle cues—how the clothes hung loose, the frayed hems, and the woman's glances to the side—could have led her to make up a similar story about them. She even recognized the last as the reflexive need of a mother of young children to make sure they didn't wander or do anything stupid, even when she knew them to be safe in someone else's care.

Such people did need every last scrape of money they had. Memories of others' thoughts showed her how they also needed to spend it sometimes on nice things, on treats. They used the word "splurging." She had no ill will towards such people, and knew these impulses had been the main source of income for her clan.

Interesting how the thought of her clan didn't fill her with the same pain as it did a few weeks ago. Getting the three children back filled her heart enough. Thinking of the deaths of specific people still bothered her, and she firmly shoved the memories of Pasha and Keino and her parents away.

She tapped a hand on the bar to get the tender's attention. This reminded her of Colby's request to help Ivan last night, which displeased her the moment she realized it, but she lost nothing by performing this small gesture, and might possibly gain something. Unlike with Ivan, who would do nothing for her in return.

"Do you need another refill?" The man smiled at her, reaching for her mug. Despite his expression, she noted apprehensive tension in his shoulders. After the incident last night, perhaps he expected her to complain about something.

She hadn't noticed the state of her mug, and peered into it. "Yes, actually, but I wish to tell you of a problem: you have a pickpocket working your tavern. I saw him last night and he is returned tonight. Two of your employees help him stay unnoticed." Without gesturing towards him, she described the man and the two employees.

The bartender blinked several times in shock while she spoke. "Thank you for calling my attention to it, ma'am. I don't get to pay as much attention to the room as I'd like, and I appreciate when my customers help out." He took her mug and refilled it from a kettle, then went into his back room.

"And how do you feel now?"

Chavali shrugged and sipped her tea.

The woman laughed. "I expected nothing less. You said you're staying in town for a few days?" At Chavali's nod, the woman stood and dropped several coins on the bar, more than twice the price of the tea. "I have business here myself. If you're interested, I'll be back tomorrow night, and I'd be happy to share tea with you again, Chavali." She left, winding swiftly through the room and slipping out the door as the bartender called one of the crooked waitstaff to the back, probably to fire her.

As the front door shut, Chavali frowned. She didn't remember telling the woman her name.

Chapter 9

Black fabric hung over the windows of Garrian's home, a modest two-story house with a small garden in the front. The place appeared to be well tended and had a minimalist wrought iron fence separating the property from its neighbors and the street. Chavali led the others through the open gate and up the stone path to the oak door.

One rap of the metal knocker had the door opening and Garrian's assistant peering out, then smiling in recognition. "Chastity, right on time. Come in, please. The Seran is in his office. Can I get you anything to drink?"

"No, thank you." She took Harris's arm and followed the assistant down the hall and around a corner to a door. Despite the paintings and other artwork scattered along their path, the house felt plain. Nothing struck Chavali as personal. This place didn't qualify for the term "home," only "house."

The assistant stopped at a door and knocked. He opened it without waiting for a response. "Your appointment is here." He let them into a room claimed by the possessions of the man standing behind the desk, flipping through a book with small writing in columns. Bookshelves covered the walls, stacked with books, papers, and random knickknacks. Papers cluttered his desk, strewn about haphazardly. Several wooden crates sat stacked in one corner and on the two wooden chairs intended for guests.

"My apologies for the mess," Garrian said distractedly. "My wife's death came at the same time as other emergencies."

"We are sorry for your loss."

Colby stayed outside the room, keeping the door open by leaning on it. Portia took one look inside and followed his example. That left Harris and Chavali in the room with Garrian, both making an effort to play the part of a married couple.

Garrian looked up at the words, brows knitted together. "You came to the funeral yesterday."

"Yes, I apologize for my timing. Sometimes, better judgment comes only after the fact."

He waved the matter off and returned his attention to his book. "What can I do for you?"

Harris stepped forward and offered his hand to shake. "My name is Harris Milden. I'm hoping to talk to you about my sister." Chavali noted his accent, though a little forced, sounded much more Shappan now. Portia did good work.

Garrian looked up again, now more confused. "Sister?" He stared at Harris's hand.

Harris's sad smile faltered. "Elise. She was your clerk, wasn't she?"

Still blank, Garrian nodded. "Yes." He shook Harris's hand

tentatively. "You're her brother?"

"Half-brother, actually. My mother died before she was born." Harris slipped his arm around Chavali's waist, holding her close. It exasperated her, but she kept that out of her expression.

Garrian flipped the book shut. "I had no idea she even had living relatives."

"That explains it," he said to Chavali with a nod.

"Yes, it does," she agreed. "We came to Ket for other reasons," she said to Garrian, "and thought to stop in and see her. We had her address, of course. She wrote home sometimes. It turns out someone else lives there now."

"It's kind of strange," Harris added. "I hadn't seen her in so long, that learning she's dead... It hasn't really hit me yet, I guess."

Garrian's eyes flicked between them, watching Chavali pet Harris to comfort him and make small sympathetic noises at him. "If I'd known, I would have sent a message of some sort."

She turned to watch Garrian's reactions. "You were not very close, then?"

His face flickered with an expression too fleeting and complex to decode. Yet, she knew fear well enough to see that he had some. "No, not really." He paused and looked down at the chaos on his desk. Picking up a stack of papers, he shook his head. "She had ideas, but my wife—I wasn't interested." Garrian lied well, but not well enough to fool Chavali with that. Still, the fear persisted, which intrigued her. "Elise's death was a tragedy, of course. I had no idea she felt so much."

"Your wife has passed," Chavali offered. "It's not wrong to admit you had feelings for Elise."

He shook his head, still not looking at either of them. She figured anything coming out of his mouth would be a lie from the way he shifted on his feet and refused to make eye contact. "No, I was only fond of her. I really don't know what I can tell you."

"You can release her belongings to me," Harris said. "I understand you've kept them safe?"

Garrian thought about it for a beat longer than seemed normal, then nodded. "Yes, of course." He pushed papers around until he found a blank page and plucked a pen from its holder to scribble on it. "Take this to the docks and give it to Simon, the foreman. He'll know where the crates are and can help you get them loaded up for transport."

"Thank you, I appreciate that." Harris took the note and shook his hand again.

Chavali reached out and also shook his hand, terribly curious what inspired his fear. "I again apologize for yesterday." A woman's face at a window, peering inside, ghosted across his mind. Before she could get anything else, Chavali saw purple. She stiffened and barely had time to hiss out a curse before the spirits overwhelmed her. Unable to resist, she stood rooted to the spot while her mouth betrayed her.

"The Herald swims in a fated tide, bringing ruin on the rise. The first little fish takes a bite, the second steals an eye. The third devours whole, reaping for the blind. Oaken seed, charged to bleed, taken in the night. Empty moon sees her doom, too late to put it right."

The last word hung on the air with everyone staring at her. Chavali sagged against Harris; with his arm already around her, he had no trouble catching her. Then her head split open and Colby's horse danced on it while madmen slammed pickaxes into it. In truth, it felt much, much worse than that. She would have crumpled to the floor if not for Harris.

"Chastity? Are you alright?" Harris remembered her fake name in a moment of crisis. Later, she would be impressed.

"What was that about?"

"I'm sorry about this," Portia said. "She's got a condition. It's nothing. We'll be on our way. Thank you for your help."

Chavali wanted to scream at them all to shut up. Every sound grated on her raw agony. She clapped her hands over her ears, screwed her eyes shut, and gritted her teeth. There would be no tea mixture to soothe the spirits and drain the pain away. This would be worse than the first time it happened to her. At least then, she didn't have to explain, and Mamá had things to try until they got the combination right.

This was the first prophecy she delivered as Fallen. Between mourning her clan, Eliot's training, stealing moments with the children, and the other hundred things she'd been doing, it didn't even occur to her that it would happen again, and so she never bothered to get the herbs she needed. So stupid, she had been so stupid to not think of it. Others always took care of it for her. She had to take care of these things herself now.

Someone picked her up and carried her out of the room. They went out into the cold, which hurt, and the bright light, which also hurt. The sound of the wind hurt. Voices and creaking carriages and jangling harnesses and even the crinkle of the cloth of the person carrying her hurt. Breathing hurt.

"What happened?"

"I don't know."

"Chavali?" Colby's voice rumbled painfully, letting her know he was the one carrying her. At least the chill meant she didn't have to worry about skin contact. Until he put two fingers on her neck and all his concern and confusion scraped at her. She cried out and he jerked his hand away. "We should take her back to the inn, I guess."

"What do you think that was about? A herald? Fish? Did she crack up?" Harris sounded as worried as Colby.

"I doubt—"

"Quiet, please," Chavali ground out. "Dark and quiet." Someone draped a heavy cloth over her head, holding it tight over her eyes and ears. Colby walked, his gait now smoother. It had been so long since she suffered this without her tea, she forgot how it faded from the initial spike after ten minutes or so. The agony eased to a less debilitating headache, and she cleared her throat. "Stop, you can stop now."

Colby paused, then turned and hurried for a short time. Chavali chose not to complain and felt it when he ducked into a shadow. He set her gently on her feet where she could lean against both him and a wall, partway down a shaded alley, and pulled the cloth away from her face. Rather than staying standing, she slid down to sit on the ground with his help.

His eyes flicked over her face. "Are you alright?"

"No. I will be." She put a hand to her forehead and pressed.

Harris crouched down beside Colby, mirroring his concern. Portia loomed behind them, arms crossed and frowning. "What happened?"

"Please, speak gently. My head is still in pain." She wished she could have something to drink, even plain water. "It will go away in a while." As little as she wanted to explain, they deserved to know about this.

"Prophecy. It does not happen often, and it is not kind to me when it does. Being used by—" She stopped herself from saying "the spirits," knowing no one believed in that sort of thing. No one except her and her clan. "It is not pleasant and my mind must heal from it."

"Prophecy." Harris looked at her with fresh fear. He must be thinking about what she could actually do to him if she wanted to.

"Yes. With accuracy. This is why I died. To keep this—" Gift. Curse. Burden. Damnation. Honor. Duty. "—thing from someone who wished to control it for his own ends."

"Wow." Portia's hands now dangled at her side. "That's a lot bigger of a deal than why I died."

"What did it all mean, though?" Harris asked. "None of that made any sense to me."

Chavali shook her head. She stopped right away, because it hurt. "Metaphor. All of it. A herald is some kind of messenger, a harbinger, the first of many. Swimming is arriving by water. Ruin is something bad, coming by water, or in water, or something like this. The fish could be people, creatures, ideas, anything that can come and devour. Three times, three waves, three something. The first is the least, the third is the worst.

"Of the rest, I will guess the 'empty moon' means the new moon, and a woman will be taken and killed then, or perhaps by then. I have no idea what 'oaken seed' means. Some kind of clue to her identity, I expect. Bleeding probably means injury, maybe torture or incidental to an abduction. Since this came while I touched Garrian, he is involved somehow. Whether he is a victim or a fish or happens to have a connection to one of those, I have no idea."

Harris smirked. "He sent someone to spy on us, so I'd say victim is out. No trusting him, then. I want to have a look around the docks for sure now."

"Are you up for that?" Colby still supported her, his warmth a pleasant counterpoint to the chill of the ground and the stone behind her.

She *wanted* to go someplace soft and drink tea and be pampered and lie there while the headache ebbed. She didn't deserve any of that. This problem could have been managed, with no more than an hour or two of effort on her part. "So long as I do not have to run anywhere, or deal with very loud noises, I will be fine."

Colby helped her stand. "If we have to run, I'll carry you."

She pulled her mittens on and took a few unsteady steps. Harris stepped up before Colby could, and took her arm. "Illusions, mind-reading, soul stealing, and prophecy. Interesting collection of talents you have."

"Soul stealing? You weren't faking about that?" Portia walked behind them with Colby taking up the rear.

A glance back at Colby made Chavali frown. These people were her new family, and she needed to deal with them fairly. Lying to them—or, in this case, continuing to lie—needed a good reason. With Harris bound to the Fallen, she had no good reason anymore. "I may have exaggerated my abilities to a certain degree in an effort to gain your cooperation."

Harris opened his mouth and shut it. Then he chuckled. "I guess you're not actually as scary as you seemed the other day."

A commotion on the other side of the street made them all turn to look. Chavali recognized Ivan as the person helping his wife to her feet. A young man had gotten tangled up with her, probably from a collision of some sort. Harris turned away from it and kept walking, but Chavali caught a glimpse of the young man's face and recognized Garrian's spy. Later, she might grudgingly admit that helping Ivan might have had some overall positive effect somehow. Maybe.

Several moments later, Colby closed the distance and murmured to them both, "Drune's spy is following us again. So is someone else, someone new."

Hoping Garrian's spy hadn't noticed her seeing him, Chavali nodded. "We are doing what Garrian expects us to do, so we might as well ignore them and do it."

"Agreed," Portia said. "Keep up the married act, and we're all strolling down to the docks to collect Harris's half-sister's belongings. Nothing suspicious going on here."

"Why are they all following us separately?" Harris muttered.

"Who knows."

Chapter 10

Ket's deep water port had moorings to accommodate four large boats at once and a dozen smaller ones. Wooden ramps wide enough for wagons ran down from the warehouses at the top of the low cliff to a wide platform at the water's edge, built so the waves crashed into the rock face underneath it. Harris pointed out Lover's Leap in the distance, where the cliff wall climbed up much higher.

Chavali's pounding headache kept her from thinking much about any of this. She let Harris pull her along without resisting him, focusing on not snarling at anyone. Portia asked around for Simon. Men with better things to do than give directions pointed them at a quay where a team of laborers moved cargo off a ship.

The foreman stood out among the workers. He directed traffic and checked crates and papers without doing much physical work of his own. Despite that, he had the same build and muscle as the rest, and wore the same type of clothing: bland, simple pants and shirt that protected against the cold without being restrictive or bulky. If any of them fell into the water, their boots would be the only thing to cause a problem with getting out again.

Harris and Chavali followed Portia down the ramp and up the quay. Colby stayed by the warehouses, watching everyone and everything, playing the part of a bodyguard again. The docks had been mounted to not sway with the water, a fact Chavali appreciated. Clomping boots did enough to her head without having to walk on an unstable platform.

"Excuse me," Portia called out as they got close. "I'm looking for Simon."

All their heads turned, and several gave Portia an appreciative once-over. The foreman smiled with a similar sentiment, then barked for his men to get back to work. "I'm Simon," he said as he walked towards her.

They shook hands. "Seran Garrian sent us." She jerked a thumb at Harris and Chavali.

"Ah." Simon's smile faltered, falling into a more professional greeting. "What can I do for you?"

Harris held out the letter. "I want to have it all shipped to a small town east of Todan. Can you handle that for me, or do I need to get someone else to take care of it?"

Simon scanned the letter, scratching at his scruffy beard. "Says here the Seran will pay to have it shipped, so you're in luck." A loud splash behind him made all of them look, and Simon grunted. A crate had fallen into the water. "Can't turn my back on these idiots for even a minute. If you don't mind coming down this way, let me get the details from you."

The three of them followed him to the stack of crates. Simon handed Harris a piece of charcoal with the letter. "Use the crate to write on," he suggested, then he turned to shout at the workers, directing the retrieval.

Harris nodded and wrote out enough information to get Elise's belongings to Eldrack. Chavali leaned on the crate, holding her head. The one she rested against had similar dimensions as the others: as tall as her, perhaps three feet wide, and four feet deep—big enough to hold any number of things. Portia turned her back on the commotion and appeared to be doing nothing more than huddling in her cloak against the wind and staring out over the water.

Something seemed wrong to Chavali about all of this, but her headache kept her from thinking much. Simon seemed honest, the docks all looked fine, the two moored ships appeared to be normal, the crates didn't seem unusual, and the men all had the right look for their job. She noticed someone lurking up on the cliff, not far from Colby. It had to be one of their spy shadows, and that merited no concern. So long as they did nothing suspicious, the spies had nothing to report.

Simon got the crate straightened out and turned back to them. "Sorry about that. Is there anything else I can do for you?"

"Is there any way we could have a look inside these crates before they get sent?" Harris handed the paper back and put his arm around Chavali, pulling her close.

Scratching at his beard again, Simon shrugged. "We're getting ready to tear down and rebuild the warehouses, so it's going to be a while until I can get to this."

Harris waved the subject off. "Don't worry about it. There'll be plenty of time to go through it when it gets there. Thank you for your help." They turned and left Simon to get back to work. "They're smuggling something," Harris muttered to her as they reached the ramp. "I saw a mark I recognize on one of the crates."

"We should see where the marked crate goes?"

"Agreed." Harris explained to Portia and Colby, and they found a place to wait. No one would notice them except the spies who watched while they settled behind some old crates and a barrel. "I can see why smuggling would be tempting here. Simon runs the place and there isn't much oversight."

"The workers aren't very smart," Portia said, "so it would be easy to get them involved without them knowing it. Simon probably hand picks the dumbest for moving that stuff."

Colby frowned. "I don't approve of any of this, but does it have anything to do with Elise?"

"She was Garrian's assistant," Harris said. "Maybe she noticed something funny and confronted Simon about it. Threatened to tell Garrian."

"It's as plausible as anything else at this point." Portia nodded her chin toward two wagons, getting loaded with the crates. "What's the mark? Do you see it on any of those?"

Harris squinted, peering at the activity. "There, that one has it. They're putting it on the closer of the two wagons. There's another one." He noted the symbol on four of the five crates the workmen loaded onto that same wagon.

Chavali's headache lessened as they waited. She didn't need Harris's support anymore when they slipped out to follow the wagon. It trundled up the streets, moving in bright daylight without attracting attention. The driver stopped in front of a wine shop and two bulky men came out within half a minute to greet him, sign papers, and move the crates from the wagon to the shop.

"I've never seen wine shipped in boxes that size before," Portia whispered from the hiding spot they picked to watch the unloading. "Cheap stuff comes in barrels. Expensive stuff gets sent in small quantities to avoid large losses when crates get damaged. Middle of the line stuff might come in larger lots, but they still only stack them one bottle across."

Colby glanced at her. "How do you know that?"

Portia grinned. "I may have been raised on a pig farm, but that doesn't mean I stayed there for my whole first life. I can get us a look inside the shop without raising suspicion. We might need some subterfuge to get to their cellar."

"We could come back after they close and break in," Harris suggested.

"We're not doing that."

The three of them all looked at Colby. Chavali rolled her eyes at him. "What do you suggest? Walk in and ask to see the smuggled goods for no reason? Do you think they will put their hands out and say 'Oh, yes, you caught us. Please, put us in jail to pay society back for our misdeeds.'?"

"No." He scowled. "Of course not. I just don't like—"

"Being false, yes, we know. You have made this exceptionally clear." She wanted to slap him. "Portia and Colby can go distract whoever minds the shop while Harris and I sneak in through the back."

Portia nodded. "We should watch for a while first. See who comes and goes. Wait until there are other customers for the best possible distraction."

"In that case, we should get something to eat." Harris gazed off at a tavern down the street. "It's been a while since breakfast. I'll go with

Chavali, you two can go when we get back. That way, we can all keep an eye on the place and each other."

Chavali ignored Colby's grumpy scowl and hurried down to the tavern with Harris. Dim light filtered in through greasy windows smudged with soot, tables and chairs had cracks filled with glue and gouges scratched out, and the smell of burnt bread hung thick in the air. Two steps in, Chavali turned around to leave. Harris stopped her with a pleading look.

"It's the only place nearby," he apologized. "It's probably not as bad as it looks. And smells."

Chavali's lip curled but she went to a table anyway, eyes flicking around the other patrons. No one here had enough money to go elsewhere except her and Harris. "They may appreciate if we bring food to them. Assuming it's edible."

"Relax, honey," a gravelly voice said from behind her. "The plague at the docks hasn't made it this far yet, you're safe." The owner of that voice wore a tight dress that hugged all the wrong parts for her shape. Her light-colored hair hung in limp, greasy curls and creases in her face under a thick layer of cosmetics pointed to a hard life.

"What plague at the docks?"

Deaths at the docks. She heard about that at the inn and should have remembered. Damn the spirits and their timing.

The woman smirked. "Must be from out of town. Bodies been turning up down by the docks, one here, one there. My cousin's husband works down there, says he found one of them. Man had a look on his face like he cracked up, and bloody foam around his mouth. They say these people are catching something down there that eats their mind away until they go crazy. Nobody knows what it is or how they catch it."

"They are replacing the docks because of it, yes?"

"Yep, that's what everyone says. No worry about that here, though. Our kitchen is clean as a whistle. You want something to eat?"

Chavali found the comparison lacking, as she knew how whistles worked. She sighed and ordered food anyway.

Chapter 11

A few hours later, when Chavali's headache had cleared, the wine shop had four customers at once. This might be the best chance they would get, and Portia led Colby inside while Chavali and Harris slipped around the back. The door was locked, but Harris pulled a set of tools out and stooped to the level of the keyhole, showing some of skills he picked up in his time on the streets.

Two soft clicks announced his success. He cracked the door open, then pulled it wide enough to peer inside. She followed him when he crept in, and kept the door from slamming shut behind her. They stayed low and moved slowly to let their eyes adjust to the dim inside light. Chavali saw neatly stacked papers, wine bottles in racks, and cupboards—nothing of interest.

Harris tugged at her sleeve and pointed, drawing her attention to a cellar door. Doubled over, they scooted to the door and Harris popped it ajar. When nothing happened, he peered inside and beckoned for her to follow. They went down a wooden staircase with an unobstructed view of a cellar. It reminded her of the tavern basement in Cloverdale.

Wine racks filled with bottles covered the walls, and more racks stood in rows. A wide path from the bottom of the stairs went to the center of the room, presumably for unloading crates. The size of that empty space struck her as odd. Surely, this type of business needed to fill as much of its space as possible to have a wide variety of stock.

They walked through the racks, checking for anything unusual. Harris stopped at the drain in the center of the empty space, squatting down to take a closer look. "Would you grab a bottle of wine and open it?"

Surprised by the request, she quirked an eyebrow and opened her mouth to question the wisdom of drinking now. Before she spoke a single word, a man stepped out from behind a rack they hadn't reached yet, holding a loaded crossbow pointed at her. She raised her hands and took a step back. "This may not be the best time for such things."

"Stand up and keep your hands where I can see them." His voice rumbled, deep and full of menace.

She saw Harris show his surprise to her, then put his hands up and smile as he turned. "Take it easy, mate." He dropped the Shappan accent he'd worked so hard on.

Chavali grasped his intent. "Simon sent us. He is worried."

"About our patron."

The man looked them both over skeptically. "I don't know either of you."

"I'm Harris, this is Chastity." He still remembered to use the fake name. Despite his stupid fawning grins and how easily her rear distracted him, he impressed her in some ways. "We're not from Ket, that's why you don't know us. We work on the other end. Simon asked for outside help is all. Nothing to get ruffled over."

The crossbow wavered and Chavali put her hands down. "He challenged us to track everything down, to see if it is secure. This location has many faults."

"It's too obvious," Harris agreed, also putting his hands down. "We just got here today and we already figured out the chain." Thank goodness she had Harris down here with her, instead of Colby. He would've been shot by now. Twice.

"We can help fix these problems. They are not disastrous." A crash upstairs grabbed her attention. Did Colby and Portia get into a fight?

The smuggler swung his crossbow up to point at the door a moment before it burst open. "Stay where you are," a male voice boomed at them. "Run and you'll be cut down." Men in armor and the uniforms of the City Guard poured through the doorway and clomped down the stairs.

Chavali grabbed Harris's arm because she saw him reach for his bow. "Do not resist," she hissed at him.

That didn't stop their new friend from shooting a crossbow at the first guardsman, hitting him in the side. He ran for cover while reloading. "Fight back, you twits!"

Chavali saw the inevitable conclusion here, and pitied the smuggler for not being able to. Several guards followed the first. She and Harris stood by and put their hands up again, this time getting them roughly pulled behind their backs and bound there. Both were forced up the stairs at sword point, then outside and into a covered wagon. Colby and Portia already sat inside, also tied up, along with three others and a guard watching over them.

"I'm telling you," Colby said, "we didn't do anything, and we're agents—"

"Keep your mouth shut," Harris whispered to Colby, cutting him off.

"And I said no talking," the guard snapped. "Next person to open their mouth gets a fist in it."

One of the other men in the wagon started to complain, then the guard followed through on his threat and no one else spoke. After another minute or so, a whipcrack echoed and the wagon lurched forward without any additional people loaded in. That smuggler must have fought to the death. Idiot. Had he merely surrendered, he would be alive now and could have escaped the harshest judgments by giving up his fellow criminals.

The wagon stopped and more guards unloaded everyone, hauling them all inside a building marked prominently to identify it as a Ket City Guard station. A guard shoved Chavali forward, making her stumble, which caused Harris to drop his shoulder and try to rush the perpetrator. Guards stopped him before he got anywhere, and he collapsed under their efforts to dissuade him from continuing to resist.

They pulled her away from the rest of the prisoners and shoved her in a small room with nothing but a single chair bolted to the floor and a harsh white magical light blaring down on it. A female guard patted her down and took her belt with her knife. She tugged at the feather. "Is this attached?"

"Yes, it is grafted into my skull."

The woman frowned at it. "You're not supposed to keep anything but clothes." She reached for her blade.

Chavali's heart stopped. "It is only a feather, a decoration."

"I can't let you keep it. Sorry." She drew her sword and raised it.

Taking a step away, Chavali shook her head. With her hands tied behind her back, she couldn't think of any way to resist. Except one. She narrowed her eyes, glaring at the woman. "Do not cut this. It is not what it appears to be, and neither am I. Trying to damage it will earn you a lifetime of torment. A very short lifetime. You are only trying to follow orders. I understand this, and I would not have your soul cursed for it."

The guardswoman paused and searched her face. She gulped at what she found. "Well, um. I suppose you're not going to stab anyone with it. You can keep it. For now."

"Thank you."

The woman nodded and pointed for her to sit in the chair. White bindings sprang from the legs, wrapping around her ankles. The guard untied her hands, and she obligingly put them on the armrests. More white cords wrapped around her wrists. As soon as that happened, the guard left with her belt, the sound of the door shutting behind her firm and final.

Calm, she needed to stay calm. She flexed her fingers, vexed by the situation. Those stupid spies following them around must have called in the Guard. Probably, they saw her and Harris sneak around the back and assumed something illegal would happen. If she could get her hands on one of those imbeciles right now, they would regret it.

About ten minutes later, the door opened and interrupted her stewing. The woman who entered didn't wear the uniform of the Guard, but carried that authority on her shoulders. Her short, straight hair had a precise cut and style, her boots gleamed from polishing, and her clothes fit her snugly with crisp folds. Face an impassive mask, she marched into the room on a metronome beat and clasped her hands behind her back.

"Who are you?" The woman's voice rang clear and clipped.

"No one of particular consequence." Chavali shrugged with disinterest, not remotely intimidated by the woman's act. If she'd been asked with less overt hostility, she would have suggested checking the medallion resting on her chest, which they missed when searching her. The main reason not to lay in not learning where the Guard placed their loyalties. "Who are you?"

"Guard Lieutenant Orrien, the person conducting this interview. I ask the questions. You answer them." She brushed her shoulder, removing an imaginary speck of dust.

Chavali smirked, amused by the show. "I see."

Orrien pursed her lips and looked off at the wall. "What is your name?"

"Chastity."

After several beats of silence, Orrien gestured for her to continue. "And your family name?"

"Since you have given me only one name, I feel it's fair I give you only one, as well. If you tell me what I am accused of, I may reconsider this."

"Do you really think you're in a position to make that kind of statement?"

"Do you really think you are in a position to object?"

Orrien narrowed her eyes and stared at her. The intense glare had probably served her well in the past. "Breaking and entering, resisting arrest, and unlawful tax evasion."

"Interesting. No, this is not worth my family name. How about if you tell me why your men chose to raid that establishment at that time?"

At this, Orrien slapped her hands on Chavali's arms where her sleeves had been pushed up, and forced her angry face into Chavali's space. The spirits surged across the contact, telling Chavali that Drune's spy tipped them off, and that she had no proof of anything. Also, Orrien found her arrogant and obnoxious. "I told you, I'm the one asking the questions."

"Then perhaps you should ask about Simon."

"Simon? What about Simon?"

Chavali laughed. "How long have you been investigating this? A few days?"

Several months. If you know more than me, you must be involved.
"Very funny." Orrien pushed away from her and paced across the room, back and forth. "If you have so much information—"

The door burst open with Seran Garrian rushing through, breathless. "This woman has no involvement. I've been having her and her associates followed, because they seemed suspicious, but they aren't. My employee will testify to the fact they arrived in the city recently and have no connection to the ring." He took a few seconds to catch his breath while Orrien gave him a skeptical looking over.

"As you say, Seran Garrian," she said with a curt nod of her head. Obviously displeased, she stepped around the chair, where Chavali couldn't see what she did. The bindings loosened enough for Chavali to pull her hands and feet out of them. "You're free to go, Chastity. Any statement you care to make regarding your presence in that basement would be appreciated."

Chavali remained in the chair, holding the armrests and watching Garrian. He owed her nothing, yet he hurried here and made sure to have her released as soon as possible. Perhaps it came from a sense of duty to Elise and her "brother."

He seemed anxious as she continued to sit there, his eyes flicking from her to Orrien several times. "Oh! I almost forgot. I overheard that there's trouble with your other prisoners."

Orrien sucked in a breath and hurried out. Garrian stepped into the room and offered Chavali a hand to stand up.

She crossed her legs, laced her fingers together over her lap, and looked up at his face. For the moment, making a point felt more important than grabbing his thoughts. "Why did you do this?"

He lowered his hand and frowned at her, then he peeked out into the hall and looked both ways. Shutting the door, he leaned against it and rubbed his face. "I cared about Elise." Chavali couldn't see how this had anything to do with the subject, but didn't interrupt. If he had something to say, she would let him say it. "After she'd been here for a while, she started seeing someone, and she changed. It took me a while to really notice how her behavior changed. She showed up late sometimes, or seemed distracted. Then I noticed she'd left some of my ledgers out, which was unlike her.

"I flipped through them and noticed some irregularities. I began to suspect she was using my business as a front for something, and with a little digging, I discovered that someone was smuggling goods through my warehouses. I confronted her about it, asking what was going on, how she could betray me. She told me she did it because she loved me and was only using the other man to get what she needed. Apparently, she was trying to pay off some debts I'd accumulated because of my wife's sickness."

He hung his head. "Maybe I should have—I don't know. When I told her I appreciated the thought but wasn't interested, she went crazy. A few days of her throwing herself at me and me rebuffing her advances later, she jumped off Lover's Leap. It's my fault she's dead, and...I didn't want her name dragged through the mud with the smuggling thing. I thought if I just kept quiet, it would go away."

The story sounded believable. It all made sense. She didn't buy it. Something about his grief and confusion struck her as fake, like his grief for his wife. Still, suspicions could be wrong and needed facts to corroborate them. Standing up, she decided they needed to keep an eye on this man. The next time she had a chance to sample his thoughts, she would take it.

"I appreciate your consideration of Elise's memory. My husband will, as well. He has been released?"

"Yes, he and your friends should be waiting for you. One of them is an agent of the Crown, apparently?"

Of course, Colby wouldn't have been shy about that. Chavali nodded. "He is our friend and came in case anything needed to be smoothed over."

He nodded in understanding, staying between her and the door. "Before you go, that thing you said earlier, in my office? It sounded... weighty. Important."

To buy herself time to think about how to word an answer, she crossed her arms and pursed her lips, averting her eyes from him. Portia's quick thinking gave her someplace to start, and she only needed to carry it through. "I have a condition. It comes in flashes and sometimes I speak strange meaningless things, like I am dreaming. Harris is very understanding, and I am lucky to have found him."

This satisfied Garrian, and he opened the door for her, then escorted her out. "I hope you both find the closure you came looking for."

"Thank you." She hoped so, too. Would Garrian be happy when they did? She didn't care. Pushing open the last door between herself and freedom, she found Colby, Portia, and Harris waiting. Harris rushed to her side and embraced her while the other two went for the door, looking relieved. Since Garrian watched them, she leaned into the hug.

Harris pulled away and took her chin in his hand. "Are you alright?" *Damn, I like the feel of your body against mine. I could really get used to this act.*

"Yes, I am fine." Even though she knew she ought to return the concern, especially with the fresh bruises on his face from the swift beating he received outside, she pointed at the door. "We should go." His disappointment fortunately cut off when he took his hand away to hold the door for her. Neither had anything else to say until they caught up to Colby and Portia, though he did pass her belt and knife back to her. "I think we should go to Lover's Leap."

"Why?" Harris had his hand around her waist. When she squirmed, he let go. "It didn't look that interesting."

"I spoke with Garrian. His intent was to make me go away, but instead, he has given me suspicions. We should go take a closer look at the spot. Perhaps we find nothing, but I wish to be certain."

"We don't have anything else to go on at the moment," Portia said, "so we might as well take a look."

Chapter 12

The sun sank in the sky, nearly touching the horizon when the four of them first caught sight of the spot. The light outlined a figure standing at the edge of the cliff. Wisps of her long hair fluttered in the breeze coming up from the water. The rest of it and her dress clung to her body so closely, she appeared to be soaking wet.

Colby pointed. "Do you see her?"

Portia and Harris both nodded. Chavali said, "Yes, and I think it's Elise." The shape matched the image she saw in Garrian's mind.

"Maybe the jump didn't kill her," Harris said.

"Then where's she been for the past few months?" Portia asked. "Swimming? Living on an island?"

Chavali didn't understand this any more than they did. She hurried forward and sucked in a breath when Elise disappeared. Did she jump? Again? Her feet hurried faster as she ran for the edge. Stopping a pace before she fell off the cliff, she dropped to the ground and peered down at the water. Nothing, no sign of her at all. She expected to see a body, or cloth disappearing below the surface, or something.

Behind her, Harris said, "What's this?"

"What's that?" Portia pointed out over the water. Following the finger, Chavali saw something hazy and indistinct in the distance. The fading light offered only a vague impression of a smudge on the horizon.

"I do not know."

"Don't. I *don't* know."

"Is this really the time—" Chavali growled under her breath and pushed the irritation aside. "I don't know. Something shrouded in mist, perhaps."

"Some islands attract mist."

"Ladies." Harris sounded somewhat impatient. "This might be more interesting than that." Crouching a few steps behind them, he held up a silver chain with an odd-shaped pendant dangling from it.

"What is that?" Chavali scooted over to him and put a finger under the silver pendant. The shape confused her: half a heart with a jagged break down what would be the middle. It had been made on purpose with the break. "Why would anyone want such a thing?"

Portia bent to peer at it. "Lovers sometimes do that. One half for each. When I've seen them, they normally have initials or a name, or a word or something. This is blank."

Such a gesture struck Chavali as stupid and overly sentimental. It fit the location. "Not branding it means... A secret affair?"

"There would be no way to tie it to him for sure. Especially if he was smart and got one for his wife, too."

"He told me she was infatuated with him and he rebuffed her. I would expect to find both halves were that truly the case."

Colby stared out over the water as the sun reached the horizon, spilling gold across its flickering surface. "So many lies causing so much trouble."

Chavali rolled her eyes and let go of the pendant. "He also laid the blame for the smuggling at her feet. Which I doubt, given it's still active."

"Without someone to doctor the books," Harris agreed, "it should collapse. The new assistant could have been involved before and stepped in when he got the new job."

"Or it's all Garrian." Chavali shrugged. "He has, so far I can tell, lied about everything. Getting us released feels out of place, unless he feared we would reveal something. Did any of you hear what happened to the other prisoners?"

"One of them hanged himself," Colby said. "I didn't hear about the other two. We should get back to the inn. The temperature is dropping with the sun."

Harris tucked the pendant into a pocket and they hurried to the inn. Chavali ate mechanically, her thoughts churning over the day's events. So much happened, including a prophecy, which needed to be taken seriously. If that woman really had been Elise, and she really was wet, and she really did disappear beneath the surface so quickly, did that mean she swam on a fated tide, making her the herald? The herald of what?

"Chavali?" Colby's voice interrupted her thoughts. She looked up from the table, where she'd been staring for some time, to see Portia and Harris already gone and him standing beside her. "You haven't responded to anything for the past several minutes. Are you alright?"

She waved him off irritably. "Yes, you can go."

His eyes went flat and he turned on his heel, leaving her there without another word.

Now drawn into the moment once more, she noticed the tavern had become busy, full of customers. She took up an entire table by herself, and since she had finished her meal, she stood to move to the bar. It surprised her to see that strange woman sitting near the end, one empty seat between her and the wall. The woman did say she would be back, but with everything that happened today, Chavali forgot about her.

"May I sit here?" She stood beside the stool next to the wall, and hopped up onto it when the woman nodded. "How does your business go?"

"As well as can be expected under the circumstances." The woman had a mug of hot tea already and sipped at it. "I wasn't sure you'd come over."

The bartender walked over and set a mug of hot tea in front of Chavali without her asking for it. He gave her a smile, which made her look around the room. She didn't see that waiter and waitress, nor did she see the pickpocket. He'd thrown them out based upon her statements, and now showed his gratitude with promptness.

Occasionally, people surprised her by being unexpectedly sensible. Not often, but it happened. She returned the smile, genuinely pleased. He nodded and moved away to help other customers, and she gave her attention to the woman. "I was not sure you would show up."

The woman grinned. "Certainty is in short supply until it isn't."

Chavali snorted at the absurd statement. "Naturally."

"May I ask about your business here?"

Knowing they had spies following them made Chavali hesitant. "It's uninteresting."

"Really? Maybe I can help with that. Have you seen the island off the coast? It's often covered with a thick layer of mist, but you should be able to make it out in the distance during the day."

Strange that this woman who somehow knew her name should bring up something she encountered so recently. It could be coincidence. "I did not realize it was an island."

"It was originally set up as a penal colony, called the Lost Island. The rulers of Ket have been staunch members of the Order of Spilled Blood for several generations."

Chavali's lip curled. "So, naturally, they cannot execute people, yet must still deal with the most heinous criminals."

The woman cocked her head to one side. "Do you find their beliefs so abhorrent?"

"I find their beliefs ridiculous," Chavali huffed. "If the Creator truly made us, then She knew we would be inclined to kill each other and to eat meat. These Spilled Blood people are stupid. At least I can understand some of the other Orders. Knowledge is a powerful tool that can be a weapon, for example. The Pure Seed followers want to keep the races from being diluted or perverted. The Creator's Path and Feminine Divine Orders also make sense to me."

"Yet, you don't follow any of those." The corners of the woman's mouth quirked up. Chavali couldn't decide if the approval in the small smile mocked her or not. "Why not?"

She picked up her mug and sipped at it, not sure how to answer the question. In her clan, they followed their traditions because they were traditions, and not specifically out of a desire to please the Creator. None of them examined the "order" they all followed much, preferring to live their lives without such serious contemplation of matters that had no real effect on anything. Then, an hour after her predecessor died, the clan elders cut her forehead open, chipped a hole in her skull, and stuck the feather in it. In that moment, she understood the ways of her clan much better.

"I do not think we will find salvation in denying ourselves the pleasures of life, or in performing a self-imposed duty. If the Creator wants us to do or stop doing something specific, She should have said so plainly. Instead, She left us to scramble about and make up our own ideas, like beggars on the street. Whatever earns us a bit of favor becomes the greatest sin, and we follow it obsessively, and try to persuade others it will also bring them good fortune."

How strange she should be so honest with this woman. She had no reason to do so, yet found herself explaining something that had sat with her for some time, festering along with a thread of doubt about the Creator's existence. Like everyone else, she had the memory of the Creator stamped indelibly in her brain since birth, yet she always found it surprising how much more fervently other people clung to it and let it shape their lives.

"So what is the greatest sin we all know we have been accused of?"

She stared down at her half-empty mug, the brown water still and no longer steaming. "I don't know. I think it's sitting still: never changing, never growing, never learning new things. But I don't know."

The woman leaned over and whispered to her. "No one really does." Setting her own mug down, she slid off her stool and smiled. "Tend your dreams, Chavali. They're not just nightmares." As before, she left too much money to pay for her tea, and walked away briskly.

Chavali watched her go, too confused to stop her. How did she know about the nightmares? What did that mean, to "tend" her dreams? No more of this idle chatter. Tomorrow, when they met again, she would ask for a name and get some answers.

Chapter 13

A white stone keep straddled the road, its doors thrown wide open. Chavali walked inside, expecting a party. For the past several days, she had been making hats for this party, knitting them with her own two hands out of feathers. One perched jauntily on her own head; the sack under her arm held the rest. This would be the most fun she'd had in some time.

Through the doors, she found a courtyard covered in slabs of blood red stone. Chalk drawings on the stones reminded her of her parents, and her brother and sister, and Keino, despite being nothing more than stick figures. They would meet her here, and everyone would wear a hat. A table at the other end of the courtyard held cake. They would all eat cake, and it would be fun.

She carried the sack to the table, seeing the same chalk drawings repeated on each stone, with minor variations each time. The lines were white, gray, and black, the shades used in random nonpatterns. Even here, her mind wouldn't let her see colors.

The table had a space for the sack, and she set it down where it belonged. It immediately slumped to the side and fell open, spilling the hats all over the stones. When she looked down, her own hat fell off her head and got lost in the pile. She crouched down to try to find it. Her hat was different, special, precious. It must be found at all costs. Frantically tossing hats aside, she couldn't find it.

Plants sprouted up between the stones, each of them unique in both shape and arrangement of grays. Buds on their tips opened, revealing blooms in the shape of mouths with jagged teeth. Those wide, gaping mouths spewed a stench in the air, of foul, rotting things. The flowers bent over and swished around in the hats, sending them flying in every direction on diseased zephyrs.

How dare they? She straightened and stomped on a flower. The wide mouth opened and swallowed her foot to the ankle. Whipping to the side, it knocked her to the ground. Other flowers leaned in and held her down, their teeth nibbling at her flesh without taking bites. The hats all landed on her, soft and light, a swarm of feathery butterflies.

It felt almost pleasant, aside from how it made her skin crawl. She squirmed, trying to break free. Her head stayed stuck fast while her limbs thrashed around. The one flower bit her foot off, a snapping crunch echoing off the walls. The rest took it as a signal. The flower teeth sank into her flesh. The hats jumped up and down, their feather quills growing sharp, blackened spines that stabbed a thousand tiny holes in her flesh.

Chavali's eyes snapped open and she sucked in a breath. The hat nightmare. She rubbed her eyes, then peered around in the early morning gloom, wondering what woke her and spared her the indignity of being devoured and defiled (not to mention the part with the wagon wheels). Portia lay on the next bed, still asleep. Nothing seemed out of place. She stood and checked out the window, finding the first hints of dawn coloring the sky and a few thin clouds passing by a crescent moon.

Just once, she wanted to not stomp on the flower in that dream. For as long as she could remember, she'd been having that and a handful of other dreams, and never once could she change anything about them. Though her terror at them had receded since childhood, she still didn't enjoy waking to that every single day.

Sleep wouldn't come again, so she got dressed and left the room. She sat in the darkness of the closed tavern at a table in the back, thinking about that strange woman and her words. Her thoughts wandered to the Lost Island. What happened to it that it "used to be" a penal colony? What did Ket do with its prisoners now? If Lady Mardis followed her family's tradition of abhorring killing, then they must have some other way to handle truly dangerous people.

What did the "oaken seed" mean? A child of an oak? Garrian's wife had an oak for a family tree. Did she have a child no one knew of, or did it mean her? Except Merilyn was dead already. A prophecy wouldn't speak of the past, only the future. A secret child, then. Perhaps a sibling. With Merilyn dead, maybe this other person no longer had her for a protector or keeper. Someone who knew could take advantage of that.

Everything pointed at Garrian. Except he didn't strike her as a large fish in this pond. He had the feel of a man in control of a small corner of the city and knowing better than to venture far from it or take too large a bite of anyone else's dessert.

The lights flickered on, distracting her from her thoughts. "Oh," the bartender's voice said a short time later. "Up early, ma'am? Can I get you anything?"

"Juice or tea, whatever is close at hand." She waved to show how little it mattered to her.

"Certainly." He poured a cup of dark berry juice and brought it to her. "I didn't get a chance to thank you for that tip about the pickpocket."

She shrugged, uninterested. "I like the service here."

The bartender beamed with pride. "I try to treat all my customers as individuals, not just plates and charges and tips." His face fell and he leaned against a chair. "My staff are supposed to do the same, to be my face when we're busy. It's distressing to discover when they're not."

"Money will always motivate those who would otherwise be honest." The point struck her as true. Greed and profit had to play a part on all of this. Someone ran that smuggling ring and profited from it. The fact that goods still moved through the port and into the city spoke to Elise's innocence. Simon struck her as the obvious choice, since the crates required him to guide them to their destinations. Yet, it felt too obvious. Someone else must be involved, someone able to set up a wine shop as a front.

"So true." The bartender sighed. "Can I get you some cheese or fruit? Hot breakfast won't be ready for a while."

Chavali's stomach growled, making her smirk. "Yes, please. I will wait for my friends to take a meal, but whatever you have on hand now would be good. Thank you."

He brought out a small plate with apples, grapes, and chunks of cheese. She sat and pondered everything Garrian told her about Elise, not sure what truths lurked behind his lies. It could be simple and embarrassing without being nefarious. Even if he had an affair with her, refusing to leave his wife could have sent Elise over that cliff. People did stupider things over emotions than that all the time.

Eventually, the others joined her and they shared breakfast. A tense murmur ran through the small crowd. It seemed that everyone talked about the same thing, so Chavali didn't bother getting up to absorb it. Instead she stopped their waitress and asked about it.

"Folks are saying Luna Mardis was taken in the night. That's the Lady's daughter. Plucked right out of her bed in the Lady's estate. Her guards are out in full force, looking for clues, which means they don't know anything yet."

Chavali thanked the young woman and frowned. Harris, Colby, and Portia all echoed the expression. Before any of them could discuss the possibility of a connection with Elise and their investigation, the door banged open and six armed men filed in, scanning the room and settling on Chavali. These men wore the uniforms of City Guards, except for a few bits of trim making them seem higher ranking or otherwise more important.

The lead guard walked directly to their table and gestured for them all stand. "Ladies and gentlemen, your presence is requested by Lady Mardis, at her estate." Closer, Chavali noticed the men had a patch on their shoulders depicting a family coat of arms: an acorn with a wreath.

"Requested?" Colby's eyes flicked across the room. "This doesn't look like a 'request.' "

The guardsman held up his hands. "You're not under arrest." He left a beat, then added, "Yet."

"I see." Chavali stood up. They had no other leads to follow this morning, so none of them had anything better to do anyway. Deciding to be annoying as a kind of retaliation, she picked one of the other guards and took his arm. "You know, this city is splendid," she gushed. "I have never seen such architecture, and the coast is beautiful, especially at sunset. Are you from here? Of course you are, and a strong, handsome man like you must know everything there is worth knowing. You must tell me all about it. What should I be certain to see and do before I leave? I don't want to miss anything!"

The poor man glanced back helplessly at his comrades. He stammered and said "um" a lot as she dragged him out of the inn. She caught the sound of snickering from his fellow guards before they left, and had him flustered and tongue-tied all the way to the Lady's estate with a combination of flattery and questions about the city he couldn't know the answers to.

Lady Mardis's estate perched on a rise in the north part of the city, with a view of both the ocean and most ofKet. It sprawled across a large swathe of land, surrounded by towering trees and a wrought iron fence. Everything about it, from the wide drive past a marble fountain to the white stone of the three story building to the precision of the grass and placement of flowers, spoke of wealth. Guards at the gate—emblazoned with that acorn and wreath image on their chests—made Chavali and her captive escort wait until the rest caught up, giving her time to pester them with her excited, single female tourist routine.

These men standing at the gate had more discipline than her escort, and stood at attention despite her. They didn't even glance at her rear (at least, she didn't notice either of them doing it). The others arrived before she had a chance to truly test their patience, and all of them were swept through the gate and into the house.

The inside mirrored the outside for opulence: grand and stately with orderly, uncluttered decoration. Textured tile flooring carried them from the entry, down a tastefully decorated hallway, and into a large sitting room with tall windows and a plush rug under chairs, couches, and a coffee table. Everything matched, of course, in style and tone, and probably color, as well. That same acorn and wreath design appeared on some of the vases.

Chavali sat on a couch, finding it less yielding and comfortable than it looked. Guests were probably not meant to linger here, but rather to handle business and be on their way. Mardis didn't expect them to stay long. Whether that meant they would be politely interrogated and arrested or only questioned and released, she couldn't guess.

Lady Mardis swept into the room a few minutes later. As Chavali suspected, this was the woman with the brocade cloak at the funeral, now dressed and with her hair swept up in a fashion that felt casual. Casual, that is, for a very wealthy person interested in impressing people. "Welcome to my home. I hope you weren't interrupted from anything important." Her voice spoke of calm command brimming with worry.

"Only breakfast," Chavali told her dryly.

Harris mostly hid a smirk behind his hand. Portia coughed. Colby stared at her in disbelief. "We were nearly finished anyway," he added quickly. "What can we do for you, Lady Mardis? The invitation seemed somewhat...urgent."

Mardis pursed her lips as she glided into the room, the skirt of her fur-lined brown dress rippling across the rug. "This is about my daughter, Luna." As she got closer, Chavali noted a pendant around her neck with yet another instance of that acorn and wreath. She also had a peculiarly neutral expression, one utterly devoid of emotion. Chavali could do that, too, and did when she needed to hide something important. "She was abducted sometime last night."

"We're very sorry to hear that, Lady," Portia said. "What does it have to do with us?"

Mardis clasped her hands together. "I'm hoping you can tell me where she is."

Colby held up his hands, showing them to be empty. "I hope you don't think we're involved somehow?"

"No, not at all. I've had someone following you, and I know none of you left Cander's Lodge last night."

"That explains the third person following us around," Harris said with a roll of his eyes.

Mardis stayed blank. "Why did you go to that wine shop, and what are you doing in Ket?"

"Acorns," Chavali said, suddenly realizing what else they were. Never mind the frustratingly impossible to read woman standing in the room. "Oaken seeds are acorns. That last part is about her. Or her daughter. 'Taken in the night' fits."

"Oh!" Portia sprang to her feet and hurried to a vase. "This is your family's symbol, right?"

"Yes." Mardis finally showed something: alarm. Her hand went to her pendant, protecting it, and she took a step back. "It has been for several generations. What 'oaken seed'? Taken in the night? What are you talking about?"

Chavali waved dismissively in her direction, finding the woman to be a distraction. "It makes sense."

"That means we have until the new moon to find her, right?" Harris looked up at Mardis. "When will the next new moon be?"

Mardis narrowed her eyes, sweeping her gaze disapprovingly over all four of them. "Another week, I think. What's going on? Did you know something would happen?"

"Apologies, my Lady," Colby said. "My colleagues aren't used to interacting with nobility. We encountered something we believe to be a prophecy, and it seems to concern your daughter. Chavali, could you repeat it for the Lady?" With a subtle nod towards Mardis, he made her think he wanted her to be polite.

Chavali stifled a roll of her eyes. "The Herald swims in a fated tide, bringing ruin on the rise. The first little fish takes a bite, the second steals an eye. The third devours whole, reaping for the blind. Oaken seed, charged to bleed, taken in the night. Empty moon sees her doom, too late to put it right." At least he didn't say where it came from. Leaving such a detail out must not disagree with his idiotic need to be honest.

"Charged to bleed?" Mardis dropped into a chair, covering her face. "My poor Luna. Why would anyone do this?"

"Did you find a note?" Harris asked. "People kidnap nobility for ransom all the time, don't they?"

Colby gave him a flat, disapproving glare. "I wouldn't say 'all the time.' " He went to Mardis's side and produced his Crown medallion for her. "If we can help, we will."

"No note." Mardis touched the medallion, then pulled her hands away and didn't cover up her grief and fear anymore. Uncertainty and despair clung to her. "You can go see her room. Maybe you'll find something my people can't."

Harris hopped to his feet. Colby stood and left the room with him. Portia leaned forward. "Has anything been removed?"

"Her personal guard was found dead outside her room, the body was moved to the basement until it can be examined."

Portia got to her feet and nodded. "I'll have a look at that, then."

Chavali still sat, watching Mardis, more interested in her now that her facade had cracked. "Is there anyone you know of who would want to take your daughter?"

Mardis rubbed her forehead. "I am the Lady of Ket, I do have enemies. That said, I can't think of anyone who would actually kill one of my guards to get at Luna. These people may have wrong-headed ideas, but they're political enemies, not personal ones. None of them are monsters."

The woman didn't need to hear Chavali's response to that. She, of all people, knew the pain of losing kin, and had no reason to be callous to Mardis. "She is sixteen, yes?"

The Lady nodded. "She's discovered boys recently."

"Is it possible a boy came for her, and the guard was killed by accident?"

Mardis took a deep breath and lowered her hand, recomposing herself. Her shoulders raised, her hands clasped together, her head lifted. The transformation made her a queen on her throne, yet her face still betrayed her desperate anguish. Once that mask slipped, putting it back took more effort than she could—or, perhaps, would—make right now. "I doubt it. If she went willingly, she would have stopped and summoned help rather than leave him to be found. Luna isn't a rebellious chit."

"Is there anything else unusual that has happened around her or you recently? People lurking about, happenings at your holdings, business gone wrong, anything."

Mardis's nose twitched. "Besides the four of you? Nothing comes to mind."

Chavali smirked, acknowledging the point. "Why did you have us followed?"

"I saw you at the funeral." She lifted a finger to point at the feather, and a smile ghosted around the edges of her mouth. "If your goal was to be seen having a strange conversation with Sera Drune, you succeeded. Why are you here? Someone coming to town armed with a prophecy and an agent of the Crown who gets herself tangled up in a smuggling ring is not an average traveler."

Judging this conversation as best closed, Chavali stood and smoothed her dress down. "My business is the Crown's business. We will do what we can to find your daughter."

Mardis stood, too. "I understand. And thank you. I'll instruct my guards to cooperate in whatever way you need."

"We appreciate that." Chavali went upstairs to find the two men going through a teenage girl's suite of rooms. Blood on the tile outside the door showed where the guard died. Oddly, there wasn't much—just small, tacky puddles with smeared edges. She remembered stabbing her wrist to kill herself, and that single wound made at least as much blood as these four put together. "Have you found anything?"

"The room was neat and tidy when we got here." Harris shrugged as he flipped through a book. "No sign of any kind of struggle."

"She could have been subdued in her sleep." Colby lifted the pillow at the head of the bed and peered under it, then checked behind the headboard. "But I don't see any actual sign of that."

"Either way," Harris said, "there's nothing here pointing us in a particular direction to find her."

Chavali scanned the room, not sure what to look for. The girl preferred light colors, but not frilly things, and had a rack with two plain, functional swords. "Perhaps it would help if we determine how an attacker got in."

Colby straightened and checked the room over, a sheepish look on his face. As well he should. With his past, he should have thought of it first. "The windows that can be opened are all shut." Moving to one, he tapped the lock. "Secured from the inside. Unless there's a secret passage, they used the door."

Giving the room his own once-over, Harris stroked his chin. "No hinged furniture, no unexpected indents or seams in the carpet, no spaces of wall left curiously blank. I'll check the closet." He disappeared into the small adjoining room.

"Milady?" A woman in a servant's uniform stood behind Chavali, giving her a strained smile. "The Lady asked for someone to come and see if you need anything."

Chavali saw nothing remarkable about this woman, another average person in her thirties with the same look of these people native to the Ket area. She offered her hand to shake, and the woman blinked at it before taking it. "Did anyone see anything here that you know of?" She prolonged the contact by adding her other hand, making the gesture more about comfort and familiarity than a simple greeting.

"I don't think so, milady." Her mind focused on the feather, on Chavali's exotic olive skin tone and her accent. None of that helped in any way.

"What do you do here?"

"I tend to clothes and linens, mostly." *Why are you still holding onto my hand?* "Clean them up, get them washed, bring them back and put them away."

"Do you recall seeing anyone unfamiliar around the house or grounds recently? Besides myself and my friends, I mean."

The maid frowned and looked away, her mind conjuring up a fuzzy image of a figure in the distance. "I don't know, milady. Maybe. A day or two ago, I thought I saw someone, but when I really looked, they were gone."

"Are you sure you didn't get a good look at them? This person may have killed the guard here. You knew him, didn't you? Close your eyes and try to imagine this person."

The maid gulped and complied, conjuring up a different image, of a figure in a cloak. They entered the house while the maid chatted up a guard on her break. She got a better look than she thought, and Chavali swiped the image while the maid stammered through a basic description. Something about this cloaked woman struck her as familiar, though she couldn't say why. Perhaps she'd been at the funeral.

"Thank you," Chavali told her kindly, letting go of her hand. "You have been very helpful."

Colby cleared his throat. "Before you go, can you point out something in here we could give to a bloodhound to track her? Something that wouldn't have been cleaned since she last wore or used it?"

The maid pointed out the girl's hamper and left them with a curtsy.

Colby flipped it open and grabbed a sock.

"Since when do we have a bloodhound?"

Colby gave Harris a grim smile. "My horse can handle the job."

"Really." Chavali's eyebrow quirked up. The horse had a queer way about it, and Colby trusted it too much. At some point, she would take the time to prod the beast. This mission would probably not be that time. "We should trace the most likely path out of the house, yes? See if there is anything to see."

The two men nodded and took the lead, one with a guardsman's eye, the other with a criminal's. Between them, they found the door Chavali saw in the maid's mind. They questioned the nearby guards. Neither saw anything of note. Portia rejoined them as they finished that task.

"Here's what I can tell you. He was disabled before being killed. They punched him in the face, then cut his ankles and elbows. All the cuts were shallow, intended to disable, and none of them could have killed him, even if he went untreated for an hour. Well, maybe if he was a bad bleeder. At any rate, he didn't get left that way long enough for it to matter. He had bloody foam in his mouth, and—"

Chavali interrupted her, remembering a similar description. "And a look on his face, of madness or terror?"

"Yes, actually." Portia frowned. "How did you know that?"

"That poxy wench at the restaurant," Harris said, brightening with recognition. "She said that's what's happening to people down at the docks. The corpses turn up like that, and everyone's calling it a plague."

"That does not make sense," Chavali said. "It's too convenient for him to succumb to that kind of illness at exactly the right time for Luna to escape or be taken."

"There were lingering traces of magic," Portia said. "Any mage should be able to pick that up. I don't think it's a disease at all. That they're redoing the docks because of it says to me that the disease angle is a cover story for something. But I don't know what, and it could be coming from anyone involved in any of this. The traces don't tell me much, just that magic was used, and a vague idea of what kind. Best I can offer is that someone killed his mind, which then killed his body."

The idea sent a shiver up Chavali's spine. Telepaths affected minds, and the Order of the Strong Mind consisted of telepaths. At least one of them had already shown to her that he would do whatever it took to get whatever he wanted. Colby's deep frown said he had thoughts along similar lines. He was there, at that compound in the mountains. He saw what they did. He knew how she died.

"Are you sure?"

Portia shrugged. "No. It's an educated guess."

She still had some uncertainty to cling to, at least. "We should go, then. I don't think we will find anything else here."

Chapter 14

Karias arrived at the gate as they did. Horses didn't do that. Chavali had a thought to pull off a mitten and find out what she might learn by touching it. Perhaps she would do it on the ride back to the tower. There would be nothing better to occupy her.

Colby patted the great beast and murmured to him, holding up the sock. Karias managed to convey rolling his eyes, further supporting Chavali's suspicions about him. The horse trotted up the drive to the house, sniffed around, then came back and sniffed the sock again. He nickered and nodded, and they followed him up the street.

"Wait," Chavali said before they got very far. All four of them stopped and looked at her. "If we find her in a den of kidnappers or murderers, we may need more help. The guards have their duties, but the idiots trailing us do not."

Harris grinned. "I'll be right back." He ran off down a side street, disappearing from sight.

Chavali looked directly at where she knew one of them crouched and beckoned to him with a finger. The man they originally caught stepped out of his hiding spot, head hung, and shuffled to her. "I'm just doing my job," he offered before she spoke.

"Yes, and now you will do it closer to us."

A woman's squeak of surprise rang out as one of their other shadows hopped out of her hiding place, rubbing her backside. Chavali waved for her to come, and she did, scowling. Harris reappeared shortly, urging two more men forward at knife point.

"He really is more useful than he looks," Portia observed.

"Agreed." Chavali surveyed the three men and one woman, all of them dressed to blend in most groups of people, with no distinguishing marks or items displayed, and with average appearances. "As has been made clear," she told the four sulking spies, "we are aware of your presence. At this time, we may be able to locate the Lady's daughter. We would appreciate your direct assistance should it turn violent or if our presence or actions summon the City Guard."

"That's it? You're not going to do anything...er...unpleasant to any of us?"

"Not unless you refuse or otherwise give us a reason to." It would be somewhat telling if any of them did refuse, but all agreed with no further coercion. If any of their patrons were involved, these people didn't know about it. She considered forcing them each to divulge who they worked for. Really, though, it didn't matter. For whatever reason, four different people in positions of power felt compelled to have them followed separately. Something was rotten in the city of Ket, but she didn't particularly care, unless that turned out to be the real reason Elise died.

They followed the horse to a different neighborhood, one a few steps down in wealth. The townhouses of the row they walked past were all the same, with a few differences in trim or color or landscaping. "Sera Drune owns several of these houses," one of the spies noted. They didn't know who this one worked for. "She rents them out."

"That doesn't mean anything," Drune's spy (the woman) snapped. "She doesn't kidnap girls, and she's not responsible for what her tenants do!"

The first spy shrugged. "It would be easy for her to use an empty house. You know as well as I do that she's vindictive. This whole thing with the docks has her in a huff."

"Are you pointing fingers?" Drune's spy stopped and put her fists on her hips, getting in the other spy's way, and in his face. "Because Jore pushed for the renovations pretty hard from what I hear. She paid off plenty of people to make it happen."

"I don't think we need to go airing all of our bosses' dirty laundry," Garrian's spy said with his hands up, trying to placate the other two.

Both Drune's spy and Jore's turned and stared at him. Before anyone else could say more, Chavali stepped into the middle of it. "As fascinating as all of this is, I don't care. We are here to find Luna Mardis, not to indulge your petty squabbles. Will you all agree this is the goal? To find Luna and see her safely home?"

The one who stayed out of the argument gave Chavali a nod of approval. "She's right, of course. Luna is still a child. Let's think of how scared she must be, at the mercy of people who would murder a guard in the night to take her from her home."

"This is it," Colby said, his voice a harsh whisper. He and the horse stood in front of a townhouse, nothing remarkable about it compared to its neighbors. The spies all went quiet and scanned the neighborhood.

Harris slipped up to the door and set to work on it.

Garrian's spy nudged his chin towards a different house. "I'm going to talk to the woman peering out through the curtain. She may have seen something."

Drune's spy crossed her arms over her chest in a sulk. "I'm coming in. This isn't Sera Drune's doing, and I'm going to be there when that's proven."

"I'm coming in, too," Jore's spy agreed. "I want to see the evidence before anyone—" He gave Drune's spy a mild but significant look. "—*accidentally* spoils it."

"As am I. Luna knows who I am, and seeing me may help her remain calm." Something about the way the last spy said that gave Chavali the suspicion his involvement with Luna didn't strictly have the Lady's approval. He was young, at least, in his early twenties, so entertaining the affections of a sixteen year old girl didn't fall too far outside acceptable. Also, if he had frequent opportunities to meet with her, he must work for Mardis.

"Fine," Portia said, reaching behind her back and revealing a dagger. "Just don't cause a problem. Get in my way and I'll burn you to a crisp."

Colby pulled his large sword from the sheath strapped to his back, ready to use it. Harris put his tools away and grabbed his own long knife. Seeing so many loose weapons (the spies all carried small blades), Chavali chose to twine her fingers through the spirits, preparing to construct an illusion if she needed to. Harris turned the knob and Colby shouldered his way in. Harris and Portia followed right after him, then Chavali hurried inside, the three spies behind her.

Chavali saw Colby punch a man in the face, knocking him senseless, and Harris swept the legs out from under another, sending him to the floor. Portia turned to a different room, her empty hand tracing half a circle in the air, then throwing something at a different man. A dart of red force hit him squarely in the chest, tossing him at the wall. He hit it hard enough to rattle the scant furniture and landed in a heap.

She still had so much to learn about all of this. Chavali didn't think she contributed much by calling up an image of crackling lightning arcing between her hands. At least it caused the last man to scream and run straight into the three spies, who made quick work of him. She'd never seen blades move so swiftly through the air, killing the man before he hit the floor. However incompetent they were at shadowing without being seen, they made up for it with efficiency at death-dealing.

Portia stooped to check on her victim while Chavali moved into the other room. Harris knelt over another dead man, checking his pockets. The other man squirmed in Colby's grasp, pressed against the wall by a hand around his neck and elbow in his gut. Colby held his blade aside as a threat.

Chavali dismissed the lightning image and strode to his side, grabbing the prisoner's wrist. "Who do you work for?"

He thought some rather colorful things about her and Colby's lineage, and what they should do to themselves and possibly each other. Colby, of course, held on loosely enough so he could breathe and speak. And spit in Chavali's face.

She flinched, then wiped the spittle off. "If you have nothing useful to tell us, we have no reason to let you live."

I'm not gonna live anyway. "Screw you."

"Whoever he works for will kill him if they find out about the failure," she told Colby.

Listen to the lady.

Colby frowned. "We'll have to take him to the Guard for a trial."

Kill me or let me go. The man snorted. He opened his mouth to offer a new curse on Colby's ancestry.

"She's up here," Portia called out from the stairs, interrupting the prisoner. "No other guards. Unconscious."

The three spies lunged for the stairs, wedging themselves together at the bottom step. Wriggling and kicking and shoving and grunting commenced. Chavali ignored them. "Tell us this much: what were you hired to do?"

"Watch a girl and make sure she doesn't escape." Clear in his mind, she saw he had no idea about the girl's identity, and hadn't seen her face.

"He speaks the truth, and is of no use to us. Kill him or let him go. Anything else is a waste of time." Chavali let go and ignored Colby as she walked away, expecting some kind of dramatic look from him.

On her way to the stairs, she heard Harris say, "You're choosing 'let him go? At least let him use the back door and keep what he's got on him. Sending him out the front with nothing... You might as well kill him yourself. Your way would at least be painless."

The former bandit understood what the former guardsman didn't. Colby's sentimentality and obsession with truth and justice didn't fit in this world. Even his death—rescuing halfbreed children from execution by Pure Seed zealots—spoke to this. And still, he learned nothing. Chavali rolled her eyes and hurried up the stairs to find Mardis's spy tenderly brushing Luna's hair out of her face and the other two inspecting the room. Portia worked at untying the girl's bindings.

It was odd, Chavali thought, how easy this turned out to be. Did they not expect her to be found so quickly? Was their goal unrelated to her? "Are you certain this is actually Luna, and not someone under an illusion or shapechanging magics?"

Portia looked up and pursed her lips. "Good thinking." She murmured something under her breath and her eyes flared with red light. Scanning the girl, she frowned. "It's her. There's a few lingering traces, but nothing like that. She must have been subdued with magic. It explains why she's still out cold."

"It's not a lookalike, either," Mardis's spy confirmed. "I'm sure of it." Chavali didn't care how he knew that. "From what I can tell, she wasn't harmed at all, just knocked out and tied up and brought here."

"They probably didn't have time to do anything yet." Portia's eyes lost their glow and she resumed untying knots.

Was this hubris or incompetence? Chavali's eyes flicked around the room. It had nothing but the bed, and no signs of neglect. Stepping back into the hallway, she wandered, peering around and sniffing the air. It seemed the only parts of the house with actual furniture were the downstairs and the one bedroom, and both had only exactly what they truly needed for this particular operation.

No one used this place as a headquarters or hideout prior to this night. Tenants had occupied it recently, but didn't now. Stooping in the corner of an otherwise empty room, she found an abandoned block of painted wood. Even if she didn't have memories from other minds to point to its purpose, she would recognize a child's toy block anywhere. She tucked it into a pocket, thinking she might as well keep it for Danel or Haizea.

"I'm just saying that Chavali's got a point." Harris's voice drifted up the stairs as Chavali returned to the ground floor.

"And I'm not surprised to hear you say that." Colby sounded exasperated, and she caught sight of him as he hauled his prisoner to the front door by the scruff of his neck. "We're not letting him go or killing him. We're taking him to Lady Mardis. If she wants to let him go or kill him, that's up to her. We don't decide who gets to roam freely and who gets to die and who stays behind bars." He met her eyes, and she could see he wouldn't be swayed.

Uninterested in the fight that doing otherwise would create, Chavali said nothing and revealed nothing.

"I'll meet you back at the estate," he growled. Giving his prisoner a shove, he went outside.

Harris watched him go, then shook his head in disapproval. "Black and white," he muttered.

"Yes, very much so."

His eyes flicked over to her, and the start of that stupid little smile formed. "He would've turned me in at Atrica."

"Yes, I expect so." His eyes swept down and up her body blatantly. She ignored it. "He is a much more capable fighter, though, so I expect you would actually be dead."

"Fair point." That look on his face, she'd seen it too many times not to recognize it. Right now, he had thoughts about all the various things he could imagine doing to her, most of them without clothes.

She stifled down a roll of her eyes and changed the subject. "The girl is fine. This operation strikes me as odd. You?"

He rocked on his heels, attention diverted. "Ransoming nobles is tricky work. Not something to do with no experience in kidnapping. No one starts with breaking into a high end place and swiping a high end target. These guys," he waved in the general direction of the nearest dead body, "are amateurs."

"I agree. We have stumbled into something unexpected." She turned at a creaking of the stairs to see Mardis's spy carrying Luna down them. Portia and the other two followed.

Garrian's spy jogged up to the open door and peered in. "The nosy neighbor down the street said there was a family living here until about a week ago. They moved out and it's been vacant since. She didn't notice anyone coming or going last night, but did see someone yesterday, walking around the property. Didn't get a good look, thought it might be a woman, bundled up against the cold."

"Interesting." Chavali followed Mardis's spy out, gesturing for the rest to come along, back to the estate.

Harris tried to walk beside her and strike up a conversation, but Portia nudged him away and leaned in to whisper to Chavali. "Drune's spy sent a message. I'm not sure if she used magic or a device, or what, but I heard her muttering and noticed the tiny flare of power. If Drune's not there by the time we get back, I'll eat my boot."

Grateful for the interruption, Chavali took Portia's arm, looping hers through it. "The others may have done the same, yes?"

"Certainly. It's not that hard to do over relatively short distances. Anyone with money to throw around could set it up. Only takes a bit of prior planning."

As they reached the estate, a carriage pulled into view and through the gates. Chavali and Portia, walking together behind Harris, shared a smirk. The guards let them through without a hassle. Drune went inside before their procession arrived at the front door. Colby's horse stood nearby, pretending to be normal by sniffing the grass and trees. The guards at the door opened it for the group and they walked in to see Drune and Mardis in the entry. Both women held themselves stiff and used sharp gestures until the moment they noticed the parade.

Mardis swooped in, at her daughter's side in a moment. Drune's spy sidled to her employer. The other two spies tried to melt into the background, but Chavali knew they stuck around. Harris leaned against the wall, staying out of the way. Chavali expected to be interrogated and stood in the open with Portia.

"Is she alright?" Mardis touched her daughter's face tentatively, then looked to her employee.

"Yes, Lady, she seems fine. I think she'll wake up soon—she started making noises on the way."

Mardis took a few steps away and called for a servant. Colby and two guards clanked down the hall, returning from wherever they stashed the prisoner. The combined noise woke the girl. Her eyes fluttered and she moaned softly. Mardis's spy shushed her and murmured things too quiet to be overheard.

Luna breathed in deeply and smiled at the spy, then looked around. Her eyes fell on Drune and widened in fear. A half-second later, she screamed, pointing at Drune. Guards rushed to the spot.

In the resulting chaos, Chavali noticed several things. Luna's fear seemed genuine, so did Drune's surprise. Mardis whirled around in a panic. Her spy curled around the girl, protecting her and backing away from everyone. The guards had three different targets: Lady Mardis, Sera Drune, and Luna (or perhaps the spy).

The first guard to reach Lady Mardis stabbed at her instead of leaping to her protection. The Lady had enough skill to dodge it, taking only a superficial cut to her side. With that, Chavali drew her knife, let go of Portia, and threw herself at the closest guard. She crashed into him hard enough to shove him a few steps aside. Her action sent Portia, Harris, and Colby into the fray.

Colby ran to Mardis, leaping between her and her guards. He parried away three attacks at once, while also forcing the Lady to move back and grabbing a handful of Chavali's skirt. She found herself yanked backwards and closer to him, just in time to avoid an armored elbow to the face. Drune's spy moved to protect the Sera while Harris and Portia fought their way to Luna and her protector.

Two guards rushing Drune both stopped at the threat presented by her spy and looked around, confused. The rest of the guards, eight of them, attacked in two groups of four. Colby chopped his blade into a neck, nearly severing a guard's head. A fountain of blood spewed from the injury. His foot shoved another guard away at the same time, and the armor under his shirt stopped a blade from chopping his own arm in half.

For all of his annoyances and baggage, the big man could fight. Chavali threaded her fingers through the spirits, calling up darkness to obscure Mardis and herself. It surprised her how eagerly the spirits provided that. The whispering in her mind grew louder, almost intelligible but for the number of voices, and inky blackness issued out of the floor to surround them both.

Chavali lunged out of her shadows with her knife, finding a lucky gap in a guard's armor and slicing through his elbow. He howled with pain and backed out of the fight, dropping his sword and clutching at the wound. In the time it took her to do that, Colby hacked another man in half. The two confused guards split up and helped fight off the attackers, making quick work of them.

Of the attacking guards, only Chavali's victim still lived when the fighting stopped. Garrian's spy held him on his knees at knife point. A beat passed where everyone panted, still vigilant, then Colby lowered his sword, hurried over, and grabbed Drune's arm.

"You're not going anywhere."

"She's the one that attacked me," Luna shrieked, pointing at Drune.

Chavali dismissed her darkness, banishing the voices with them. "Are you alright?" she turned to ask Mardis.

The Lady put a hand to her mouth, surveying the carnage. Seven bodies lay on the floor, with severed parts lying about, and a lot of blood. Her other hand stayed on her side. "By the Creator," she hissed, her face pale and eyes wide with shock.

"She made me drink," Luna insisted, panicking and burrowing into the spy's chest. "She tied me up and made me drink something, it was her!"

"I did no such thing," Drune huffed, her chin raised in defiance.

"Take her and the guard to the cells below," Colby ordered. "Her, too," he pointed at Drune's spy.

"Luna, are you alright?" Mardis recovered enough to ask that, her eyes averted from the death splayed across the floor.

"We should move to some other place." Chavali took Mardis by the arm and pulled her to the nearby sitting room.

Chapter 15

Colby had the scene in the hall under control. Portia and Harris brought the spy with Luna into the room, where her mother sat on the couch and took the girl into her arms. Harris held his arm and winced, but if he chose not to call attention to it, Chavali wouldn't either. No doubt, if she did, he would take it as a sign of interest in him, instead of a sign she wanted to not let him get her killed.

From the hallway, they all heard Drune protesting her innocence, angry and outraged. Chavali wanted to speak to her very soon. "Luna, are you sure Drune did this?"

The girl, too hysterical to be helpful, nodded and cried into her mother's shoulder.

"It's alright, Luna, it's all over." Mardis rocked her daughter and murmured other soothing words to her.

"I hate to interrupt at this moment, Lady," Portia said, "but your own guards tried to kill you. I think we need to discuss a few things."

Mardis sighed and offered her daughter back to her spy. "Adem, take her up to her room and see to it she's protected and has everything she needs. Get her father to help her calm down."

"I'll take care of it personally." The spy bowed and accepted the burden, removing her from the room. He covered Luna's eyes so she didn't have to see the hallway and disappeared.

Chavali focused on Mardis, vaguely registering when Colby entered the room. The woman sat there, staring at nothing and breathing deeply, her hand gripping the arm of the couch tight enough to turn her knuckles white. For an ardent member of the Order of Spilled Blood, so much violence right in front of her probably shook her to the core.

The room stayed quiet for several long seconds, until Portia asked, "Could the kidnapping have been a ruse to set up that situation?"

Chavali crossed her arms and considered the prophecy. They still had no firm ideas for the Herald or the fish, but the last parts of it seemed to be falling into place. "We need to question the guard, and Drune. Before we go do that, this house has been in your family for several generations, yes?"

The Lady took a deep breath. "Yes. The Mardis family has been here for about a hundred and fifty years."

"Perhaps the oaken seed refers to the house itself, which was breached and has bled. The specific timing of this attack could have been subject to several events, explaining why it gave only a deadline." Yet, although that made perfect sense, she'd never had a prophecy about something so banal before. Who cared if the house had blood on the floors? Granted, had they not been here, the situation would have turned out much differently.

Chavali shook her head and turned to go, but something made her stop again after a few steps. She couldn't explain it—a feeling, a twitch, a *something* that, in some ways, reminded her of the impulse she had back in that burning building. It made her stop then, too, and not get killed by a falling, flaming beam. This time, it didn't carry that same weight of life or death, but it mattered. Somehow.

Since the spirits had to be responsible, she heeded it. Why, though? What did she need to say or ask about? The latest conversation with that strange woman at the inn came to mind. "What do you do with your prisoners here? The dangerous ones, the kind the King would condemn to death."

Mardis straightened suddenly. "Why do you ask?"

"Because I have heard you follow the Order of Spilled Blood, which means you cannot kill, and if you are a true follower, you would not let anyone do it in your stead. I am interested in the fate awaiting that guard, and Drune, if she has tried to commit treason by assassination. It will help us question them."

Accepting the reason, Mardis nodded stiffly. "We send them to an island in the ocean, a penal colony. They have to work together or they starve to death."

"The Lost Island?"

"People call it that, yes."

Chavali's mouth went thin, irked she had to draw this out piece by piece. "Why do they call it that?"

Mardis went still. Some would fidget, but the Lady of Ket did the opposite. She stared straight ahead and said nothing for what seemed a long time. Chavali nodded for the others to leave the room, which they (thankfully) did. "My mother told me that there's a legend about it. A sort of prophecy, I suppose, but I don't know where it came from. The Lost Island is a place we're not to go for any length of time. We send our condemned there, and they manage however they can. I'm sure they don't last long.

"The guards who go are rotated and instructed not to leave the ship. They have a mage and archers to defend themselves. I'm sure it seems hypocritical. It's not, not really. There, they have a chance to atone for their sins before death. Here, a mob would rip them apart, or we'd have to house them in some horrible place for the rest of their miserable lives."

Chavali made a significant effort to hide her disdain. Showing it would help nothing. "What is the prophecy?"

The Lady waved a hand dismissively. "They're supposed to return somehow. As I said, we take precautions. It can't happen in my lifetime."

"Do you know the exact wording?"

"No."

A prophecy without the wording? Useless. No, worse than useless. Having nothing would be better. At least that way, no preconceived notions and poor translation efforts got in the way of dealing with events. "Thank you for the information." She kept the sarcasm to a minimum and left the room before saying anything regrettable.

Now she wondered even more about her mystery tea companion's choice of words. If the Lost Island 'used to be' a penal colony, yet Ket still sent their damned to the place, what had it become?

Portia stood in the hallway, waiting for her. They headed to the basement in silence, where Colby and Harris already waited with the prisoners. Odd that the Lady had cells in her home, but perhaps she rendered judgments here sometimes. Each small room—twelve in all, in two rows with a ten foot wide hallway between—had solid walls on three sides and bars for the fourth, granting no real privacy from the guards, only from fellow prisoners.

Harris leaned against the wall casually. Colby stood straight-backed and grim. Both had liberal amounts of blood spatter on their clothes. The first cell on the left held Drune, gripping the bars and glaring at them all. Harris pointed to two of the cells further down the hallway for Chavali and Portia's benefit.

"I'm telling you," Drune snarled, "I have no idea what just happened. I wasn't expecting it, and didn't set anything up!"

"Give me your hand." Chavali beckoned to Drune, who pulled her hands back, crossed her arms, and scowled. "Should I take this as an admission of guilt?"

"Who are you, really? You're not working for Garrian."

Unperturbed, Chavali returned Drune's hard stare, turning it into a contest of wills. "Someone who can make your life very unpleasant, should I wish to. Do they not say the Lost Island is a damned place?"

Behind her, a rustle of cloth and creak of leather and muffled clink of chainmail told her Colby found this uncomfortable. Too bad for him.

Drune's eyes went narrower, her mouth thinner. "You can't have me shipped off there without evidence, and there isn't any, because I've done nothing wrong."

"If you have nothing to hide, you have no reason to refuse my request. I merely have an unusual gift, granted to me by the Creator to do Her work, to sense lies. It functions best through skin contact." Chavali held out her hand.

The Sera's nostrils flared, her mouth pursed in distaste. She stuck her hand through the bars. "Fine. I had nothing to do with the attack upstairs today, and have no interest in seeing harm come to Lady Mardis or any member of her family." Her thoughts showed her constructing the words a moment before they came out of her mouth, with the intent to not leave any doubt about her innocence. No hint of duplicity lingered about her, no consideration of protecting lies or omitting anything. "I did not do anything to Luna, and, prior to this morning in the hallway upstairs, I hadn't seen her in a while. At least a month, maybe more."

"Why did you have me followed?"

Rolling her eyes, Drune huffed. "I thought you worked for Garrian and were trying to set me up or threaten me." *I still want to know what he's up to and why he opposed the renovations at the dock so much. As if it was all about the cost. I'm not that stupid.* "If you have other questions, I suggest you ask him."

"I see. Thank you." Chavali let go of her hand and waved dismissively. "Let her go. She is not involved." Luna must have been in shock or confused to finger Drune so adamantly. The girl did, after all, have a traumatic experience and was only a child. Some slight between them—she could well imagine Drune being unpleasant to a child—may have tainted their relationship early in Luna's life.

"Is that what you can actually do?" Harris slipped up behind her and whispered into her ear as she headed down the hallway and away from Drune. "See the difference between truth and lies?"

"No."

"Are you going to ever tell me the truth?"

"Perhaps."

He grinned. "I'll take a 'perhaps' over a 'no' any day of the week."

Chavali rolled her eyes. He didn't see it. Drune's spy leaned against the back wall of her cell, arms crossed and bored, an eyebrow perking because she did see it. Chavali beckoned for the woman to approach her, which she did after only a moment's pause.

"Do I stand or fall according to my employer's fate?"

"Give me your hand and tell me if you had anything to do with the attack upstairs or the kidnapping."

The spy obeyed. "Your man didn't search me very well, you know. I could stab you in the gut." *No one ever finds the slim knife on the inside of my thigh.*

"But you will not, because this would be stupid. Unless you are guilty, in which case I can see how it might seem to be a reasonable choice. Except you would still be in the cell, and your fate would not change." Chavali smirked. "Well. He might kill you in retaliation instead of letting anyone take you to that island, but I cannot see how that is truly an improvement."

Too smart by far, lady. You're weird, but my kind of weird. The spy laughed. "I had nothing to do with the attack upstairs or Luna's kidnapping, other than by defending Sera Drune and trying to help find Luna. I'm sure it was a setup to put the girl in that particular house." *And when I find out who did that, they're going to regret it.*

"She can go," Chavali told Harris. She passed Colby's rescued kidnapper in another cell to find the guard sitting on his hard wooden bed, cradling his hurt arm, head hung and staring at the floor. For this man, she chose to go to him, not seeing a reason to make him get up. "You understand there are others who will kill you if you attempt to harm me or escape, yes?"

He sucked in a breath and looked up, blinking as if she shone a harsh light on him. "Yes, ma'am."

She opened the door in the bars and stepped in, sitting beside him. The guards all seemed professional and devoted to their task earlier. The fact that eight of them turned aside from their duty bothered her a great deal. Certainly men had their loyalties bought and sold all the time, but she expected the Lady had the resources to screen the men she employed for this purpose, and to pay them well enough to prevent this. Mardis seemed the type of woman who could inspire loyalty in her servants.

Without preamble, she took the man's good arm, yanked off his glove, and grasped his hand, lacing her fingers with his. The contact surprised him, and he squeezed her hand. *Are you a confessor? Some kind of soothsayer? Am I to be tormented with kindness before going to my fate?*

"Why did you attack Lady Mardis?"

He squinted and frowned, gaze dropping to the floor. Memories boiled up, of Drune and money exchanging hands. He and the others were supposed to kill the Lady on her next journey to Todan, to visit the King. Drune paid them to do it. They'd all get assigned to her for the trip, and in that foreign place, they'd kill her and make it appear to be an accident. *When I saw Drune, I knew we had to act right away. It was so much money, I couldn't resist.*

The memories made no sense, in light of Drune's lack of involvement. How could he remember an event that never happened, and remember it so vividly it had to be true? "When did Sera Drune pay you to murder Lady Mardis?"

Again, he remembered all the same things. Money exchanged hands.

Sera Drune. Planning for the trip. Panic at seeing Drune today. His brow furrowed as he tried to dig deeper into them and recall a date or time. "I... I don't know." *Was there snow on the ground?* When he accepted the money, he could see snow. When he thought of Drune, the trees had green leaves and the air felt warm. The planning had disjointed parts, like it had been stitched together from different pieces of cloth with the same pattern. The pieces lined up almost perfectly. Almost.

Someone meddled in this man's memories, and he couldn't see past or through them. He could tell; the memories made him uncomfortable. If she knew some way to clean them up, she would do it. This man did not deserve to suffer. And yet, he would. Because someone chose him to. Someone decided he suited their purpose and would be used as a pawn in their game. This someone wasn't Drune. She would find out who it was.

"I am sorry for you. This is a wretched thing." Her pity put her hand on the knife at her back.

A well trained bodyguard, he noticed the movement. *What are you — Oh.* His eyes met hers. *There's no hope.* He sighed and nodded, shoulders slumping. *Yes, do it. Please. I don't want to go there any more than you want to send me. The shame on my family will already be enough without that.*

Could she do this? To kill someone who didn't fight back in the name of pity and release? Harris, she knew, could do it and not think much of it. It didn't make him a bad person, not really, it only shaped how he looked at things, what options he kept available. Algie could, too, but she hardly wanted to consider herself an equal to him.

You don't want to, I can see it your eyes. You're not that kind of person. That's not a bad thing. "It's alright," the guard said quietly, his voice rough. "I don't think I can do it, either."

If he frightened or attacked her, she could do it. She could defend herself, but not kill an unarmed, docile man. Did that make her weak? Pulling the knife out, she held it in plain sight and stared at it. Colby couldn't do it, either. Or maybe he could, but wouldn't. If only this man had been cut down upstairs. She lifted the knife halfheartedly, a gesture somewhere between offering it to him and offering to slit his throat.

I wish I could find another way. She tried to pull her hand away, but he held on tightly. *You understand. I need that right now. Please don't go.* "Stay a little longer?" He meant to have her hold his hand while he bled out, an idea that terrified her. She didn't want to feel it when a person died. She didn't want to be a witness to his last thoughts.

"Take it and I will go." She tugged on her hand again, this time more frantic. "I can get another."

No, stay. He thought about trying to overpower her, about taking the knife and stabbing her with it. Riding on her fresh fear, he yanked her hand, jerking her closer. She lashed out with the knife. *I'm sorry. Thank you. You're lovely and strange and I hope this doesn't stain you too much.* Blood sprayed from his neck where she'd slashed him deeply. *Dizzy. Cold. Weightless.* He slumped over and fell to the floor, finally releasing her hand.

Chavali shook, from head to toe, and dropped the knife. The clatter brought Harris to the cell—he must have been close by. He came to her side and put a hand on her shoulder, saying something she didn't hear. The guard—she didn't even get his name—thanked her. He wanted that, preferred it to being left on an island to struggle and rot.

She looked at her hands, covered in blood, then looked at Harris. He took her chin in his hand, checking her over. *Did he hurt you? No, he didn't. What happened?* "Chavali?"

Wiping her hands on her dress, she jerked away from his touch. He backed off, giving her space. "I am fine." Her eyes caught Colby peering into the cell, taking the scene in and finding it repulsive.

"You killed him."

"Look at her," Harris said, "she's shaking like a leaf. He must have done something, scared her."

Chavali closed her eyes and made fists. Being shocked and confused wouldn't change anything. Later, back at the Tower, she would discuss this with Healer Kelly. The girl would help her deal with it. Until then, they had a job to do and it needed to be done. With effort, she pushed all of this aside.

When she opened her eyes, she found Colby still frowning down at her. "This isn't justice, it's vengeance."

He didn't and couldn't understand. She scowled at him and stormed out of the cell. "Believe what you wish."

"Chavali." Colby grabbed her arm as she brushed past him. "This has to stop. I won't let you lie, cheat, steal, and murder our way through this."

"Let me?" She couldn't resist his grasp and didn't bother trying. "Your insufferable obsession with honesty threatens to jeopardize our mission at every turn, but *I* am the one causing the problem. Yes, this must be it. Chavali cannot control herself. She needs a tender or she will run rampant, doing whatever she thinks must be done and damned be the consequences. Obviously, she must kill whoever resists or refuses."

He wanted to slap her, she could see it in his eyes. "You just murdered an unarmed man in cold blood!"

Of course that's what he saw. It was even true, to an extent. "You, of course, think this island nonsense is some kind of justice."

"It's better than murder. It's better than the lies to you tell yourself to sleep at night."

Chavali now wanted to slap him, too. "The one person I *never* lie to is myself. Which is more than I can say for you." Yanking her arm away almost sent her to the floor, because he let go, his face twisted with fury.

"Whoa," Harris said, stepping between them with his hands up. "We're on the same team here."

Portia stepped up next to him. "We should all calm down, clean up, get something to eat, and talk about this later."

"Let's split up," Harris suggested. "Take a walk or something. We can meet back up at the inn later and go over everything."

Chavali crossed her arms, glowering at Colby between their heads. "Fine." She let Harris put an arm around her shoulders and steer her out of the basement. Servants already swarmed the hallway, cleaning up the bodies and blood. They skirted around the commotion and hurried out. She ignored Karias's interest on the way to the gate and through it. Harris turned her up the street and they walked.

He said nothing while she seethed. That ass judged her. How dare he? Not only did she get to remember his thoughts draining away with his life's blood, she had to have Colby sitting up on his giant horse, looking down at her. He reminded her of Keino, always thinking she needed to be managed or handled. Except Keino wouldn't assume the worst of her. Colby didn't know what happened there; he saw the knife and the blood and the dead man, made a guess, and reacted. Ass.

Chapter 16

As Harris presumably intended, the brisk walk settled her nerves and cooled her anger. They walked all over the city, eventually slowing down. He took her past the forested graveyard, reminding her of Drune's thoughts on Garrian. She stopped and leaned against the fence, staring at the trees.

"Do you want to talk about it?"

"No. I want to punch him in the face."

"I can relate." Harris grinned. He pulled her knife out from behind his back and offered it to her, hilt first.

Chavali snorted, took the knife, and changed the subject. "Drune suggested we speak to Garrian about the docks. I don't really understand how these things all connect, but they seem to, somehow."

"Yeah, I'm getting that feeling, too. It doesn't make sense, but it does."

Movement attracted Chavali's attention. She looked up to see Garrian's spy hurrying down the street. He must have been following them still. Odd, since the other three weren't. More odd, now that she thought about it, she hadn't seen Jore's spy since the guard attack. Then again, that had been a major event, and if he reported it, he may have been called off to do other things. Especially if he reported that the four of them were not responsible for it. They might not be worth following anymore. Except to Garrian.

"We should go see him now. Garrian, I mean." She pointed at the spy.

"Are you sure? You're still kind of covered in blood."

Looking down at herself, she saw her dress had smears, spatters, and a spray, but she could cover that up. His clothes weren't much better. "Worry about yourself. I will hold my cloak closed. It seems important now."

Harris didn't disagree and they followed the spy, who seemed unaware of their pursuit. His destination became clear when they reached Garrian's street. The pair didn't bother shadowing him all the way there. Instead, they waited a few minutes after he turned the corner, then strolled up to the house.

A servant answered the door, her eyes wide and frightened as she scanned the area behind them. "The Seran isn't seeing anyone right now."

The fear intrigued Chavali. She gave the woman a sympathetic, confident smile, wondering what put all the tension in her shoulders. "We are here to help, he asked us to come."

"Oh dear." The maid beckoned them inside, demanding they hurry. "He's going mad." She shut the door right behind Harris, clipping his boot in her haste. "At least, I hope he's going mad. He's in the office."

Voices came from deeper in the house, too many to make out what any of them said. "What is he doing?" Chavali put a hand on the woman's arm (her sleeve lay between them) to try to calm her.

"He's barricaded himself in his office, calling all his people back, but not letting anyone in to see him. Twelve guards, all his assistants and clerks and everyone, sitting around inside. He doesn't want anyone outside, because some woman is coming. Won't say who, just goes on about 'her.' " The servant ushered them to the office, passing a sitting room full of people all chatting or playing cards.

Harris knocked on the door. "Seran Garrian? It's Harris, Elise's brother."

Chavali thanked the maid and shooed her back to her duties. She had a thought to say something, but a scraping sound came from the other side of the door, then it cracked open. Garrian pressed one wild eye to the gap and it darted up and down each of them. "You can talk to her," he muttered. Flinging door open, he grabbed them both, hauled them inside, and slammed the door shut again. He then barricaded it again with a heavy wood bureau.

That bureau had been against the opposite wall the last time they saw it, and papers and books he must have swiped off its surface lay strewn about the floor. Remains of a meal sat on his desk, and the smell of urine mixed with sweat and dust. Garrian's fear crawled over him, twitching his fingers, keeping his eyes open and wide, forcing him to stay on his feet and pace. His hair stuck out, wild, as if he'd run his hands through it several hundred times.

"You have to talk to her." He pointed an accusing finger at Harris. "She'll listen to you, she has to."

"Who?" Harris kept his eyes on Garrian, which Chavali deemed a wise choice.

"She's coming back, don't you see? I saw her." He paced the length of his office in four long strides and returned, and kept going back and forth, back and forth.

"Who's coming back?"

Chavali noticed the window had only a curtain over it, which seemed odd in his current state. She leaned over and peered out through it, but saw nothing. "Is it your wife? Merilyn?"

"No, no, of course not. I didn't kill Merilyn." Garrian's hand dipped into a pocket. His fingers rubbed against the outside of his thigh, then he pulled his hand out again.

Chavali glanced at Harris and caught him doing the same with her. They shared a look, passing a message along the lines of 'he's cracked, so we need to get as much information as we can before he does something really stupid.' "You killed her?"

Garrian stopped pacing in the middle of the office and pressed the heels of his palms over his eyes. "It wasn't supposed to happen like that." Pulling his hands away, he pleaded with them. "It wasn't my fault, I swear. You have to tell her I didn't want that. I loved her, I couldn't help myself." Again, his hand dipped into and out of that pocket.

Taking a hesitant step forward, Chavali offered her hand to him. She had an idea what he might be talking about and wanted confirmation. "We will speak to her for you, but you must be honest with us. Tell us the whole story, the real story."

He shied away, pulling his hands close. "No, don't touch me. Fish! Fish. Oh, Creator save me, it's all about fish. Her eyes, you can see it in her eyes." He rubbed his own eyes again. This time, when his hand went for the pocket, he grabbed his pants there and squeezed. "I wanted her, but she didn't want me. Why didn't she want me? It's so unfair."

"The maid's right," Harris whispered as Garrian resumed pacing and muttering, "he's mad."

Chavali nodded. "We need whatever is in that pocket."

Harris kept his attention on Garrian. "I'll distract him, you pick his pocket."

"I do not have this skill."

"You don't really need skill for this, but we can swap it. That's fine with me."

Chavali took a deep breath and stepped into Garrian's way. "We will speak to her for you, but you must do something for us." Behind his back, Harris crept up.

Garrian reached up and grabbed two fistfuls of hair, yanking on them. "Is it too late? It might be too late."

"No, it's not too late." She kept her hands out, placating without touching him. "Listen to me, Garrian. David. She will listen to us, you must simply tell us the truth. Tell us how she died. It's important, David."

Harris dropped his hand slowly into Garrian's pocket. Garrian didn't notice and released his hair to cover his face again. "She wanted to expose everything. I worked so hard for so many years, and couldn't keep up with it all. Besides, who doesn't see the ways to take a little? No one got hurt, and it was all for Merilyn. Until it wasn't anymore."

When Harris pulled his hand out, a necklace with a pendant dangled from it. They both instantly knew who 'she' referred to. "Until it was about Elise," Chavali prompted.

Garrian panicked, waving his hands wildly and shushing Chavali. "Don't say her name," he croaked out in a harsh whisper. "She's coming for me."

"She found the irregularities in the books and came to you, not the other way around." Chavali didn't bother asking it as a question. The moment she saw that broken heart pendant, she understood exactly what happened. "You tried to coax her into your bed to keep her loyal. She rejected you, throwing down the pendant when you met her at Lover's Leap, hoping to romance her, to seduce her. Enraged by her rejection, you strangled her with the very symbol of it and threw her body off the cliff."

Garrian crumpled to his knees and seemed suddenly more lucid. His eyes glistened with tears. "No, I didn't kill her, not with my own hands. I swear it on my wife's grave. She knew, even. Merliyn wanted me to be happy, and she was so frail. We thought to bring someone into the house with us so we could have children. But I didn't kill El— Her. It was the people running the smuggling operation. They wanted to silence her and keep me in line."

"Wait," Harris said, frowning as he dropped the pendant into his own pocket. "What does any of that have to do with Drune, the renovations at the docks, or the dead bodies showing up?"

"They had to stop using my warehouses and move everything out, all because Drune demanded action on the disease." Chavali pitied him for how he blubbered everything out. "I couldn't argue about anything but the costs without revealing myself. I don't know anything about the disease, though, I swear on the Creator I know nothing."

The man seemed genuine, yet Chavali still didn't quite believe him.

It seemed so convenient. Why would that man in the wine shop basement—or others of his type—leave behind such an obvious bit of blackmail as that pendant? She didn't think pressing on it would help, though; not yet, not directly. "We discovered the smuggling because they had to ship it someplace deeper in the city. If it went straight into the warehouses, we may not have noticed."

"That's why the wine shop seemed weird," Harris said. "I thought it must have a sub-basement tunnel they took the goods through, but it must have been a makeshift stop on the path the goods were taking. They cleared some space out, waited for nightfall, and moved things in small quantities."

Garrian nodded through his hands, once again covering his face. "They bribed the owner to use it temporarily, same as they bribed me to use my warehouses."

Many things clicked into place now, but Chavali still didn't understand the dead bodies in the water, or the kidnapping. "Did you bribe Lady Mardis's guards to attack her, or have Luna Mardis kidnapped?"

"What?" Stunned out of his self-pity for the moment, Garrian looked up at her, face pale and shocked. "No! I would never do that."

Chavali arched an eyebrow. "Yet you took bribes from smugglers."

He held up his hands, begging her to believe him. "It was only about money. Who does smuggling really hurt when it's only about avoiding taxes? Merilyn's illnesses were expensive to treat. She required specialized care and food, and it wasn't easy to afford all the time. With the extra money, I could manage it all and still keep up appearances for my position."

The window smashed, a large rock flying through it and ripping the curtain down. Chavali ducked away from the flying glass, shielding her face. She heard Harris grunt. "The Seran is under attack," she bellowed towards the door, hoping at least one of the people milling about in the house would hear her.

Straightening, her hand went to her knife to face the figure who dove in through the broken window. The figure hit the floor and rolled to her feet, leaving a spray of water in her wake. The drops spattered Chavali in the face, a few landing on her tongue. Salt water. The woman turned to face them. Chavali recognized her from Garrian's mind yesterday, the one she saw a confusing flash of.

Bits of kelp and seaweed clung to her torn, soaked dress and her wet, limp hair. Her abnormally pale flesh had a deathly blue tint, and her eyes were strange, as if her pupils floated in pools of murky water instead of whites. She paused for only a moment, taking in the room, then focused on Garrian and lunged at him.

It had to be Elise, which made no sense. Then again, Chavali, Colby, Portia, and nearly all the rest of the Fallen agents died, too. Was it really so farfetched that someone else found a way to return from the other side? No, not really.

Elise shrieked in rage, clawing at him with jagged fingernails while he flinched away and huddled on himself. Someone tried to open the door, discovering the bureau blocked it. Harris pounced on Elise, sinking a dagger into her back. Chavali raced to the door to heave the furniture aside.

"It's a strange woman," she told the guards trying to force their way in. "She came in through the window!"

Behind her, Elise turned her attention to Harris, kicking and clawing at him, still screeching her rage. He stabbed her again, which only seemed to anger her more. The blade stuck in her side and he drew another. Before he could attack her again, she flung her hand out, hitting him across the face so hard he stumbled to the side. She grabbed the knife in her body, yanked it out, and stabbed him in the chest, leaving the blade there.

"I am the Herald of the Lost," she growled as she turned to face Garrian again. Her voice warbled strangely, as if she spoke through water. "I come to judge and punish the people of Ket for their ancient sin. You will be the first to feel my wrath!"

Four guards heaved the door open and thundered in, weapons ready. One went to Garrian, shaking in a lump on the floor, while the other three advanced on Elise. Her water eyes darted from one to another, then she turned and dove out through the window, still screaming. Two of the guards turned and ran out. The third knelt to check on Harris.

Chavali rushed to his side also, taking his hand. As much as he annoyed her with his attraction, she had no wish to see him die. He'd proven himself worthy of friendship, a commodity she'd found to be in short supply all her life. "No dying," she told him firmly.

"Don't talk," the guard ordered. "Save your strength. I'll get help."

This is what I have to do to get you to take my hand now? Get stabbed in the chest?

She snorted and leaned in to whisper to him. "I will not enjoy hauling your body back to the tower so you can be one of us in full. Maybe I will leave you here anyway, for being an idiot. Even I know better than to let go of the knife when I stab someone."

He grinned, weak and laced with pain. *Good one. You should interrogate Garrian more before he's bundled off by his guards. Stay close.*

Harris was right. She reached into his pocket (which he enjoyed, of course) and pulled the pendant out. "That," she said as she turned to face Garrian, being checked over by his guard for injuries, "was not a woman killed to send a message to you. That was a woman full of rage. At you." Vaguely, she noticed other people standing at the door, watching. "She came here to murder you, for the crime of murdering her." Holding up the necklace, she stared at him, hard and cold and ready to kill him herself if Harris died for trying to defend him.

Garrian, his face streaked with angry red lines where Elise's fingernails scraped him, burst into noisy tears. "I killed her. Like you said. I ran the smuggling ring, she found out. We were already having an affair. I thought I could convince her to stay quiet because of it, but she threatened to expose me, to expose it all. We met out there because no one goes out there, and she was angry. With me. I gave her the necklace, trying to buy her affection and silence. She threw it in my face, and I strangled her with mine, then threw her body off the cliff."

The audience sucked in a collective breath at the revelations. Chavali noticed the spy among the spectators and pointed to him. "You, be useful, go get the Guard and act as a witness to all that has happened here."

"Chastity, please, I swear on my own life, I never meant to hurt anyone. I had nothing to do with any kidnapping plot, or attack on Lady Mardis. Please believe me."

Chavali sneered. "The fear of death has put honesty into you, I see."

Colby wouldn't approve of how they reached this point, but he would appreciate the fact they got here. Her attention returned to Harris, whose thoughts had a hard time with coherence through the pain. "I will not leave you until you pass out, Harris. That is the only incentive I will offer to remain conscious."

Pretty good incentive.

Chapter 17

Ket had no healers with the skill of the women at the Fallen tower, or so everyone said. There, Harris would be back on his feet within an hour or so. Here, he had to be bandaged and sent to Cander's Lodge to rest. They kept him from death, but did no better than that. It took Chavali an hour to free herself of the City Guard and their pointless questions and demands and idiocy. If she knew how Garrian could confess to the murder of someone who tried to kill him after he killed her first, she wouldn't tell them.

Back at the inn, she checked on Harris to find him asleep, as he had been when she let go of him earlier. His thoughts until that point had bounced around, showing her more of his past than he probably wanted her to know about. They could talk about it later, at the tower. Still covered in blood, now with Harris's added to the mix, she took the time to clean herself up, wondering where Portia and Colby got to. At this point, that argument felt wrong and stupid. Neither of them should have let their tempers flare, not there and then.

Given what he thought happened in that basement, it made sense for him to be upset, of course. Even with what actually happened, he had a right to be upset about it. *She* was upset about it. And about her reaction to Harris nearly dying, and Elise's appearance, and everything Garrian said and did, and many other things. So much happened here in so few days, she wanted to crawl into bed and sleep until it faded away.

Her stomach rumbled as she dressed in clean clothes, so she turned her back on the bed and trudged downstairs, into the press of the evening dinner crowd. The bartender would let her order food at the bar, she felt certain of that, so she sat down at the end, the same seat as before. Within a minute, she had hot tea and an order for a meal in.

Staring into her steaming mug, she recognized she needed to do something about Colby. In her clan, when someone bothered her, she told them to their face, in front of other members of the clan, then talked it out with her parents, and then never had to deal with it again. Except for Keino, but he had been a special case. Colby was not Keino.

It surprised her that she felt it necessary to point that out to herself. Obviously, Colby had little in common with Keino. The two men couldn't be more different. One strove for honesty and justice with every fiber of his being and thought of others before himself. The other sulked and groused when he didn't get what he wanted. Of the two, Colby certainly deserved the second chance at life more than Keino. Even if she did miss him and wish he would walk in through those doors to come irritate her with his ideas about what she should and shouldn't do or think or feel.

Mourning a dead man had no place here. The living needed her attention. And whatever Elise had become. She called herself the 'Herald of the Lost,' putting weight and importance on the words, making it a title. There could be no doubt she was the herald in the prophecy. Those water-filled eyes bothered her more now that she had a chance to think about them. Swimming, indeed, and on a fated tide. Her coming—whether it was always going to be Elise or she happened to be in the 'right' place at the 'right' time—could not have been averted, even if they'd known about it soon enough. Nothing good would come from Elise now, and she needed to be stopped.

"My goodness, you look as if you've seen a ghost."

The voice stirred her from her thoughts and chilled her to the bone. She pushed her empty plate away and gave her attention to the mysterious woman once again sitting beside her. "What?" Studying her face, Chavali saw no sign of humor, which further disturbed her. Did she mean Elise?

"The stories say ghosts are restless spirits of the dead, unable to move on for one reason or another."

Chavali sipped at her tea, bothered that she didn't understand the conversation. "Ghosts are not real. They are stories to frighten children and fools."

"Yet you believe in spirits."

Scowling, Chavali shook her head. "Spirits are not real, either." She couldn't imagine a bolder lie to spill from her lips.

The woman laughed. "Of course not." She flicked a hand up and touched the feather sprouted from Chavali's forehead with a grin. "You would know, wouldn't you?"

Pulling away from her, now thoroughly spooked, Chavali held up her tea between them. As shields went, it had no real value, but it made her feel a little better about the situation. "You never told me your name."

She looked off at the wall, thinking about it. "No, I don't suppose I did. Not that it matters. Names are forgotten, lost to time. Warnings, too." She picked up a mug of tea Chavali didn't notice the bartender setting down. The man had a way of slipping in and out without being spotted. He had more skill with it than those four spies.

Chavali glared at her cup, in no mood for cryptic word games. "What warnings?"

"Have you ever thought about why no one can agree what the greatest sin is?"

Although she liked the woman initially, this visit made her want to strangle her. "Because it is not in the memory we all share from birth."

"Why do you suppose that is? That memory is oddly and specifically nonspecific, isn't it? We don't even know with certainty that the Creator is female, we just assume so."

A keen interest in decoding the memory popped up in the minds she sampled from time to time. Usually, she noticed it in passing while examining other thoughts. A few times, she used it to help while telling a fortune. She'd never met someone who insisted upon pulling her into the conversation before. "I am not interested in this subject."

"No? But it's fascinating. Makes you wonder what the Creator is really like. If she, or he, or it desperately wanted us to all stop doing something, why not come out and say what that thing is? Why give us all the capacity to do it in the first place? Why trample over the ancient beliefs that came before? I've often wondered what the Creator has to gain by being so vague. It's so little to go on. Might as well not have that kind of instructions."

Chavali narrowed her eyes, not sure she heard all of that correctly. Ancient beliefs? Granted, she never did feel as certain about the Creator's dominion as anyone else she met. "Keep talking of these things, and someone will accuse you of atheism."

The woman shrugged. "There's no crime in asking questions. Not with the Lost stirring. Not with what's in your dreams. Someday, they'll devour you, Chavali. Remember that and learn to tend them before they can." She dumped coins on the bar again and slid off her stool.

Too stunned by the direct and precise warning to act, the woman had already reached the door when Chavali got up to follow. She hurried through the tables and ran outside, hitting the cold air with a gasp and snapping her head around wildly. The woman must have ducked out of sight. It would be easy to do here, with people walking in both directions and alleys to slip into, despite the fact Garrian's spy over there couldn't manage it. Why follow her now? Did he have a grudge for making him indict his own employer? Drune's spy lurked in sight, too.

Chavali might have gone over to harass either or both of them, except she saw Karias trotting down the street, someone slumped over his back. She recognized Portia's cloak and hurried to meet them. "What happened?"

Portia's eyes fluttered and she moaned. Chavali pointed straight at Garrian's spy, then curled the finger around and beckoned him to her. Never mind why he kept following her, she needed help right now.

The spy didn't hesitate—he jumped and trotted to her side. "Who did this to her?"

"I don't know." Portia taught her to say that. "Help me bring her inside and put her to bed." With his assistance, they pulled her down from the horse, carried her up to the room, and laid her on the bed. Several small injuries stained her clothes with blood. "Can I trust you to bring a healer for her?"

The spy sighed and nodded. "I'm not here for my boss now, I'm here for myself. I don't care why you've come or what you're doing; I want to know what's going on in my hometown. I think you're the best chance for getting to the bottom of all this now. I'll take care of her, I promise." He grinned. "It's not like I can hide from you if you want to hunt me down, right?"

Chavali huffed in muted amusement. "No, you cannot. If I am not here when you return, do not panic. I must also tend to that horse."

The spy flipped a salute with two fingers and hurried away.

Leaning over Portia, she touched her forehead, checking for a fever and sampling her thoughts. They raced around, too chaotic and bizarre to be useful. None of it made sense. Chavali grabbed her cloak and mittens, asked a waitress to keep tabs on Portia, and went back to the horse.

He stood there, head high and imperious, waiting for her. She hesitated for a moment, then reached out a hand and touched his nose. The spirits swarmed on him and acted strangely, recognizing a brother, or something along those lines.

How am I going to get her to climb on my back so I can take her to Colby? I know she wasn't much of a rider before, and only knew horses in the form of wagon-pulling beasts.

"Ah ha," she said triumphantly. "I knew it. You are more than a mere horse." Something about his mind even felt familiar, as if she'd met him before. Also, she felt an undercurrent riding along with the coherent words, of pain and distress.

...Er?

"What are you, Karias? On second thought, never mind. We need to get to Colby. Is it far?"

I...how—?

"Stop wasting time being surprised. You know where he is, yes? And we must find him. Bend down and I will ride."

You can read thoughts? Wait, you're right. Never mind, yes. We'll talk later. For now, yes, let's go. Karias bent down and she climbed onto his back. With no saddle, she struggled until a pair of hands supported her from behind.

"May I go with you?" Drune's spy pushed her the rest of the way up. "I know something else is going on, and I know you know I know, and all that. Let me come along and help." Strange how both of these people now chose to be active participants instead of observers. Equally interesting: she didn't see Jore's spy. Mardis's probably still fawned over Luna.

Might as well bring her. I didn't see what happened, but Portia barely made it out alive, and Colby was captured. You'll need all the help you can get.

"Agreed. Come and let us hurry." Taking her hand, which revealed she wanted most to find out what happened to Portia and if it had something to do with the deaths, she helped the spy up to sit behind her and held onto Karias's mane.

When he wanted to run, Karias could really run. The large horse pounded through the streets, dancing around wagons and carriages with unexpected grace. His thoughts focused on avoiding hazards and not harming anyone. As they went, she got the feel of his mind. That sense of familiarity increased until she recognized it as the other stream of thought she noticed in Colby's mind when she first met him. He had that same sort of undercurrent. The man and the horse had a connection, and the pain she sensed came from Colby.

Horse, indeed. This was no mere animal gifted with intelligence. The spirits knew what they found in him, and that made him some kind of spirit, or something along those lines. A spirit possessing a horse, perhaps. Such things didn't happen or exist, but neither did her connection to her spirits.

She needed to be careful around Drune's spy, making sure not to spill either of their secrets. Who knew what people would do if they found out. One person already tried to take her for the prophecy gift. The thought of him made her mouth run dry. She slammed the door shut on those memories before they could swarm out.

Karias stopped north of Lover's Leap. That ragged cliff began here, shooting up in a pillar of dark rock with gentle waves lapping against the base. From this spot, they could wade out into the water where it met wild grasses lying dormant in the cold. Chavali and the spy slid off Karias's back and peered around. Chavali kept her hand on the horse's neck, noting he now cast about for Colby's scent.

"Find your master," Chavali told the horse, over-enunciating as if she spoke to a dog.

I'm going to assume you're doing that for this other woman's benefit and not get offended by it. Karias snuffled the air and the grass.

Chavali smirked. She pulled her hand away, letting the horse wander as he saw fit. "Remarkable creature, yes?"

"I don't know much about horses," Drune's spy said, poking through the grasses, "but I've never seen one that big before."

"A large man needs a large horse. Who knows where he got it. The mind staggers trying to imagine his parents." Chavali shrugged. "You know, I don't think I heard your name."

"Lynley. You're Chastity, right?"

"Yes. Well met."

Karias chuffed a snort and kicked into a trot. The two women followed him off the grass and into frigid, knee-high water slapping the rock. Chavali pulled off her boots and socks, leaving them behind with her cloak and mittens. They would come back this way, of course. She grabbed up her skirt and held it out of the water as she sloshed along behind Lynley.

"How, exactly, is the horse sniffing out his master across water?"

Chavali smirked at Lynley's back. "Horses are remarkable creatures." She guessed he had some ability to follow the link between them. It couldn't be strong enough to lead them unerringly to each other or there wouldn't have been a delay at the water's edge, but it probably gave a good idea of general direction and distance.

Karias stopped and pawed at the water next to a hole in the cliff wall. It didn't look big enough for any of them to get inside. When Chavali got closer, she saw it extended several feet underwater. Good thing she made the effort to keep herself dry. She sighed and put a hand on the horse's flank.

"I do not know how to swim."

It smells like there's dry rock inside. I expect it slopes upwards. Watch out for the dip in the ground right in front of it.

"Not my best skill, either," Lynley said, oblivious to the horse's comments. "The most important thing is to not drown."

She's so helpful. I'm so glad you brought her.

It amused Chavali to discover the horse had a similar sense of sarcasm as herself. "I will keep that in mind."

Lynley stepped in front of the cave, immediately slipping and disappearing underwater.

See? There's a dip right there. Oh, and it's probably slippery.

Snickering, Chavali took her hand off the horse as Lynley popped her head above the surface again. She pushed water out of her eyes and spat, then sucked in a lungful of air. "Didn't expect that."

"Is there a way for me to avoid this?"

Lynley surged forward, arms out and feeling around. "Not really, but if you hop to here, you should be able to keep your head above the surface. Here, I'll give you a hand."

"We will find him," she told Karias. She registered him nodding as she grabbed Lynley's hand and used her help to avoid the deepest part of the cave entrance.

I hope you're not too attached to this guy. He's probably dead. You seem like a good person, so I'd hate to have to watch you deal with that.

Chavali didn't want to listen to those kinds of thoughts and let go of Lynley's hand as soon as her feet found the rock. Now in moving, chilled water up to her shoulders, her teeth chattered and her whole body shivered. They pressed ahead, finding the ground sloped up.

Only dim light managed to reach them, reflected off the surface of the water. She saw him clearly in the gloom as they crested the rise. Colby lay on the slick rock, eyes shut and twitching, his whole body shaking, his clothes gone but for his pants. His wrists were bound by a rope tied to a finger of rock without slack. Oddly, his sword lay on the ground nearby, taunting him.

Old, faded burn scars attested to how Colby died before becoming Fallen. A handful of new burn marks accompanied them, angry red welts puckering his flesh. Someone hit him in the face a few times, too, splitting his lip and giving him a black eye.

Both of them rushed to his side. Lynley pulled a knife from her sodden boot and cut the rope. Chavali had no way to truly help, so she picked up his head and lay it in her lap, brushing his face. A nightmare plagued him, she could tell that without touching him. The images in his head carried so much pure, bloody violence, she flinched away from them. "Colby, wake up. We will need your help to get you out of here."

"Damn. Someone cut his ankles so he can't walk. And his elbows, too. Look at that. Those are—" Lynley turned at a change in the light.

Chavali followed her gaze and saw a strange person a few feet into the cave. How did this woman get past Karias? Perhaps she swam, because her hair and face dripped. Something about the dripping bothered her, though Chavali couldn't put her finger on it. Odd also how the woman's hair and nose reminded her of Sera Drune. Both had that same severe, sharp look.

The woman stared straight at both of them, and then her face and hair changed. Chavali knew illusions well enough to recognize one fading when she saw it. The woman used some kind of illusory gift to mask her appearance. In this situation, watching her raise a thick blade and charge them with a growling sort of scream, Chavali had no thought to spare for what that might mean.

On her knees, Chavali had to scramble to set Colby's head aside without hurting him more, pull her own knife, and get to her feet. Lynley jumped to engage the woman, leading with her dagger. Given that distraction, Chavali chose to twine her fingers through the spirits, crafting an image of Eliot entering the cave. Her idea turned out to be more complicated than she expected. Water needed to appear to be displaced. Spray needed to fly in the air—salty spray at that. What color did the ocean appear? She had no idea.

Illusionary Eliot rose up out of the water. Sound, it needed sound. More splashing filled the cave. Lynley stared at him, confused. The strange woman ignored Eliot and stabbed the spy in the neck, ripping the blade to the side. She turned and pounced on Chavali before Lynley hit the water.

In a panic, Chavali flung her arms up protect herself. The woman's forearm (covered by her soaked sleeve), hit Chavali's forearm (also covered by a wet sleeve), the blade stopping mere inches from her face. Never mind Colby's head, she had to keep them both from dying in this forsaken place. She rolled to the side and kicked out, grabbing a fistful of hair and smashing the woman's head into the rock. The woman bounced back up with a gash across her temple and fury in her eyes. She lunged at Chavali again.

Chavali smacked the hand with the knife to keep it away, sending the knife skittering across the rock. In that moment of contact, Chavali got a flash of what this woman wanted to do to her, and had no intention of letting any of that happen. Determined not to be strung up and used as a toy for a torturer, she threw a punch at the woman's face, kicked her in the gut, and grabbed her fist when it got close.

A curious thing happened when she got a good grip.

For ten years, Chavali thought she knew how the spirits behaved. They forced prophecies on her from time to time. They connected with the auras or spirits or whatever of other people she touched and formed a conduit to their thoughts. They allowed her to manipulate them into creating illusions from her imagination. Her predecessor in the clan explained all of this, and she had been as prepared to handle it as any fifteen year old could be.

This woman's mind pushed on Chavali's, and the spirits pushed back. Never once had they done such a thing before. She felt it happen. Like the man who murdered her clan and tried to take her, this woman sent a tendril into her mind—a stained, oily questing finger. This woman, however, had less skill. The spirits couldn't stop him, but they could stop her.

Chavali gripped the woman's fist, refusing to let her pull away. The spirits surged across the link, letting her rip away the woman's memories. Several flashed by while the woman shrieked and flailed. A wild thrash hit Chavali across the jaw, stunning her enough to let go, and the woman dove into the water without trying to retrieve her knife.

Scrambling to her hands and knees, Chavali grabbed Lynley, floating face down in the water. She turned the spy over and hauled her up. Nothing could have saved her. The blade cut too deep. Her eyes stared, glassy and blank. No thoughts spilled from her.

She sat back with a heavy sigh and pushed Lynley's eyelids shut. Such a stupid waste. Colby moaned, the first noise he made since they found him. Turning her attention to him, she saw his eyes flutter, trying and failing to open. "Colby, it's Chavali. You are safe for the moment. Open your eyes."

He groaned. His shaking worsened. She knelt beside him and tried to think of a better idea than slapping him. Nothing came to mind. Her hand cracked against his cheek. Thankfully, his eyes snapped open. He groaned and tried to get up. With his hamstrings and elbows cut, he couldn't manage more than rocking enough to hurt himself. His grunts and groans echoed in the cave.

Letting him do it with a mostly stifled roll of her eyes, Chavali pushed Lynley back into the water, figuring floating would be the easiest way to get both of them out. "Relax. Karias is nearby and I will get you out."

"Chavali?"

"No, I am a water monster, come to devour your soul." She stared at him in surprise when he whimpered and curled into a ball. The dream had been bad, but she didn't think it would continue to affect him on waking. Perhaps the helplessness compounded it.

"Ah, no, I am only joking. Yes, it's Chavali. Lie still. You are free. The healers here should be able to handle these injuries, they are... I believe they can be healed." She picked up the knife and, knowing it to be rude and cruel to her family, stabbed it into Lynley's body to transport it. Next, she grabbed Colby under his arms and dragged him to the water.

Bloodanddeathandbloodanddeathandbloodanddeathandbloodand death... Along with these words, she saw more of his dreams in disjointed flashes of horror. New memories of being burned now mingled with his memories of dying in fire. With this on top of that woman's memories, she found it difficult to think.

She pushed every last bit of it aside as hard as she could. "You have to lie flat, Colby. You need to float on your back, or I will never get you out of here. That woman is gone. Karias is close, waiting in the water to take you to dry clothes and a warm bed. Think of food. A meat pie, perhaps, or fresh bread with that sweet butter you like smeared all over it. Honey drizzled in a cup of hot tea. Cakes frosted with sugar and lemon. A leg of turkey, dripping with juices and as big as your fist. Or maybe my fist. Your fist is very large."

Her voice cut through his repetitive thoughts, giving him something else to latch onto. He pictured the foods she mentioned and started adding his own: pancakes filled with fat, juicy blueberries. "Chavali. You came for me."

"Your horse insisted. Otherwise, I would have taken a long bath and gotten some sleep."

Liar. He made a coughing noise, the best he could do for laughing right now. "He can be like that."

"Yes, I gathered. Come, lie flat. Float. I can kick you if it will help."

It took him several seconds, then he relaxed enough to let her push him out of the cave, and she changed her grip so she didn't have to listen to his thoughts anymore. He went through the opening feet first, and she saw Karias take a mouthful of his pants.

"Take him to the shore, I must also get Lynley." The horse whuffed as she turned away from them both and went back for the corpse. Without Colby's body in the way, she noticed an oddly smooth rock in the wall. She padded out of the water and ran her fingers along it. The rock moved and she pushed it. Some sort of spring mechanism released it into her hand.

Someone had hollowed it out and used it for storage. She removed an envelope, Colby's Crown Medallion, and a handful of gold coins. With no reason to take the empty stone, she put it back, sliding it in until it clicked and stayed. How curious that someone bothered to set something like that up in a place like this. It didn't matter, though.

Chapter 18

It took doing to get both Colby and Lynley onto Karias. The water helped. Colby passing out did not. As soon as Chavali sat down beside her things, the strange woman's memories flooded her mind. Perhaps the spirits kept them at bay until she could take a moment to breathe. Each had little more than a flash, a glimpse of something.

A red hot fireplace poker made the new burns on Colby's chest. An enchanted knife reached out from a shadow and slashed through boots, biting into Colby's ankles. Her mind thrust into Portia's, learning little but riling the mage into a fight nearly to the death. Portia only got away because Colby punched the woman and Karias got close to braining her.

The only other memory she took made her flinch and wish covering her eyes would make a difference. This woman, whose name seemed to be 'Pale,' knew the man Chavali would never forget, no matter how long she lived. He put slime in her head, he murdered her clan, he took the three children, he forced her to the point of killing herself.

And now, he had a name: Robin. Such a pleasant, friendly name for such a vile, despicable man. In Pale's memory, he had sky blue eyes and light brown hair with a reddish tint, his face open and inviting. Pale thought of him fondly, as a mentor. She believed he had all the right answers, and followed him without reservation. Which made her incredibly dangerous, more than she seemed in that cave. If she got word to Robin about Chavali, he would stop at nothing to find her again, and this time, he'd be even better prepared.

With a shaking hand, she picked up the envelope. Karias nickered at her, a reminder his master needed help sooner, not later. She nodded and tucked the letter inside her cloak. It took only a minute to pull her socks and boots on, then her cloak and mittens. A single thought circled around in her head: find Pale. By herself. Somehow. She had no idea where to start.

Worse, she also now knew Pale could craft illusions, better than her own. It must have been her giving the money to Mardis's guards, disguised as Drune. Any one of them could then finger Drune when questioned. She must have worn the same illusory disguise to kidnap Luna. But why take the girl? She still didn't understand that. Especially given how easy she had been to find and free.

While they walked, she glanced behind, worried Robin might be shadowing her. Someone lurked back there, flitting from shadow to shadow, and she imagined it must be him. Garrian's spy said he'd stay with Portia, and she believed him. Mardis's wouldn't bother hiding, she thought. Not anymore. It could be Jore's, or someone new. Or Pale. She already shivered from wearing cold, wet clothes; it worsened as she imagined a rock or other weapon aimed at her head. Spikes of anxiety shot all the way to her fingers and toes with every alleyway and shadowy corner they passed.

"I must go see Lady Mardis." She didn't really want to hear whatever the horse had to say in response, but pulled off a mitten and touched his neck anyway.

I'll take Colby to the inn. Someone should recognize him and be able to get him to his room. That man who helped you with Portia seems trustworthy enough. What about this woman?

Chavali frowned and looked around. For once, fortune favored her, as she recognized one of the patrolling guards from Garrian's house. "Stop, we will let the Guard do some of the work."

I won't let them delay me any longer than is truly necessary.

Smirking, she lifted a hand and waved to the guardsmen. "Leave after we get her down. I will handle it."

Thank you, I will.

"We were attacked down by the water," Chavali told the two men the moment they arrived. For good measure, she pulled out her medallion and showed it to them. "They fought her off enough to let me get the last word in with my foot. This one is dead, her name is Lynley and she works for Sera Drune. The man is hurt and unconscious, but will be fine. The attacker, I know little of. A woman. Beyond that, I cannot say."

"Ma'am, we'll see to the body." The two guards pulled her down. "As for the gentleman—" Before he finished speaking, Karias trotted away. He turned to chase the horse down.

Chavali put an arm out to stop him. "I will handle that. Take to Sera Drune my regards, please. Lynley gave her life to save ours. She is a hero and should be treated as such in death."

The guard watched the horse go with disapproval, but didn't push past her. "I'll need you to come with me to answer some questions."

"There is no time. I must report to Lady Mardis before this attacker has a chance to leave the city." She wheeled and hurried away, not giving him a chance to grab her. Without looking back, she ducked down the next alley and jogged through the city.

Once the burst of speed borne of her desire to lose the Guard wore off, she had to slow down. Her wet clothes made the running too much work. Wheezing and panting, she tripped over nothing and sprawled face first on the sidewalk of a street with respectable homes. She scraped her palm, banged her knee, and jammed her shoulder. Too worn down to get back up, she went limp and lay there, catching her breath.

A nearby door opened, and a male voice called out, "Are you alright?" He sounded cautious. He also sounded familiar. "I saw you fall. It looked painful."

Chavali had no interest in dealing with some random stranger. She pushed herself up on her hands and knees, finding her arms weary enough to shake. "I will be fine," she told him, her voice betraying her exhaustion.

"Chavali?"

She blinked in disbelief at the person rushing to her side. "Ivan?"

"Goodness. Here, let me help you up. Ah, you're soaking wet! You'll catch a cold. Here, come inside and warm up."

"I have to get—"

"Inside," he cut her off. "Whatever it is you need to do, it can wait until you're fit for it." He half-carried her to and through the door, into a warm home. From the worn rug on the floor of the entry and its plain walls, she got the impression they didn't waste money on fripperies.

"You don't need to do this."

Ivan smiled and took her into a room with a well-used couch and matching chairs. "No, but it would be wrong to leave you out there in this condition. Besides, you were right. I forgot how much I love my wife, and needed a kick in the pants to remember. Jody's a bit skeptical, of course, but I'm trying. We'll get it sorted out in time." He turned away from her and called out, "Jody, can you come help?"

Jody appeared in the doorway and her brow lurched up in surprise. "Chavali?"

"She's collapsed outside in damp clothes." Ivan grinned at his wife. "Ah, you'd know what to do better than me."

"Too right, I do." Jody put her hands on her hips with a smirk and watched her husband help Chavali down onto the couch. "Go fetch a soft blanket and I'll put some tea on. We'll put your clothes over the fire to dry off."

In no way would she tell Colby that his insistence on helping this man paid off. Chavali leaned into the yielding cushions and sighed. She considered arguing, but didn't have the energy for it. "Thank you."

Jody nodded and left her alone for a minute. Chavali pulled her cloak and boots off while she waited. Ivan's feet clomped on the stairs to announce his return. He shook out a fuzzy blanket and handed it to her. When she pulled her dress up, he turned and fled the room. It took her until Jody returned with a steaming mug to pull all her clothes off and settle in the blanket.

"It's safe now," Jody called out, sitting beside Chavali and helping her steady the cup in hands that refused to stop shaking.

Ivan ducked in, gathered up the wet clothes, and slipped back out without a word.

"He thinks I'll accuse him of having wandering eyes if he sits with you." Jody smirked again and shook her head. "Of all the things he's been a pain about, that isn't one of them. But at least he's thinking of my feelings."

"That seems a victory."

"I'd say so, yes. I'm guessing you're responsible, at least partly, so thanks for that."

Chavali snorted into her cup. "I may have made a few suggestions that he may have taken to heart."

"I'm glad you did." Jody smiled and sat back. "Funny how it's easier to help other people than it is to help yourself, isn't it?"

"Why do you say this?"

"You told me all about how your husband gives you so much trouble, and didn't seem to have a solution for that."

"Ah." Chavali looked down at her mug, not particularly interested in sorting this subject out right now.

"Maybe you need to accept that he has a thing for horses and work around it. You know, the funny thing about marriage is that it's a balancing act. So long as both sides give as much as they take, it works out, one way or another."

Although their relationship only rose to that of 'colleague,' the observation struck too close to true for Chavali to brush it off. She did have to deal with Colby in some fashion, no matter how little she wanted to. With so many Fallen, it would be no particular hardship for Eldrack to make sure not to assign them together, she thought. A conflict of personalities serious enough to threaten the success of missions surely gave such requests weight with the Administrator.

Yet, her clan always considered her 'difficult.' They said as much to her face, along with whispering it behind her back. Was it fair to ask to be kept apart when the fault lay equally on both their shoulders? Eldrack had enough to worry about without his Fallen running to him over every petty misunderstanding and squabble they could clear up on their own if they tried. 'Administrator' had nothing to do with tending children.

"You're thinking awfully hard." Jody put a sympathetic hand on her shoulder. "Maybe it would help if you talked it out?"

She huffed, considering how to preserve the marriage fiction while discussing this. Had these people not taken her clothes, she could collect herself and leave anytime. "We are not a good match, put together by chance and duty. His ideals and morals are different from mine. We agree on close to nothing."

"That's awful. But 'close to nothing' isn't the same thing as nothing. Why don't you focus on the things you have in common? You fell in love for a reason, didn't you?"

It occurred to her to be thankful Jody didn't ask about his bedroom habits or skills. She also hated the woman for forcing her to deal with the subject. Especially when she had to take such care with every word. "We work together, for the same employer, and are both devoted to this job. We have both suffered losses and been through...trials."

Jody made a small noise of sympathy. "That must be difficult. Maybe he's spending all that time with his horse because he doesn't want to offend you somehow."

No, he spent all that time with his horse because they had a bond, one that transcended death. She needed to push off the horse topic. "It's more complicated than that. Our quarrels are about methods. He...does not like the way I prefer to handle things, and he is vocal about these complaints. And in such complaints, he often assumes the worst, rather than the best."

"We've talked a lot today, Ivan and me. I kind of forgot what it was like, to talk out our differences and try to be constructive when I have gripes. I spent so much time being angry at him that I never really said anything. We'd argue about something stupid, when we should have been figuring out how to have more time together."

Chavali sipped her tea to avoid glowering at the woman. She knew this, knew the keys to making a relationship work. She'd seen so many failures in other people's minds, she understood them. And yet, when it came to her own life, she made all the same idiotic mistakes as everyone else.

Either she gave up and flicked her wrist to be rid of Colby, or she made an effort to get to know him and find some way to work with him. Trying to be rid of him tempted her. His arrogance grated on her nerves, along with the insistence upon total honesty being some great virtue. Every time she did something he considered 'dishonest,' he twitched his mouth in disapproval, at the least. And then came the arguments, distracting both of them from the mission, from what mattered. If he could just see that being so uncompromising never solved anything, then he'd be much happier, and so would everyone else around him.

With that thought, she knew she had no intention of bothering Eldrack with this. Turning away from him now would be cowardice. The Seer of the Blaukenev Clan was no coward. She faced life eyes forward, unblinking and refusing to submit to anyone. Submission was for the weak and foolish.

"Yes," she sighed, "I know. It's merely difficult to see the stew when you are sitting in it."

Jody laughed. "I'd say it's hard to see the forest for the trees, but yours is better."

"I thank you for the tea and your time, but I should be on my way. My business is urgent." Her clothes hadn't dried yet, but had warmed a great deal. With the short break, she felt able to handle the rest of the trip, so long as she didn't push herself too hard. The couple bade her a good night and wished her good fortune.

She plunged into the night again and hurried as much as she dared. The guards at the Mardis estate let her pass without challenge, and she found herself back in that same sitting room, waiting for the Lady once more.

Since she had free time, she pulled the envelope out and rubbed a thumb across it. Pale had a reason to hide it there, an important reason. Her hands shook as she opened it. She elected to believe that had nothing to do with apprehension and everything to do with her clothes still being damp. A piece of parchment inside had been folded in half.

On one side, tidy handwriting in black ink covered a small portion of the ordinary piece of paper:

R-

City has turned out to be a brilliant choice. So much going on, all the time. Assignment nearly complete. Technique works. First success

The way the last sentence didn't end, Chavali assumed the letter hadn't been completed, despite a 'KP' at the bottom for a signature. Given the name Pale, she must have written it, and 'R' must mean Robin. So, Pale came here on instructions from Robin, trying to accomplish something specific. Given what she knew Robin could do, and what Pale tried to do to her, and their relationship, she had a feeling about what went on here with the guards.

Lady Mardis glided into the room, her mouth drawn down into an unhappy frown. "Is it true you murdered one of my prisoners?"

Chavali shrugged. "It would be more accurate to say he killed himself. This is not why I have returned." She explained what happened at the cave and produced the note, only leaving out any mention of Robin to avoid explaining how she knew that. "Can you tell me, Lady, what measures do you take to prevent the type of behavior we saw from your guards earlier?"

The Lady sat halfway through the explanation, straight-backed and unyielding—a pose of discomfort with the entire subject. "They are well paid, well treated, and evaluated psychologically, as well as being rotated in their duties and given lesser duties for several years before being posted to the house by recommendation of their superiors."

"Does it strike you as reasonable that eight of these men were bribed and carried out an attack on you and your daughter?"

Mardis furrowed her brow. "No. I could, I think, see a single man able to fool my people and get close. Eight of them at once seems farfetched."

"I think they were subject to an attack on their mind, one that implanted a suggestion and falsified memories. That guard had clear memories of Drune giving him money and a planning session with the other men that I think were faked. Beyond that, he had terrible confusion and horror at what he'd done. Which all speaks to someone manipulating his mind."

"Then who can I trust?"

"I seem to be immune to it."

"That's something, I suppose." Mardis scanned the room. "Where are your companions?"

"Injured, all three of them. They returned to our inn to rest."

"I can have a skilled healer sent to them."

"I would appreciate that. So would they, I am sure."

Mardis got up and summoned a servant, giving an order to have a healer sent. The young man ran off to take care of it. "Can I offer you something to eat or drink? I can have your clothes cleaned and dried before you leave, too. It's too cold to wander around like that, and you've been a great help. It seems the least I can do."

"I appreciate that, thank you." As it turned out, the Lady did not intend to share this food or drink with her, nor to sit with her while she waited for her clothes. Instead, Chavali sat in an informal dining room with a cup of hot tea and a bowl of soup, wearing a borrowed fluffy white robe. The servants scooted around her, not stopping to chat. At least the soup tasted good—the tea had an odd minty flavor she didn't care for.

A while later, a servant delivered her clothes, clean and dry. She heard a commotion as she finished lacing her boots up and peeked out the door to see Harris swaggering down the hallway. He grinned and waved when he saw her. She smiled back, pleased to see him on his feet.

"Colby decided to stay with Portia, she's more exhausted than hurt at this point. I came to collect you, in case you decided to hide here for a while to avoid talking to either of them. Or something like that." He moved in to hug her.

She stayed an arm's length away, avoiding the intended embrace by bending down to readjust her boot laces. "I did not think they had healers good enough to handle your wounds here."

Harris shifted, then crossed his arms to cover the awkward moment. "Apparently, Mardis has the services of the real deal, and that woman is pretty good at her job. She fixed Colby up in a snap, and the gaping hole in my chest didn't take her much longer. How are you doing?"

"I am fine. People keep throwing themselves in the way so I do not get hurt. It's the least irritating thing anyone does around me. Come," she beckoned for him to follow her out. "There are still things I do not understand, but I doubt we will find them here." As the words left her mouth, she caught unexpected movement out of the corner of her eye, near the steps to the basement.

"Did you see something?" Harris looked that way, too.

"Yes." Grabbing his arm, she hurried to the basement. Who would be down here? That one kidnapper Colby refused to kill or free should be there—she remembered seeing him earlier. Did they bring Garrian here? Neither fit what she thought she saw, though. At least, she didn't think they did. Familiarity tugged at her mind. She slipped in a puddle, catching herself on Harris's arm. How did water get on the floor here?

They ran down the steps, a sudden foreboding weighing on her. Flying through the doors, they followed the trail to the second cell on the left. Garrian lay on the floor in a pool of water slowly seeping into the stone. His body lay drenched and lifeless, his face twisted with horror and pain.

She and Harris stared at his corpse for a few beats, then turned to each other. "Elise," they both said at the same time. "Where did she go?"

Harris shook his head, then pointed to the floor. "Wherever this leads."

They turned and ran back up the stairs, Harris in the lead. He tripped over a servant already on her hands and knees with a sponge and bucket, cleaning up the water. Chavali stopped in front of her and watched him duck and roll with the fall, coming up on his feet. She bent and grabbed the servant by the front of her dress.

"How much have you cleaned up already?"

The teenage girl shrank away from her and tried to ward her off with the sponge. "Not much, ma'am, I just started!"

"Where?"

"At the base of the stairs up." The girl pointed at the servants' stair not far away. "It goes up, I just—"

Uninterested in whatever else the girl had to say, Chavali shoved her away and dashed for the stairs, Harris right behind her. At the top, they found a watery streak across the tile floor, heading down the hall. Two guards littered the floor, both soaking wet, both unconscious or dead. They didn't stop to check.

"How could you abandon your duty," a female voice screeched. They knew that voice. "How could you be so blind about your sins?"

The water trail took them through an open door, to a well appointed bedroom. In the middle of it, on a plush rug, Mardis struggled for her life. Elise straddled the Lady's hips, both hands covering her face. Water shot out of her body, all of it directed at Mardis. The Lady tried to pull Elise's hands off, but couldn't get a grip.

This time, they took Elise by surprise. Harris leaped at her, blade out to sink into her back. Chavali rushed them both, crashing into the bodies. Elise rocked with the impact, but kept shoving water at Mardis, spraying it out of her hands. "This isn't about you," she screamed. "Let me deliver this justice!"

"Can't do that," Harris grunted, yanking his blade out and stabbing her again. Her wounds ran with diluted pink blood.

In their favor, Elise seemed more interested in killing Mardis than defending herself. Chavali grabbed her own knife and stabbed Elise in the leg, then the gut. Harris got her one more time with his dagger and the water stopped spraying out. Elise slumped, still bleeding pink, and fell off Mardis. Harris stabbed Elise in the neck.

The Lady had stopped struggling, and Chavali dropped her knife to check the woman over. "She is not breathing."

Harris muttered a curse and dropped his own blade. He patted her face, then put his ear next to her mouth. Pulling away, he felt around her chest, selected a spot between her breasts, and pushed down with both hands, using the heel. "Tilt her head back and open her mouth."

"What?"

"I've seen people saved from drowning before. Just do it!"

The command in his tone irked her, but she did it while he kept thumping her chest. "Nothing." With her hands holding Mardis's head, she also knew the Lady had no thoughts right now.

"Hang on, a body can survive this for a couple of minutes." He kept thumping her.

Mardis coughed up water and Harris stopped, pulling his hands away and giving her room. Her thoughts screamed back, jumbled and confused.

"Yeah, cough it all out, keep going. Pat her on the back to help."

Chavali let go and gave Mardis a few solid whacks to her back. She restrained the urge to ask very stupid questions, like 'are you alright?' and gave the woman space. The water came out in bursts at first, then Mardis coughed several times and lay back on the floor.

"What happened?"

Harris picked up his dagger. "Elise killed Garrian, then came up to get you. I'll go check on your guards."

"Elise?"

"This is a strange tale, to be sure." Chavali looked down at herself. Soaking wet again. Good thing they cleaned and dried these clothes for her. "Garrian had an affair with his assistant. She discovered he ran a smuggling ring for extra money to take care of his wife and threatened to expose him. He tried to kill her, dumping her body off Lover's Leap, but did not finish the job. She returned later with some kind of strange water magic, to take revenge, and called herself the Herald of the Lost. Now she has killed him and nearly killed you. Had we not arrived when we did, you would be dead."

Mardis sat up slowly, with Chavali's help. "All this because of Merilyn's illness?"

"It seems so, yes. We spoke of the Lost Island earlier. Your family is charged with what, exactly, regarding it?"

Brushing her face, Mardis sighed. "We're to beware it. Those we send to the island, the Lost, will return one day. Those we send are the worst of the worst, Chastity. The island...it's not a hospitable place. They don't survive long, and there's none who could return. My people make sure they can't escape, and the undercurrent is treacherous. Only one safe sailing channel goes there, and it's not deep enough for a full sized ship. Those who try to swim turn up from time to time, bodies smashed and drowned."

"The Herald swims on a fated tide." Chavali shook her head in disdain. That was what Elise meant. So long as the Mardis family followed the Order of Spilled Blood's mandates to the letter and ruled Ket, the Lost Island continued to gain sacrifices. Something stirred out there, and it used these people. Elise was their Herald, the first of many. How thoughtful of them—who or whatever they might truly be—to send a warning.

None of which explained Pale and the guard attack on Mardis. "Is there any way you can find out the original wording of the full prophecy given to your family on this subject?"

"I can check the old journals, but I doubt I'll find it."

"If there is a threat to the Crown, that may be the only way we have to combat it."

Mardis nodded and brushed her face again, pushing dripping hair out of her eyes. "I'll get whatever I can for you to take to the King, as quickly as possible. I've followed the directives of my family without fail, Chastity, I swear it. If that was the wrong thing to do, I didn't know."

Not knowing couldn't and wouldn't ever protect anyone from anything. Chavali learned that lesson the hard way. "I understand." She still needed Mardis's good will, and suspected a scolding would accomplish nothing of value.

"The guards are alive. Elise knocked them out without killing them." Harris leaned in through the doorway without re-entering the room. "We should get back to our friends."

"You two saved my life. At least let me have your clothes dried before you run out into the cold again."

Chavali smirked. "The robe was very comfortable."

Chapter 19

Mardis agreed to have Elise's body prepared for transport. Eldrack could puzzle over whether to bring Elise back from the dead (again?), and Chavali and Harris had no need to concern themselves over it. The 'Crown' wanted to study her, of course, to determine both what happened to her and if her body presented a threat. The corpse would be wrapped to ease transportation, but not otherwise tampered with.

The two of them sat on the floor, both in fluffy white robes, in front of a roaring fireplace. Chavali greatly enjoyed the feel of baking after all the time spent outside in the chill today. She had nothing to say and wanted Harris to keep his mouth shut. This situation had a great deal of potential to develop into an awkward, unpleasant conversation.

Naturally, he spoke. "Can I ask you something?"

"No."

"We're going to be here for another quarter hour, probably. How would you rather pass the time?"

"In silence."

He reached over and brushed some of her still damp hair off her shoulder. She glared and shrugged away. "You remind me of a whore I know."

She raised an eyebrow at him. "I see."

Laughing, he shook his head. "No, not for that. I mean she was all closed off like you are, didn't want anyone getting close. Said it made her job harder if she got familiar with people."

"I am not interested in you because I am not interested in you."

He cringed, but still smiled. "Ouch. Why don't you tell me how you really feel?"

As someone fond of sarcasm herself, she recognized it. Perhaps she ought to take this moment to speak openly and clear the air. They'd have time back at the tower, yet she suspected it would be something she avoided, either accidentally or on purpose. Might as well deal with it. "I value you as someone to whom I can speak freely, and who shares many of my views. There is, however, no space in me to care for another person."

"What about your kids?"

She sat with her back to the fire to help her hair dry, wishing she could watch the flames dance at the same time. "We are family, but they are not my children. We are clan, bound to each other as surely as you and I are bound, except I share blood with them. I could not turn them out even if I wished to, and I have no such desire."

"Huh." He scratched at his cheek, a gesture betraying superficial thought. "What's that like? Being one of us and having kids to look after, I mean."

"What kind of a question is that? Should I ask you what it's like to be a street urchin, or to be slapped around by the only adult you thought you could trust?"

He shrank back and pulled his hands in close, a young boy scolded by his mother. "I didn't tell you about that."

Chavali scowled. "It ran across your mind while you thought you were dying at Garrian's house. And no, I have no interest in hearing you speak about it. Your tragic past is in the past, as is mine. Letting it rule you is a mistake." Never mind her own difficulties with the subject.

His mouth shut and he stared at his feet. A blessed silence hung between them for a few minutes. "I don't think of it as a 'tragic past.' Especially since it only really ended a few days ago."

"If you are about to thank me for saving your life, stop now. You may have shed your problems, but you have acquired new ones."

"It's not really that different, you know. I've always had to fight and struggle for survival."

Chavali shrugged. "Yes, I know." She wanted the conversation to end, but at the same time, she also wanted to pry and find out everything she could. In her clan, she always knew everything about everyone and she wanted to have that kind of leverage over someone again. "I am curious now why you chose to pursue archery with the bandits. You told Algie you are an archer, but that was not strictly true. You are capable enough with a dagger, from your time as a street kid. Elise now lies dead because of your skill."

"It seemed safer. When I joined the gang, they had an old man with them. He was missing his leg below the knee, claimed it happened when he still used a sword. After that, he had a wooden foot, and couldn't really fight up close anymore. He got himself a bow and never got hurt again. I liked those odds. Got him to teach me before he died of sickness or age, or something like that. I've been using a bow for a long time now, and it's more comfortable. I still know how to knife fight, though. Which is good, because it's a lot more useful in a city."

"Practical and pragmatic, I did not expect this from you."

"Thanks, I think."

Chavali laughed. "Yes, it is a compliment."

The door opened. "Milady, the clothes are dry. Lady Mardis says she has nothing else for you now, and to come back before you leave the city."

"Thank you." They changed out of the robes in separate rooms, as they'd done to change into them. Within a few minutes, they went on their way, returning to the inn. She explained everything he missed while unconscious on the way.

When Harris leaned over several minutes into the walk, she got a sinking feeling he didn't quite grasp her lack of romantic interest. Until he whispered in her ear. "Someone is still following us."

"It could be Mardis's spy, watching to see if we uncover anything else." She ignored their shadow, uninterested in giving away their notice.

"What about Pale, or someone else?"

"She may know I took her unfinished letter by now. Sadly, she can change her appearance, so if it is her, we may never know."

"I think we should try to catch them. With stealth instead of boldness."

"Bah. Let them follow us to the inn. Then we can enlist Colby to help, and Portia if she is up to it."

"Yes, ma'am." He grinned in a way that made her dread what might come out of his mouth next. "You know, we *are* supposed to be pretending to be married, so—"

"No. Keep your hands to yourself."

"You're a cruel, cruel woman, and I'm blessed to have you as my fake wife."

She rolled her eyes. When they reached the inn, they went straight inside and split up. Chavali took the stairs up to get Colby while Harris used the back door to get outside again without being seen. Colby sat with Garrian's spy, watching over Portia as she slept. At Chavali's gesture, both came with her, into the hallway, where she gave them a terse explanation of the plan, and sent them off to carry it out.

For her part, she walked back out the front door, an expression of furious rage on her face and looking ready to kill anyone who came near. A prospective patron saw her and gave her a wide berth as she stormed down the stairs and up the street. Behind her, Harris, Colby, and Garrian's spy all converged on her shadow. A whistle from Colby announced their success. She returned to find Jore's spy on his back with his hands up, the point of Colby's sword resting on his belly.

"This is ridiculous."

"Why are you following them *now*, Bren?" Garrian's spy knew the man, and stood looming over his head, arms crossed and confused. "They've already shown who they are and what they're doing."

Bren took a deep breath. "I want to help. Look, I know you're agents of the Crown, and I know something fishy is still going on. I work for Konti Jore, yes, but I got into this line of work for a reason, and it wasn't to stand by and watch while Ket burns to the ground. I can help, let me help. I have information, we can pool it all and figure this thing with the diseased bodies out. I'm a patriot, Chastity, I want to protect the people of Ket."

Chavali raked a hand through her hair and resisted the urge to kick him. Crouching beside him, she laid a hand on his forehead, and was surprised to see him flinch. "Why should we trust you? It would have been just as easy to walk up and offer information, or to send an anonymous note."

Don'ttouchmedon'ttouch—...Neither of those things even occurred to me. "You're right, I should have. I followed you because...I guess because I was following you." *Let me help, I won't stab you in the back.* "Never mind. This isn't about me. It's about Ket."

"Alright, let him up. Come in and let us speak of all this."

He came willingly, and sat down at a table inside with them. Chavali had no wish to wake Portia if she truly needed sleep, so they left her alone. She explained once more what happened with Elise and Pale for all of these men, and added the summation of everything with Garrian. Bren remained silent while she spoke, his hands clasped together on the table and his eyes on his thumbs as one rubbed the other idly. Garrian's spy predictably reacted to the news of his employer's death with shock, of the stunned silence variety.

"Maybe some background information would help." Bren unlaced his fingers and laid both hands flat on the table, his eyes still on them. "Everyone is interested in what's happening at the docks, but it's Sera Melora's responsibility, as she's the Minister of the west side, where the docks are. Sera Drune is also involved, because she's responsible for overall health and welfare in the region. A disease outbreak is her problem.

"Seran Garrian's interest is because he manages the actual docks and warehouses as part of the city's infrastructure. He argued against the renovations because of cost. That put him and Drune in opposition. Now, of course, we know his real interest in stopping the renovations. I imagine he kept his goods in the warehouses and no one noticed because the journey from dock to warehouse was short. Which means that if anyone had a motive to discredit Drune, it's Garrian."

"I believe he spoke the truth when he claimed no knowledge of the attack on Mardis." Chavali watched him closely, paying attention to every little flick of his eyes and twitch of his face or body.

Colby sat back in his chair, hands laced together in his lap. His eyes bored into Bren, no doubt searching for some sign of duplicity. "What's Konti Jore's interest in the docks? She's the Minister of the east, isn't she?"

Bren shrugged. It made him appear to be holding something back. "It's part of the city and an expense. They're all interested."

"Then why were you following us?"

"The Konti saw Chastity here talking to Drune at the funeral, and to Garrian's assistant. I don't think she cared until later, though. You were easy enough to find, ma'am, so it wasn't a problem that she waited. The thing is, she seemed to think you in particular posed some kind of threat. Wouldn't tell me any details, just said it was important to follow you and not be seen. If I was seen, I wasn't to let you touch me."

Ice gripped Chavali's spine and heart. She could think of only one reason anyone would know to say that. Two, actually, but one struck her as farfetched. Few of the Fallen knew how her peculiar form of thought reading worked, and she trusted all of them to keep their mouths shut about it to non-Fallen. That left Robin, and by extension, his protégé.

"Why not?" Harris asked.

"I don't know, she wouldn't tell me. Said it didn't matter. You don't have a plague, do you?"

"No." She rolled her eyes at the idea. "Have you seen anyone new around the Konti recently? A woman, perhaps?"

"There's always new people around. She sees petitioners, and anyone in the east sector can present something. She's found a number of qualified contractors that way, for various job functions she needs performed from time to time." Bren furrowed his brow and tapped a thumb on the table.

"But one of them did not seem local," Chavali prompted. "Her accent felt a bit off, or she tried too hard to be convincing, or something else about her struck you as not quite right?"

Bren sat there, thinking and telegraphing his dislike for the conclusions he came to. "Yes," he finally said, the word drawn out and unhappy.

"She meets openly with Jore, but their conversations are hushed, or meetings take place behind closed doors and always end when someone interrupts?"

Colby switched his attention to Chavali, watching her with curiosity and surprise. Did he really think people so opaque? This wasn't tracking whisper cats. Any idiot could read people if they wanted to. Knowing how people think came down to practice and experience. Just like swinging a sword.

Bren nodded, his shoulders slumping. "You're right. I should have seen it, but I didn't. I don't know what possible motivation Jore could have to try to kill Lady Mardis."

"What about discrediting Drune? Having her exiled as a traitor?"

He sat and thought longer this time, leaving Chavali to wonder if he hoped the question would go away for ignoring it. "Of all the Ministers, Drune is the only one she actively dislikes. I couldn't say if it's as bad as hate. With Drune removed, Jore would have some say over who her replacement is, given her title. Mardis would give her recommendations weight. If Amelia is dead, her daughter would be the Lady, and her husband would act as regent until she's of age. Those two would lean on her for advice, I guarantee it. She would actually gain a lot of sway over how Ket and the surrounding region is managed."

Colby stood up. "We should take the Guard and go arrest her."

Chavali rolled her eyes. "Sit, relax. This is not the best plan. If she is innocent, arresting her will make her angry and uncooperative. More importantly, if she is guilty, we will tip off Pale. We must assume she would kill Jore to prevent her from talking. Those cells in Mardis's house will not stop her. We are dealing with someone not afraid to use torture and working on a grand scheme of some kind, not a simple petty thief or common criminal."

Settling down into his chair again, Colby nodded his acquiescence. Everyone watched him think until he finally asked, "What do you suggest?"

She directed her attention to Bren. "We should not let her know immediately the subject we come to speak of. Can you ask her to grant us an appointment tomorrow morning? I think if we leave it for the night, not only will Portia be able to back us up, but we may lead them to believe there is some other thing to speak with her about, or that it is routine."

"Without urgency, you mean, she won't suspect as much." Bren rubbed his chin, gazing off at nothing. "I'd be hard-pressed to explain why I'm delivering that request for you."

Chavali waved off the concern. "Tell her we appear to truly be agents of the Crown and are skilled enough to have noticed you. Since that makes spying on us less useful, and—as you said—I am easy to find, you decided to deliver our request rather than wait around while we stay here and eat and sleep."

"We could write it as a note," Harris suggested. "That way, you can say someone passed you a note and you had no direct contact."

"I like that plan, yes." Someone had paper and a pen, Harris scribbled out a quick note, and Bren left with it.

"I hope you know what you're doing." Colby had the look of a man who wanted to sulk but knew he had no good reason to.

The two of them needed to talk. Chavali waved a hand to shoo Harris and Garrian's spy away. Funny, she still didn't know the man's name. In truth, she didn't care. They would leave soon, and he would stay. Assuming he survived. The man had a decent heart and some useful skills, so maybe if he got himself killed, they would bring two bodies back instead of one.

She waited until the other two men left before answering Colby. "I always know what I am doing. The problem is, sometimes, no one cooperates."

One side of his mouth ticked up. "I don't have a problem with your goals, Chavali, it's your methods I find abhorrent." He shook his head and fixed her with a firm stare. "That guard didn't have to die."

Meeting his eyes without flinching, she nodded. "No, he did not *have* to die at that time, in that place, by my hand. However, I think you misunderstand the situation if you do not see why he did die there."

"Then explain to me how a cold-blooded murder can be the right answer."

"The difference between so-called just execution and cold-blooded murder is a thin line, but that is not relevant here." She placed her fingers on the table, feeling the thick, solid wood under her hands. His attention went to her hands, too. "I read his thoughts. He knew the fate that awaited him and could not reconcile his memories and what he did with what he knew to be right and honorable. He preferred death to exile on the Lost Island. Even knowing this, I still could not do it. He spared me the memory of taking a life without provocation by lunging in attack.

"Had there been something to be done for him, some way to prove his thoughts tampered with or mind controlled, I would have told him and saved him. No one benefits from the death of a good person, no matter how justified it seems. And, whatever you or Mardis may believe, it appears that life on that island is worse than a quick death. He had memories of serving on the transport ship.

"Even with all of this, I still could not merely kill him. Life is precious and dear to me. Taking my own in the first place was the most difficult decision I have ever made, because I wanted to live. Something else had to be more important. Like that guard, I thought of the options, the alternatives, and could not turn away from the rightful conclusion." She looked up to see him watching her, horrified understanding spilling from his eyes. "Now, tell me once more how wrong and monstrous I am."

For several long moments, he met her gaze in unflinching silence. "You're not half as disagreeable as you act sometimes."

After all of that, she laughed at such an absurd remark. "I am not disagreeable at all. I merely have spent enough time in the thoughts and memories of complete strangers to have an understanding of how people truly think and behave, especially when they believe no one is watching. You wish for people to be universally good or bad, because it makes things easy, but few are. Most of us have both inside and struggle to keep either from overwhelming the other."

He frowned. "I'm not a child. I know the world isn't black and white." Holding up a hand to keep her from responding right away, he shook his head. "I'm sorry I judged you like that. I should've known you'd been in his thoughts and it wasn't as simple as it appeared to be."

It chafed that she couldn't tell if it cost him something to say that or not. She suspected not. "And I apologize for losing my temper in the face of it."

"I still don't strictly approve of your methods."

"I still think you are—" Simple. Foolish. An idiot. Hypocritical. Daft. She thought all these things, but said, "—wrong about the greatest sin."

The answer didn't surprise him. "I'm glad we understand each other better now."

"As am I." She stood with him and started to follow him upstairs, but stopped when she saw the bar. The two stools on the end sat empty. Changing course, she took the seat on the end and smiled at the mug of hot tea placed in front of her. "Have you seen that woman I have been meeting this afternoon?"

The bartender blinked at her. "Beg pardon, ma'am?"

He probably saw hundreds of people every day, so she acknowledged the question as phrased poorly. "There is a woman I have met here a few times, she sits beside me? I am wondering if she has come already and I missed her."

"I have no idea what you're talking about, ma'am. You've been here alone every night, drinking two cups of tea and overpaying for both. No one sits next to you, or in the next seat, either. Do you want the second cup now?"

Chavali stared at him, confused. No one sat with her? How could that be? She considered the possibilities, finding all of them disturbing. Looking down at her tea, she shook her head and waved him away. "No, thank you. One will suffice for tonight."

All the things that woman told her were things she didn't already know or hadn't considered, so it couldn't have come from her own mind. Then again, maybe she picked these things up without realizing it, and a small part of her knew they were important, and so... She fabricated an imaginary person to bring these things up? No, that couldn't be it. Not unless being dead induced a special form of insanity. If it did, she expected Eldrack would have offered a warning.

The spirits couldn't pull off something so coherent. They swarmed in her mind, whispering unintelligible things all the time. If one of them somehow gained enough dominance to step forward, she suspected... Actually, that theory made a lot of sense. It might take a lot of energy to present itself, and therefore it couldn't happen often. To avoid startling her or being asked too many questions, it appeared as another person, someone local.

Did the spirit avoid her question about its name because it didn't remember? Perhaps the next time it appeared, she would call it by a name and see how it reacted. She had a number of things to consider for their next meeting, things to ask or do or say. For now, though, she needed sleep.

Chapter 20

"Ugh." Portia sat with her head cradled in her hands, not ready to get up.

"If you are not up to it, then you should not come. With luck—"

"You're. 'You are' is 'you're.' " She felt awful, but still corrected speech.

Chavali's lip curled. "I hate you."

"I'll take that as a compliment."

"Indeed." She smirked. "Anyway, we are not going with the intent to fight anyone. If it comes to that, we could use you, but not if *you're* not well enough to help." Tying off the laces of her boot, she stood up and stretched. "I will suggest that Colby leave Karias behind, in case you feel recovered enough soon after we leave and wish to follow."

"Good idea. A bath and a meal might help. I'm going to take care of that."

Chavali left with a wave, picking up a light breakfast and finding the three men already licking their fingers clean. Garrian's spy smiled nervously, Colby nodded in acknowledgment, and Harris grinned enough to show the chewed food in his mouth. She gave a curt wave, asked Colby to leave his horse behind (he agreed without complaint), and stuffed her face while they walked through the city.

She expected to see Bren this morning. Perhaps Jore called him off, considering he'd been spotted. The guards at the front gate of Jore's estate only asked for her name before letting them through. Like Mardis, Jore had a drive and grounds and a manor house. Befitting her lower rank, her tastes ran to the somewhat smaller and less ornate, though the attractive red brick wall around it stood a full seven feet high. They walked up the gravel drive, all three men taking notice of their surroundings. Feeling that she ought to do the same, Chavali looked around too, but saw nothing of note.

Actually, she did notice one thing. Jore's guards were not City Guards. They wore a uniform in different colors and featuring Jore's family crest: some sort of fish with its tail curled in mid-jump. Was Jore a fish? It seemed too obvious. Perhaps the little fish, then, the one whose schemes had minimal impact. Or, she might have started something that got out of her control. Pale could be the medium fish, or the big fish. Garrian had to also be a fish, yet his crimes seemed to be of minor import.

What if 'fish' meant the plural? Could one person be both a little fish and a big fish? Chavali scowled—she should have thought of that before. The spirits used fish for a reason, and this had to be it. Ket had a port, so a water-borne creature made sense. Especially given what happened with Elise. She had to be a fish, probably medium. Although she killed Garrian, that almost did Ket a favor. The more important point was her attempt on the Lady's life. Two had now done that. Who would be the third?

The guards opening the front door of the house distracted her. A servant escorted them into a sitting room, something the houses of nobility seemed to all have. Similar to the one at Mardis's estate, the large, well-appointed room had several places to sit. The servant shut the doors as she left, saying the Konti would see them shortly.

Harris dropped onto a couch with a hopeful grin for Chavali to join him. Did they still need to pretend to be married? She rolled her eyes, huffed out an aggrieved breath, and sat with him. Colby took an individual chair. Garrian's spy clasped his hands behind his back and walked around the room, examining things in a fashion that appeared to be random.

After a minute or so of this behavior, the spy saw something and crouched down to examine the floor. He ran his fingers over a spot on the dark rug and held it up with a light smear of blood on the tips. Before anyone could comment, the door opened and Konti Jore walked in.

She wore relatively simple clothes made of luxurious fabrics. The grace and gravitas of her movement had to be trained. It seemed Jore mimicked a great many things about the Lady. Chavali wanted to know if that came from admiration or jealousy, and whether she had serious thoughts of usurping the position for herself.

"Welcome to my home. I understand you have some questions you'd like to ask me?" As she paced in and took a seat, Chavali noted tension in the Konti's shoulders and something in her left hand. It might have been the note Harris wrote yesterday.

"As part of our duties here," Chavali said, "we are investigating the matter of the plague affecting the docks. It seems to have been addressed sufficiently, but we would appreciate hearing your opinions on the subject."

Jore straightened and flashed a fake smile. "I'm happy to assist agents of the Crown in any way I can. On that particular subject, I have no more information than any other member of Lady Mardis's Council. I have no responsibility over the area, so I have no specific interest to pursue in the matter."

"Yet you had us followed." It pleased Chavali to find the men keeping quiet for now.

A tiny frown flashed on Jore's face for a moment, then disappeared behind a blank facade. "I had some concerns about your intentions towards my city. Approaching both Sera Drune and Seran Garrian at the funeral in the fashion you did attracted attention."

"Would it not have been simpler to ask Sera Drune or Garrian about it?" This point, actually, she didn't understand in the slightest. Why did all four of them send separate spies? She failed to ask each of them about this so far, but no longer.

Jore's lips puckered in distaste. "We don't do things that way here."

"'That way'?" Chavali arched an eyebrow. "You mean cooperating and communicating?"

"No, of course we cooperate and communicate." Chavali spotted the little glance of her eyes to the side and a tiny movement of her hand—a sure, albeit subtle, sign of a blatant lie. Her displeasure at the assertion held no sincerity whatsoever. "We gather our own intelligence, especially when it comes from curiosity."

"I see." She didn't come here to expose corruption and incompetence, and saw no need to press on the inconsistency of Jore's statements. She'd make sure it got included in the report and do nothing else about it. "I hope you did not punish the man you had following us harshly. He is reasonably good at his job. We are merely trained to spot such people."

Jore twitched. The reaction struck Chavali as odd. Then the door flew open. "Meeting them behind my back?" The female voice sounded vaguely familiar, but Chavali couldn't place it. "Tut, you've outlived your usefulness, dear." Pale stepped into the doorway and threw a knife at Jore. Her blade hit Jore in the neck and buried itself to the hit. The Konti slumped, clawing at the injury.

The third devours whole.

Colby jumped to his feet and grabbed his blade, as did Harris. Chavali ducked down, twining her fingers through the spirits to coax out an image of the first thing to pop into her head: Eliot. He jumped out from behind a couch to rush Pale. Colby followed on his heels. Harris flung out a hand out to protect Chavali. Garrian's spy ducked behind the couch and Chavali caught his movement as he dashed to another piece of furniture, circling around to get closer to Pale.

"No, that won't do," Pale said, sounding far too confident in the face of Colby's advance. "Blue acorn waltz." She spoke in a clear voice, over-enunciating each word. "Kill them."

Eliot rushed Pale. She ignored him, apparently seeing through the illusion. Colby, on the other hand, stopped dead in his charge, pivoted on a heel, and locked his eyes—gone wide with horror at himself—on Chavali. His body shuddered in what must have been an effort to resist. That effort failed and he stalked towards her.

Harris jumped at him. Colby swept his sword in an arc, hitting

Harris mostly with the flat of his blade, sweeping him aside to crash into Garrian's spy as he tried to get involved. Pale danced into the room and cut Garrian's spy, reveling in his grunt of pain.

In their training sessions, Eliot made it clear he anticipated this kind of moment. At some point, she would face someone with advantages over her in every way: size, strength, weight, skill, speed, reach. He told her to run when she found herself in that situation. Throw tricks at them, anything she could think of to slow them down, even for a second. Her illusion of Eliot did nothing, so she let it go. An illusion of herself jumped up and ran away. Another illusion of herself stayed where she crouched. Chavali crawled until her illusion reached the door, then rolled to her feet and ran out of the room.

In the city, she could lose him if she could get enough of a head start, but in the house, she could force him to play hide and seek. Her illusion ran for the front door. She ran deeper into the house, frantically searching for stairs. Behind her, she heard Pale shriek, "It's an illusion, you idiot! Go hunt her down and take her!"

His footsteps thundered into the hall. Behind them, she thought she heard lighter ones. Right now, she had no intention of checking. She ducked through a door, finding the kitchen, and shut it behind herself. Two members of the household staff looked up in surprise. They could be an obstacle.

"Konti Jore is dead," she told them. "The woman who murdered her is on a mad rampage. Save yourselves!" With that, she dashed to a set of stairs on the far end of the room. On the way, she had to dodge an open cupboard and glanced inside. She stopped, grabbed a glass bottle of oil, and smashed it on the floor.

Hitting the stairs at a run, she darted up them, coming out in a small room with deep shelves, probably for the servants to gather things to take in one direction or the other. Right now, it had a pile of folded laundry, the remains of a meal, and a jug of water. A crash below followed by a grunt of surprise and shock told her she had no time to think. The dishes didn't strike her immediately as useful. Neither did the water. Grabbing a handful of laundry, she threw herself out of the room and ran down the hall, looking for an open door.

The first one she found, a playroom for young children, held a little boy and girl tended by a servant. Children shouldn't be used this way, and she slammed that door shut, then dove across the hall. If she had the dishes, she could throw them elsewhere to attract attention. Instead, she had a lot of cloth. And a window. She thumped her shoulder against it and nearly fell through when it swung open.

Spotting Harris out on the grounds, she waved to him. He caught sight of her and came running, gesturing for her to jump. She balked at the distance and looked down at her hands, full of cloth. Tossing it all into the air, one proved to be a sheet that she tied around the window itself.

Colby appeared in the doorway and their eyes met again for a second. "We will fix this," she told him. Then she jumped out of the window, her arms and legs clamping around the sheet until it ran out. Harris half-caught her and they looked up at Colby, watching him discover he couldn't fit through the window.

"To the back," Harris said, louder than he needed to.

They turned and ran a few steps towards the rear of the house, then Harris grabbed her arm and pulled her to a stop. He tugged her toward the front. Yes, a ruse. She took his hand and ran with him, marveling at how coherent he managed to be in his head. Everything he saw, he cataloged and considered its value for hiding, using as an obstacle, or creating a distraction, while also noting things they needed to avoid and why. Those guards struck him as questionable. *Darting through them might work.*

Then he saw Pale walking out through the front door. They both stopped and turned around, running into the trees and shrubs covering much of the grounds. Harris's mind worked furiously at different plans, each of them rejected. Off to the side, Chavali caught sight of Colby charging from the rear of the building. At least he fell for the ruse. That seemed a small victory, one they desperately needed right now. She squeezed Harris's hand to call his attention to it.

Only the threat of death kept her going now. She wheezed with the continued running, knowing she couldn't keep this up forever. Colby and Pale closed in, each faster than Chavali. She slowed Harris down. Without her, he could get away. He knew it and cursed her in his head while urging her on with his hand.

She ran into the wall, unwilling to slow down before she hit it. Harris bent to give her a hand up. A knife flew at them, and he had to drop her foot to deflect it with his shoulder. Chavali tumbled to the ground. "Go, save yourself," she panted at him. He could do it, he could scramble up the wall and get away to Portia. They could go get reinforcements and figure out what to do about Colby.

If she had to die again, it would be to save lives again. This time, one of those lives would be more directly saved, but the point remained the same: given the choice between saving herself and saving everyone else, she chose everyone else. The world would go on without Chavali. It wouldn't go on without Biholtz and Eldrack and Jore's children and the bartender and all the other nameless people in the world.

Maddeningly, Harris didn't go. He pulled his dagger again and stood defiantly in front of her, showing none of the craven bandit she first met a few days ago. "No. We're going to stop them." Idiot.

Pale and Colby advanced. He caught his breath; she slunk through the shrubbery. Standing their ground would result in Portia walking into a trap later. But she couldn't make Harris run and she lacked the skill to climb the wall fast enough to avoid being cut down.

"Did you kill Bren also?" Talking served her well many times. She might as well try it now.

"Bren?" Pale cocked her head to the side, confused. After a moment, her expression cleared. "Oh, you mean that little boy Jore had tailing you." She grinned. It dangled from the precipice of madness. "Kill him, dear Colby. Knock her out." She flung another knife at Chavali.

Harris lunged and swatted it out of the air with his arm, a thin spritz of blood announcing the cost of his action. Rather, the *most obvious* cost of his action. Colby swept his blade at them, catching Harris in the side he left open. It knocked Harris to the ground and Colby followed up with a second blow aimed at Chavali. She watched him as Eliot taught her to and rolled under the blade. It hit the bricks behind her. He used his free hand to punch her in the face. The blow knocked her head against the wall, stunning her, and she crumpled to the ground beside Harris.

Pale offered applause while Colby raised his blade to deliver a blow to Chavali's head. Harris struggled to his hands and feet just in time to get in the way and make everything worse. Colby's blade hacked into his side and he slumped on top of her.

Not fair. I want to be in this position when I can enjoy it.

"Good job, Colby. Such an obedient pet."

While Chavali scrambled to push Harris off her, he fell unconscious and Colby punched her in the face again. Everything went black.

Chapter 21

The air smelled of stone and beer and blood. Chavali groaned at the pain in her head, and all the aches from the punishment her body had been through since meeting Harris. Sharp, throbbing agony in her ankles and elbows competed with all of it. Pale must have disabled her the same way she did with Colby before. Her fingers could still move, leaving her able to craft illusions, but Pale seemed immune to them, or had enough experience to see the flaws easily.

"Keep quiet," someone hissed.

She forced her eyes open, though they wanted to stay shut. The room had only dim light, coming from a handful of clerestory windows. When her eyes adjusted to the gloom, she made out barrels and shelves. Lying on the stone floor, she could tell the copper in the air came from her own spilled blood. Like Colby, she hadn't been killed by the disabling, instead rendered incapable and weak.

A large body lay out of reach, tied well enough with rope to prevent escape by any but the most capable and slippery. Why Colby had been bound after his display of obedience, she had no idea. Questions ran through her mind, all striking her as pointless and stupid. What happened seemed obvious. How Pale controlled him, equally so. If Harris died or not, he either didn't know or ensured the man's death himself.

"Is she here?" The whisper came out so soft, her voice barely registered in her own ears.

"Yes."

That cut her options. Testing what she could actually do revealed her shoulders and knees and hips worked fine. Moving them took a great deal of effort, which she needed to save for an opportune moment. Best for Pale to think her helpless. Would a well placed illusion, one partially obscured by the lack of light, do her any good at all? Perhaps. She looked around, hoping for an idea to form.

Nothing struck her as useful. An illusory weapon wouldn't do her any good. As with Colby in that cave, Pale hadn't bothered to take her weapon—the knife and its sheath on her belt dug into the small of her back. Without the use of her elbows, that didn't help.

Footsteps—the soft swish of walking boots—drew her attention. Pale stepped around a stack of barrels with a pleasant smile. "I see we're awake. How nice. It's 'Chastity,' isn't it? Funny. I've heard a different name for you: Chavali, the Seer of the Blaukenev clan. It's the feather, you know." Pale crouched down beside her in a smooth motion and reached for the feather without touching it. "Gives you right away. Robin talks about the feather a lot. He's a teensy bit obsessed with you, with the great hope that slipped through his fingers."

It seemed best to keep her talking. Chavali swallowed, feigning more weakness than she felt. The fear, though, needed no faking. She lay there, terrified of what would come next. "When is he coming?"

"We'll see." Pale touched Chavali's hair, rolling a thick lock between her fingers. "When he finds out you're here, he's going to see how truly valuable I am. In fact, it would be ever so much better if, when he arrives, you're already under my thumb." Her eyes flashed with glee. "Then you'll do exactly what we want, and none of this resisting or killing yourself again business. I can even make you enjoy it. Won't that be nice? He'll get what he needs, and you'll think you're happy. I can make you like other things, too. Oh, Chavali, I'm looking forward to this ever so much. We'll be best friends."

She leaned in, putting a hand down next to Chavali's head to bring her face close. "Little pig, little pig," she said in a singsong voice that reminded her of Algie, "let me in."

Chavali felt pressure on her mind. As before, she could tell Pale didn't have her mentor's skill. With a touch, she might be able to turn the tables. Moving quickly, she snapped her knees up and flopped her arm over, wrenching her shoulder to get her hand on Pale's. The moment she made contact, her fingers curled around Pale's palm.

The spirits remembered her, and they remembered her mentor. Pale's thoughts flowed, of surprise and then struggle. The spirits held her at bay, but couldn't do so forever. Eventually, she would figure out how to get past them. Chavali had an idea, one that might work or might fail spectacularly. At this point, she had nothing to lose for trying it.

"Weak. Robin overcame me so quickly I barely had time to blink. You may know how to control people, but you cannot control spirits. His skill surpassed yours so much I have to laugh at you. Did you learn nothing from him? You are a child flapping your arms to get Mamá's attention."

Pale roared and reared back with her mind. Her attack came hard and fast, focused on a single point. She ground her teeth together with the effort. "You. Won't. Resist. Me!"

The spirits understood Chavali's idea and got out of the way only to push at the last moment. They grabbed the spike. Pale's thoughts came at her fast and hard, showing her many things she would have to sort through later.

Chavali blinked and found herself in an unexpected place. Instead of ground below her, she saw only churning indigo water, in every direction. Overhead, black clouds crackled with pink lightning. In front of her, she saw a bizarre creature, wings flapping to keep it in the air. It had the shape of a goat with short, stubby horns, but instead of hair, the body had glossy black scales and two leathery wings sprouting from its back. Looking down at her own body, she saw shiny metal armor covering goat legs with purple scales. The other winged goat appeared to be twice her size.

"What did you do?" Pale's voice, deeper but still distinguishable, roared.

Without bothering to respond, Chavali dove and streaked across the sky. She didn't understand any of this. Even so, she had no intention of getting caught or killed here any more than she did anywhere else. Glancing behind herself, she saw that Pale had to make a wide turn to follow and lumbered through the air after her.

Was this, somehow, their minds under the influence of the spirits? Were they able to give her a chance to fight Pale off? She would have to ask Railan about it when she got back. Because she would get back. On a whim, she turned, finding she could change direction quickly, as well as dart up and down. So, here, she was quick and maneuverable, and Pale had size and strength.

Flying directly at Pale caused her to rear up. They collided and dropped through the air. Pale scraped with her clawed hooves—they screeched across the armor. Chavali raked with her horns, but couldn't get a good angle. Somehow, she knew hitting the water would be bad and flung herself away from Pale at the same time as the other woman did the same.

"Why do I look like this? I should be a dragon," Pale screeched as she recovered from the fall, "not a—an abomination!"

Pale recognized this place. Was this what Railan did in that basement when they rescued the children? Did she fight in a twisted mindscape with those two men while Chavali, Colby, and Eliot were powerless to help? If only Chavali had been able to touch one of those men, she might have been pulled into it and able to help that way, instead of stabbing someone in the neck.

She needed to focus on the fight. Although Pale couldn't break through the armor, she might be able to find weak spots. It would be best to dart in and do something, then dart out. Just like Eliot taught her: use Pale's own strength against her.

Confident, she took the initiative and began buzzing past Pale, scraping every body part she had against Pale's scales. Nothing got through. Pale managed to stab her horns into Chavali, finding a chink in her armor as she darted past overhead. The injury left a trail of purple droplets and stung. Looking down, she noticed the droplets sizzled when they hit the water. She had to force Pale into the water, or maybe into the clouds, or face the possibility of exhausting herself. With only a few passes, she already felt winded.

She shot out ahead and took a few seconds to relax and breathe. It turned into a few seconds too long when Pale dropped down onto her, wings beating and feet pressing on her back to force her downwards.

"Did you think you could beat me here? Even with your demented goat fetish, I'm still better than you!"

Chavali would not panic. Pale's legs held her in place, keeping her from speeding up to get away. Down they went, until her wings slapped the water. The liquid scoured spots of pure agony, making her scream. Whispers in her ears told her not to submit, not to give up. She gritted her teeth as her wings slapped the water again. A light spray kicked up when she pulled them up again. Tiny specks of torture showered her. Pale grunted as the droplets also spattered her scales.

It gave her an idea. Pain, she could handle. So long as it went away later, she could live with some now. On her next downbeat, she deliberately slipped down more and sliced her wings through the water until they submerged halfway, then whipped them back up with as much force as she could muster. They slapped into Pale's wings, sharing the misery.

Pale howled and let go enough for Chavali to roll to the side and upside down and over her. Pulling her wretched wings in tight, she dropped onto Pale from above with a stomp.

"I am a Blaukenev, and I will avenge my clan." She stomped both her front hooves at the base of Pale's head, ignoring her frantically slashing horns. Chavali didn't care if Pale shredded her legs, she only cared who won. Once this woman lay dead in that cellar, Chavali would sleep for as long as it took to recover.

Bending down, she let Pale scrape her horns across the armor on her neck and bit Pale's eyes. Such shrieking made Chavali want to cover her ears. Instead, she jumped on Pale's back again, sending the other woman crashing into the water. Her own wings, riddled with gaping holes, barely worked anymore, and she wanted to curl up and rest, but she leaped into the air and flapped with all her might.

Between one agonizing beat and the next, she blinked and found herself back on the cellar floor, something warm and sticky all over her face. Metallic goo in her mouth made her wish Pale had fallen over somewhere else. She looked straight into the woman's face, her eyes popped and oozing, blood and gore dripping from her nose and mouth.

With a heaving roll to her other side, she coughed and spat the stuff out, not wanting to swallow any of it. She managed to wipe her mouth on her shoulder, though it didn't help as much as she hoped. Pale died messily.

"She is dead."

"What? How? What just happened?"

Chavali laughed. It came out as a giggle bordering on hysteria. "I don't know. But she is dead. I see your hands, they are tied by nothing more than rope. If I use my teeth to free them, are you going to help me or kill me?"

He sighed. "You know she contro—"

"Yes, I know. Is it still active, or are you in control of yourself now?"

"As far as I can tell, it's just me in here."

"Good." She wriggled and squirmed to get her face close enough, then attacked the knot of the rope. It took effort and she had to pause to rest several times over the course of perhaps a quarter hour. She lay back again, panting. "Try it now."

Colby wiggled his hands, twisting them in the rope, and found he could move them, but the other ropes didn't loosen. "At least I can use my hands, right?"

Too tired and wretched to want to do anything else, Chavali groaned. "She left my dagger." Muffled by doors and distance, she heard a voice call out his name, then for Chastity. "I have no strength for shouting now. You answer them."

"After hearing how you holler, I'm not surprised that seems daunting." He turned his head and glanced over his shoulder with a grin, then bellowed, "We're in here!"

While Colby guided them nearer, Chavali noticed every single ache, every throbbing pain, every sharp prick of agony. Her headache seemed worse than when she first woke up. The mind battle didn't leave her unscathed, but at least she lived and Pale did not. She didn't bother trying to do anything else. With rescue near at hand, she lay there, waiting, hoping someone thought to bring a healer.

Someone hit a door nearby and smash it open. Portia called out, "Is this the right room? Colby? Chastity?"

"Yes, over here. We're a little tied up."

Chavali giggled again, unable to stop herself from finding that ridiculous. Portia came into view around the same stack of barrels Pale had and stared at them both. She paused there for a beat, then beckoned to someone and swooped in. Mardis's guardsmen followed her. One picked Chavali up and carried her out, offering a few bland reassurances.

He brought her up a set of stairs and out into the hallway of Jore's manor house. Pale hadn't taken them far.

In a different sitting room than before, the guardsman laid her out on a couch and a woman with an open, friendly demeanor and thoughts of pity and sympathy healed her. A few minutes after she started, Portia and Colby walked into the room and sat down. Both waited in silence. When the healer got up and left with a pleasant smile, Chavali sat up, still suffering from a mild headache and tired, but otherwise fine.

"Harris?"

Portia nodded. "He'll live. The horse got antsy, it spooked the stableboy. He came and got me and I let Karias bring me here. The guards didn't want to let me in until the horse used his massive powers of persuasion. He sat on one of them."

Colby chuckled. "That sounds like him."

"Sure," Portia shrugged. "We found Harris first, and given his condition of having been stabbed rather seriously, I sent a couple of the guards off for help. They came back with Mardis's people, including the healer. We fanned out and searched the house, found Jore's body, a bunch of confused and scared servants, and a really strange trail through the house that led, more or less, to where we found Harris. The horse wouldn't let us leave, so we kept looking until someone suggested the basement."

Chavali rubbed her face, wanting a nap. "The dead woman down there is Pale. She was responsible for the deaths at the docks. I saw a great deal in her mind. The details will not matter to anyone but Eldrack, I think. What is important is they will stop now that she is dead."

"When we get home," Portia said with a bright smile, "I'm going to drill you on accents and speech patterns."

"Wonderful." Standing slowly, Chavali judged herself to be capable of walking. "Between you and Eliot, I will not have time to sleep."

Portia laughed as she stood. "Oh, come on, it'll be fun. I know some games for it. The kids might even want to learn that stuff."

"Wonderful," she said again, still heavy with sarcasm. "We should see Lady Mardis now, so we can be on our way soon."

Colby hung back, staying behind the two women. Karias joined him at the front door, his steady clopping a welcome addition to the procession. Chavali watched the two reunite, wondering how much Colby really knew about his mount. Whatever the answer, he hugged the horse around the neck, and leaned on him while they walked.

Mardis's guards let them through as before. Colby waited outside with Karias while Chavali and Portia went in. Chavali saw explaining all of this to Mardis as a kind of practice run for explaining it to Eldrack, but left many details out. She focused on the important parts until she realized she needed to delve more deeply into the subject of Elise with the Lady.

"Elise called herself the Herald of the Lost. Given the proximity of Lost Island and the meaning of 'herald,' it seems safe to say that whatever is there to return has begun the process of doing so."

Mardis looked at her hands the whole time. "You work for the King, you need to tell him. I don't know much more than I've already said, and I couldn't find anything in the journals I have, but I do have something you can take to him." She left the room.

Chavali and Portia looked at each other, neither knowing what to think of this. "I wish she knew the actual prophecy."

Portia sighed. "I wish we knew which fish was what, to know if we missed accounting for any of them."

Agreeing, Chavali sat back in her chair and closed her eyes. On the ride, she would have a chance to think over Pale's memories more, and the events here, and Karias, and everything else. So many dead over this, too. Three of the four spies taken, along with those eight guards and all the rest of Pale's victims, and Garrian.

Mardis returned a few minutes later, carrying a metal box reverently in both hands. Buffed and polished to a silver sheen, even along the welded edges, the box was about the size of an ordinary cat. A latch on the long side had an indentation instead of a keyhole. "My family has kept this safe for generations." Presenting it to Chavali, she continued. "I have no idea what's inside, only that in the event I ever learn the Lost are returning, I'm to have it delivered to the King. His seal can open it. With everything you've done and sacrificed already for Ket, I know I can count on you to deliver it to him."

The box weighed ten or twelve pounds, heavy enough to be noticeable. "Yes, I swear it will be delivered with as much speed as we can muster." To Eldrack, of course, and he would see it to the King, or whoever would be more appropriate.

"Thank you. May the Creator speed you on your way."

Knowing a dismissal when they heard one, Chavali and Portia got up and left with the box. They returned with Colby and Karias to the inn, where they found Harris asleep. Eager to be on their way, Chavali sat on the edge of his bed and shook him awake while Portia and Colby both packed their things to get moving.

"Hey, you're alive."

"As are you."

Harris grinned. "You ever hear the story about the prince who fell into a deep sleep and had to be kissed by his true love to wake up?"

"No." Chavali shrugged. "Nor do I care. I am, however, pleased you did not die."

"Good enough for me."

She stood. "Get up, we leave soon."

"All business. Do you ever have fun, Chastity?"

"You are aware this is not actually my name, yes? This is not a proper translation of my name. I only told Colby that so he could use it without violating his idiotic code."

Harris chuckled and rolled to his side so he could get up. "What is a proper translation of your name?"

Standing up, she smirked. "None of your business."

"Figures. If I had to pick a translation, that's what I'd guess." He misunderstood her on purpose, she could tell. She didn't mind.

"Does 'Chastity' have a meaning? I intended to ask Portia, but never did."

"Yes." The way he said it, slow and drawn out, she guessed he thought she would disapprove of it. "It means not having sex, ever."

"I see. Thank you." She left the room, not giving a reaction because she had none to give. Portia chose it for how it sounded, as did she. And yet, it applied well enough. She smirked all the way down the stairs and out to the stables. Colby tightened straps for one of the other two horses, checking and re-checking his work.

"While we ride, it would be prudent if I spend a little time in your head to make sure Pale's compulsion cannot be accidentally triggered again. Will you consent to this?"

Colby frowned and didn't answer for several seconds. "Yes, that's probably wise."

"It could wait, you could let Railan or someone else do it, I think."

"No, I think I'd rather have someone who was there do it. Thank you for offering."

She nodded and reached out to rub Karias's nose. He already had his saddle on. "May I ask what you know about your horse?"

He's aware I'm not a mere horse. We're linked, but can't share complex thoughts or communicate telepathically like I can with you. It's mostly emotions, and a sense of connection I can follow to find him.

"I'm not sure what you mean."

Since we can't share words, he doesn't know much. I'd prefer if you keep it vague for now.

"If you are being coy, you are very bad at it. He is not, of course, a mere horse."

"Ah." Colby rubbed the nose of the horse in front of him and grabbed the last saddle. "Yes, I know that. We've been linked for some time now, several years. I assumed anyone I explained it to would think I'm crazy, so I keep my mouth shut."

"You need not keep your mouth shut around me."

Be careful, Chavali. He's been hurt, recently.

"Don't be daft," she muttered at the horse. As if she had that kind of interest in such a stubborn idiot. She wanted to have as stable a clan as possible. This thing bothered him, so she offered to help with it. That's what a Seer did: she looked out for the clan. Louder, for Colby, she added, "I offer nothing more or less than what the words say. No hidden agenda."

"I appreciate that. Thank you."

I have a feeling you're going to complicate my life.

"This what I do," she told both of them with a smirk.

Chapter 22

Chavali took the box to the thirteenth floor by herself. It seemed she understood what happened in Ket better than any of the others, so she would make the report. Colby split away in Cloverdale to tend the horses and with a promise to see the two bodies safely delivered. They brought Garrian's spy's corpse in addition to Elise's, just in case. Harris parted company at the 8th floor. Portia patted Chavali on the shoulder and took her leave at the 10th.

Eldrack's office looked exactly as it did before, complete with the man behind his desk, reading from a folder. Unlike usual, Railan sat across from him, reading from another folder. Chavali paused at the door, her eyes unerringly drawn to the intriguing set of scars cutting across Railan's face. She wanted to find a pattern and figure out what happened to the woman. But not today.

He looked up and smiled, gesturing for her to take the other seat. She closed her folder and gave a less warm smile. Chavali set the box down on his desk and dropped Pale's dagger beside it as she took the empty chair. "Many things happened. Elise is dead, we have returned with her body, and also the body of a man who may be a good addition to the Fallen." Eldrack and Railan shared a look she found annoying. They expected this, she thought.

"Harris killed her." Both of their expressions changed to utter confusion, which pleased her immensely; they didn't know everything. She launched into the explanation, telling them about the affair and the dead wife and Garrian's smuggling operation, the prophecy and what happened, the Lost Island, all the way to the point of Elise trying to kill Mardis and being defeated. "She called herself the Herald of the Lost. Mardis believes this means something will 'return' from Lost Island, and gave me this box, to be delivered to the King."

Eldrack's attention turned to the box and its latch. "This is disturbing news." He opened a desk drawer and produced a seal that he fitted to the lock. It clicked open. Putting the seal away, he flipped the lid over and pulled a handsomely sculpted black stone statue of a cat out. It sat with its tail wrapped around its feet, nose lifted to a scent in the air. He set it on his desk. The material struck her as familiar somehow but she couldn't place it.

"There is more. I have learned the name of the man who slaughtered my clan. It is Robin. He had a protégé in Ket, working on a technique to implant orders in a person's mind. That person, named Pale, perfected it. She is dead, killed by me in some kind of mental battle." Remembering the letter from the cave, she pulled it out of her pocket and handed it over.

"You can do that?" Railan looked surprised.

"It seems so. I did not expect it or know what to do, but I managed.

Does it always end in death?"

"As far as I know, yes. What did you manifest as?"

"Ladies," Eldrack interrupted politely, "as much as this discussion is important, it can wait. Did you learn anything else about Robin?"

Chavali considered that, mulling over the things Pale said. "Pale worshiped him, and he told her about me. He is somewhat obsessed with me and what he almost had in his hands, or believes he almost had. Also, his eyes are blue. I do not believe he will have any reason to suspect I was there, as I used a false name, Chastity, at Portia's suggestion."

"She's got a good head on her shoulders," Railan murmured.

"Indeed. I did see many of Pale's memories rapidly, and have not yet had time to truly examine them all. If I think of anything else, I will let you know."

"Good. Can you write all of this up?"

"No. I cannot write. Colby has offered to teach me."

Railan rolled her eyes. "That ass. He knew and sent you to report anyway." She shook her head in bemused disapproval. "Don't worry about it. I'll do the write-up. We'll get together tomorrow to go over it and fill in holes or clarify things."

Eldrack's mouth twitched with a grin. "Is there anything else, Chavali?"

Sitting there, Chavali regarded the two of them. Something about them, about how few things surprised them, bothered her. She crossed her arms and narrowed her eyes as she recalled how easily Eldrack accepted her judgment about her previous mission. "It occurs to me that Harris turned out to be exceptionally useful on this mission. Without his particular and peculiar knowledge and skill set, this mission would certainly have taken much longer, and probably been less successful."

Railan's face went blank and she stood up. "You know what, I should get started on that report, and a few other things."

Eldrack's expression similarly faded to neutrality. He nodded and gave her a small wave. When the door closed, he laced his fingers together and set his hands on his desk, leaning towards her. "Sometimes, things happen for a reason."

"That is a stupid excuse," she sneered. "Besides, you are evading the subject. You were not surprised to see him. I much doubt you have no other agents with similar skills and knowledge, yet, here comes walking in this man who is exactly what you need when you need it, exactly as you expected."

"Chavali." He took a deep breath and shook his head a tiny bit. "Please believe me when I say that I told you and will always tell you everything I can when it relates to you or your mission."

The most infuriating part of that statement was how she felt exactly the same way about many things. Accusing him of hoarding secrets fell flat in the face of all the secrets she clung to. She scowled and looked away. "Fine. There is one other thing."

Out of the corner of her eye, she caught him rubbing his face wearily. "Yes?"

"Do you know what Colby's horse is?"

The question made him sit back and stare at her. It felt calculating and weighing. "He's a horse."

"I am not a child. Do not act otherwise. You know what I do. You knew I would touch him eventually."

He rubbed his chin and made a thinking face. "I don't know

anything specific, just that the horse and man are bound together in a way that transcended death. Karias is, clearly, more than a mere animal. Beyond that, I have respected their privacy. If you want to know more about him, you should talk to him and Colby."

"Very well." The man didn't know everything, but he knew enough that he might as well. If it became important for him to know exactly what Karias was, she suspected he would find out. Somehow.

She stood up. "I hope the cat means something to you." Without waiting for a response, she left the room, heading to her bed. The mission had been tiring, and the ride long. For now, she needed to rest. Tomorrow...would happen tomorrow.

Epilogue

The horse trotted up the road to Ket, its rider scanning the clear sky as the sun crept towards the ocean. It would be a new moon tonight, his favorite phase. The pitchy darkness it caused in the middle of the night wrapped around him like a velvet blanket studded with diamonds. Inside a city, it wasn't as lovely, of course. Everyone huddled around candles and fires and their magic globes to chase the monsters away.

He reached the gates a few hours before closing, not bothering to dismount when the guard challenged him. A flash of his ring and the man let him through with an apology that he waved off. No need to punish people for doing their job properly—that would be needlessly cruel and counterproductive.

His belly rumbled after his long journey, and he preferred to wait for nightfall to attend to his business here, so he stopped at the one tavern he knew had a stable of high enough quality to handle his mount. Maybe he'd leave the beast there tonight, though he wouldn't stay at the attached inn; a room already awaited him elsewhere in the city.

Inside Cander's Lodge, he took a table for himself, the cut of his fine clothes insuring a waitress came to his side the moment his bottom hit the chair. She smiled at him, in the same fake way any other waitress smiles at any other customer. Pretty girl, he thought. She reminded him of other pretty girls. But he had business here, and while he could spare the time for a meal, he couldn't justify a dalliance.

"Good evening, milord. Cook's special tonight is—"

He waved to interrupt her. "That's fine. I'm not picky, just starving. Whatever you can bring me in five minutes that's edible will get you a fat tip."

"Yes, milord." She dipped a curtsy and hurried to the kitchen.

Settling back in his chair, he let the chatter of the room flow around him. Not only did stopping here on the way mean he could eat without having to suffer through greetings and whatnot first, he also had a chance to learn what major events happened in the city recently. With a little effort, he focused his attention enough to pick out individual conversations. Everyone talked about the deaths of two members of the Lady's Council, which didn't bode well for his business.

Something about an affair and revenge for the Garrian fellow. No one seemed to know how or why the local Konti died, other than she'd been murdered. Interesting. His food arrived before he gleaned anything more. The plate held a wedge of softened cheese, a slab of bread with butter, a thick cut of meat, and a heaping pile of cooked vegetables drenched with some sort of brown sauce he suspected to be meat drippings.

The waitress stood there, biting her lip and watching him while he picked up the knife and fork she laid down with it and cut into the meat.

It all smelled heavenly, and the meat oozed with juices. Finding the inside sufficiently cooked, he smiled up at her.

"Thank you, this will do nicely." He saw she relaxed, assured of his money lining her purse. "Before you go, I wonder if you could tell me if anyone knows who killed the Konti yet? I'm a bit behind on the news, I think."

"Oh, I haven't heard much, milord. The Guard is all tight-lipped about it. They do say a bunch of strangers who stayed here had something to do with catching the murderer. Can't say if I believe that, but the bit—er, *lady* with the feather had sharp eyes and a queer way about her."

He blinked and froze with the first bite of meat on its way to his mouth. Could it be her? No, she died. Still, better to ask than to wish he'd asked. "Feather?"

"Yes, milord, growing out of her forehead." She leaned in and took him into her confidence. "If you can picture it, the feather was long and pink, with a bit of a curl to it, stuck right into her brow." The girl tapped her forehead exactly where he thought she would. "Had some kind of flowery tattoo all around it, too."

How could this be? She died. No force could bring back the dead. If there existed such a force, he needed to know about it. The odds of two women with such an unusual ornamentation... Or did he miss someone? Did that damned clan have a second group that didn't travel? Maybe she had a sister with the same gift and a similar feather. It could be more than a ridiculous ornament; the feather might be a marking to indicate the gift. Perhaps this sister had an even greater gift, so they kept her hidden away. He schooled himself to appear merely curious to get more information.

"She sounds exotic."

The waitress grabbed a seat and sat beside him, ignoring her other customers and propriety. He didn't care, he wanted to know everything she could tell him. "That's not the half of it, milord. Rude as all heck. She got my sister fired, and nearly had me out, too. Lost a night's wages *and* tips. For spilling a bit of grog on her dress!" She huffed and crossed her arms. "And yeah, foreign in an odd sort of way. Her skin tone was rough-hued, a bit on the brownish side without being a tan. Never seen anyone quite the same. And she had an accent I've never heard before, either. Spoke a little funny—stilted, like she didn't know Shappan very well."

"Fascinating. Her name must have been equally exotic."

The girl frowned. "No, actually. That was a funny thing, now that you mention it. She went by 'Chastity.' Such a mystery. The men with her were practically her slaves," she sneered. "All but carried her out on a chaise when they left first thing this morning."

Inside, he cursed himself for not discovering more about their naming patterns. 'Chastity' could very well be a name from that clan. He had no idea if Chavali would be so petty, either. At any rate, he suspected anything else this girl had to say on the matter would be prattle or bile. To get rid of her, he let his eyes glance up at the bar. "Thank you, dear woman, for the company. But I think you'll get into trouble if you dote on me too much."

"Oh!" She jumped up with a grimace and tucked the chair under the table. "I'm sorry to bother you, milord. Enjoy your meal."

If only he had left two days ago instead of today! He sighed and devoured his meal, pondering the possibility that either Chavali managed to survive somehow, or a greater prize awaited him. When he finished, he overpaid by a ridiculous amount. The girl deserved it for the incredible news she unwittingly handed him. No longer in a mood to walk, he took his horse and rode across town. At the Lady's estate, her guards did exactly what the city guard did.

He left his horse at the front door and flashed his ring again. Someone would stable it for him. By chance, as the guard opened the front door for him, he saw Luna walking up the hall and beamed at her. Such a lovely girl.

"Uncle Robin!" She ran and jumped into his outstretched arms, wrapping hers around his neck. "What are you doing here? No one said you were coming!"

"My visit is a surprise." He squeezed her tightly and set her down again. How she'd grown since the last time he saw her. Such a joy to see a lively young woman. "You must tell me everything that's happened lately. Start with this nasty affair I heard about with Seran Garrian, and end with Konti Jore's murder."

She giggled like the teenager she was and took his hand to conduct him to the nearest sitting room. "How do you always know everything already?"

"If I knew everything," he chided, "I wouldn't ask about the details."

Squeezing his hand, she pulled him to the room and all but pushed him inside. "I'll go get mother. She knows more than me anyway."

"Please do, and come back with her, won't you?"

"Yes, of course!" She ran off in high spirits. Good for her. None of this nastiness touched her. A shame about what he would do here, but she'd bounce back from it. He would help. Nothing would stop him here. Pacing through the room, he stopped at the window, looking up at the stars. They glittered brightly, just like Luna.

"Robin, I didn't believe that you were actually here." Amelia stood in the doorway, dignity draped across her shoulders. Some things never changed. She struck him as remote and unapproachable as ever, possibly even more than he remembered with that frown curling her mouth down.

"And yet, here I am. Come," he offered her the same greeting he did to her daughter, who danced from one foot to the other as she waited in the hallway. "Sit. We should talk."

Ignoring his attempt to embrace her, Amelia glided around the furniture to sit in a chair. "I thought you were dead."

"Ah, this must be very strange then." He dropped his arms and sighed. "It's a shame that weighs on your mind, especially now." Reaching for Luna, he took her eagerly offered hand and conducted her around to the chair next to her mother.

Amelia's frown grew deeper. "What's special about now?"

As much as he wished he could make her smile, he didn't come all this way to be her clown. With the unexpected appearance of Chastity, and the deaths that he suspected might include his student, he didn't have the luxury of leisure. This should have been very different. Much like Chavali had defied him before, his new prize must have found a reason to meddle in this and ruin everything. Well. Hopefully not *everything*. "Luna." To his pleasure, the girl gave him a broad smile. "Blue acorn waltz." He pulled a knife from its sheath at the small of his back and held it up for her by the sharp blade.

Amelia furrowed her brow. "I don't understand."

The girl blinked once and leaped to her feet. She snatched the dagger from his hand and whirled, plunging it deeply into her mother's chest. Yanking it out, she stabbed her mother—who gaped in shock—again, this time in the neck.

"Well done." He slipped behind the girl and wrapped his arms around her waist as she sucked in a horrified breath, staring at her blood-spattered hands. "Sssh." His finger went to her lips, keeping her quiet. "Sometimes, necessary things don't make sense. Sleep, Lady Mardis, and forget." A light touch on her mind pushed her into slumber and she sagged in his arms.

"I'll take care of everything. I promise."

About the Authors

Lee French lives in Olympia, WA with two kids, two bicycles, and too much stuff. She is an avid gamer and active member of the Myth-Weavers online RPG community, where she is known for her fondness for Angry Ninja Squirrels of Doom. In addition to spending much time there, she also trains year-round for the one-week of glorious madness that is RAGBRAI, has a nice flower garden with one dragon and absolutely no lawn gnomes, and tries in vain every year to grow vegetables that don't get devoured by neighborhood wildlife.

She is an active member of the Northwest Independent Writer's Association and one of two Municipal Liaisons for the Olympia region of NaNoWriMo.

Erik Kort abides in the glorious Pacific Northwest, otherwise known as Mirkwood-Without-The-Giant-Spiders, though the normal spiders often grow too numerous for his comfort. He is defended from all eight-legged threats by his brave and overly tolerant wife, and is mocked by his obligatory writer's cat. When not writing, Erik comforts the elderly, guides youths through vast wildernesses, and smuggles more books into his library of increasingly alarming size.

Thanks for reading! If you liked this book, please take a minute to post a review wherever you buy your books.